BEYOND DUCK RIVER

BEYOND DUCK RIVER

Angela Martin

HODDER

Angela Martin was born in Sydney, grew up around Duck River and descends from a unique mixed ancestry: Sydney Aboriginal and British.

She left school at fourteen, joined the navy at eighteen and later returned to her education, graduating with a BA from the Australian National University and a Dip Ed from the University of Canberra. Studies in fine art, philosophy and sociology followed at the University of Sydney.

She went on to work in the media, education and arts administration and is now an arts educator at the Art Gallery of NSW.

Angela's travels have taken her from outback Australia, to Russia, Scandinavia and Europe, and on a hundred kilometre journey in a dugout canoe down the Ramu River in Papua New Guinea. She now lives on the central coast of NSW and has two sons and twin granddaughters. *Beyond Duck River* is her first novel.

A Hodder Book

Published in Australia and New Zealand in 2001
by Hodder Headline Australia Pty Limited
(a member of the Hodder Headline Group)
Level 22, 201 Kent Street, Sydney NSW 2000
Website: www.hha.com.au

National Library of Australia
Cataloguing-in-Publication data

Martin, Angela.
Beyond Duck River.

ISBN 0 7336 1325 X.

1. Aborigines, Australian - Women - Fiction. 2. Australia - Social conditions - 20th century - Fiction. I. Title.

A823.3

Cover design by Danielle Cairis
Text design and typesetting by Bookhouse, Sydney
Cover image: Duck River circa 1908. Photograph courtesy of Granville Historical Society, Sydney
Printed in Australia by Griffin Press, Adelaide

To Waianya and all those who have fought a good fight and lost: nothing is lost.

ACKNOWLEDGMENTS

I would like to thank everyone who has ever welcomed me into their story. Thanks to my sons and dear Alicia and Kirsty, who have kept me going through the weekends of writing. Special thanks to my agent Selwa Anthony, who believed in this book from the start; my editor Mark Macleod; and Darug Elder, Colin Gale, for his ongoing support; Andrew Wilson; Dr Jim Kohen; and Aboriginal storyteller Pauline Macleod. Stories of Sydney passed on by my parents have breathed a special life into this book, and so last, but not least, I thank my dear mother and father.

Apart from historical instances and persons, this is a work of fiction. If characters' names depict those living or dead, it is coincidental. As a mark of respect and with gratitude, the name Miss Morphett has been used. Mrs Morphett, an English teacher at Auburn Girls Home Science School, offered working class girls hope. She was an inspiration. Those close to me may recognise a street or place name, a christian or surname: a secret inclusion, completely separate from character or story.

ONE

TO WAR

Hazel balanced precariously on the edge of a huge, varnished chair, and turned her nose up at the musty smell of the heavy curtains behind her. The room was small and bare and a strange wooden box peered at her from the blank wall opposite. She peered back and swung her legs impatiently, but the swinging and leaning toppled her tiny body dangerously close to the floor.

'Keep still!' A voice quivered and a head popped up over the top of the box.

Flouncing her legs in the air, she leant back, a timing feat that saved her from hitting the floor. Her black eyes twinkled with triumph before a blinding light froze her fluttering eyelashes.

Sound returned. Movement. Breathing and sighing. But she just sat, mesmerised by the wooden box.

A week followed before she saw the magic. It was the day Joe was leaving Leichhardt. There she was on the edge of the big chair, Joe and Alice Johnson standing as straight as the King and Queen of England, Jimmy Johnson, the student prince, standing beside her: all in their Sunday best, except for her father, who wore a strange uniform and a lopsided hat.

She examined the photograph, turned it over and wrote neatly on the back.

'Let me see!' said Jimmy, knocking the Marmite jar across the breakfast table.

'Don't snatch!'

'What's that word?' he pestered, tapping the back of the photograph, as she stood up to leave the table.

'I'm not tellin'. Ya gotta learn to read words ya don't know!'

His tiny finger pressed down on the letters. 'Rrrroy…al! The Johnsons Royal of Leichhardt! That's what it says!'

She curtsied to her father. 'May I leave the table, Your Majesty?'

'Certainly, Princess!'

'But leave the toast, Your Royal Highness,' her mother called from the kitchen.

She took Jimmy's hand. 'Come, clever Prince.'

And, despite the sadness of the day, Joe and Alice Johnson laughed.

It was late afternoon before the Royals of Leichhardt arrived at the wharf near the big ship: Alice with the same lace collar and gold brooch; Hazel the same prissy dress; Jimmy the same side-buttoned shirt, and Joe, the lopsided hat.

The Queen wiped her eyes, as the King kissed the Princess and disappeared into a sea of soldiers.

Happier Times

The Moreton Bay fig tree spread its branches over the small house and took up most of the yard. It was a part of Alice

Johnson. She had swung in its arms as a girl and she had, as a woman, sat under it, shrouded in leafy privacy.

Now Jimmy was squealing as Joe pushed him higher and higher on the swing; up and up into the shimmering leaves which waved each time he swept by. 'You look like the man at the circus,' Hazel called, as Alice watched from the kitchen window, the same window from which her mother had once watched her.

The twisting and turning of sylphlike branches, earth-brown tipped with warm green leaves, reached not only up, but out, offering shade and splendour to Seale Street. And while neighbours chatted over fences, their gazes wandered from the idle palings to the staunch tree with its roots deep in Alice's yard.

Jack Smith spoke quietly as he stood beside Alice at the open window. 'Joe's a fine man. Your mother's happy in that.'

Her father spoke only when he had something to say. He preferred books and horses to people.

Books took up the largest wall in the living room, from the floor to the ceiling: books and more books. Immaculately kept. Carefully placed. A locked photograph album on the top shelf and so many different books flowing all the way down. But Grandpa Smith had trouble keeping a hold on reverence. The candle-chandelier, lowering into the room's centre, was proof of that.

He was in the habit of draping bunches of grapes over the chandelier's branches, out of his grandchildren's reach, until the grapes ripened. And here they were once more: ragged stems with not a grape in sight. He knew who it was. He had caught her the last time, standing tippy-toed on the dining table and having a merry feast. 'Hazel, you know why they are there. If you get a sore belly, don't blame me!' And, jumping to the floor with a thud, she had swallowed a mouthful of seeds. Yet whenever Alice attempted to scold her for taking the grapes, Grandpa would only whisper, 'It's no good getting upset because her belly works better than ours.'

Joe was no firmer when it came to disciplining the children, but the gentleness of the two men left little need of it. Hazel was more mischievous than Jimmy, but she knew she wasn't to touch Grandpa's books. And she never did. Not since the day she had managed to fascinate Jimmy with the locked photograph album.

A noise had woken her and, peering from her bedroom into the candlelit living room, she'd spied on Grandpa. He was replacing the locked album. And she watched as he carefully hid the key under a book.

By morning her curiosity had raced her out of bed. 'Wake up, Jimmy!' she whispered, shaking his arm.

'What do ya want?' he mumbled.

'I wanta show ya somethin'. C'mon!'

Stumbling out of bed, he found himself being dragged into the living room, where Hazel nudged a chair up behind his knees, while pointing excitedly to the top shelf of the bookcase. 'Knock that album down,' she whispered and shoved his cricket bat into his limp hand. 'I'll catch it!'

Still half asleep, he balanced on the chair, waving the bat until the album dropped over the edge and into her arms. But it landed with such force that it sent the tiny key in her hand skidding under Grandpa's chair. 'Now look what ya done,' she whispered through gritted teeth. And with her bottom stuck up in the air, she swirled her fingers about until it slid out again. Jimmy hobbled off the chair and watched silently as Hazel did the unlocking.

Huddled over the album, they flipped through years, until a

fading photograph caught their attention. It was a girl in a funny bonnet, the wide ribbons tied under her chin. Lace-up boots disappeared under her skirt and cuff-lace hung down over her lifeless wrists.

Jimmy laughed. 'She's got no neck!'

'She looks sad.'

'That's cause she didn't want her picture taken!'

'Wonder why she's all covered up like that?'

'Must be lergic to the sun or somethin'!'

And Grandpa walked right in to their muffled laughter.

'Who's this funny lady, Grandpa?' Jimmy sniggered, before Hazel could shut him up.

Grandpa snatched the album up from the floor, snapped it shut and locked it. 'Stop that stupid giggling!' And he pushed the key deep into his trouser pocket. 'Don't touch things that don't belong to ya!' And, clutching the album, he wiped his nose.

The shock of Grandpa's distress left the culprits dumbfounded. Jimmy began babbling, 'What did you go and hurt Grandpa like that for, Hazel? You shouldna sneaked! You're a dirty spy! They shoot spies ya know! Ya shouldna made me do it! Yuv made me a spy now! We'll go to hell, we will! Ya shouldna made him shout like that! Ya made him cry!' And he sniffed.

'I didn't mean to!'

'Ya not to do it again!'

'Don't worry, I won't!'

'Ya gotta promise!'

'I promise!'

And she promised herself to push the awful incident, as Grandpa had pushed the tiny key, into a pocket and out of sight.

Grandpa was the local blacksmith and he fascinated Hazel.

Sometimes after school she would run from Kegworth Primary home to Seale Street and on up to Elswick, opposite Myrtle Street, to watch him at work in the blacksmith's shop. She knew all the streets in Leichhardt, the horse and carts didn't frighten her and she didn't have to go near Parramatta Road, or the steam trams.

Sparks flew out in all directions and hammering bounded and echoed off the walls, and steam shot to the ceiling. *Whoosh! Whoosh!*

Jack Smith half turned and gave a slight nod in the direction of his granddaughter, who'd sat herself on a stool at the wide opening of the shop. Sweat streamed from his forehead onto his sooty, black arms. Boys in the neighbourhood called him Darkie, because they weren't allowed in. Even Jimmy's presence was frowned upon, but he didn't mind, because to him it was just hot and dirty anyway. Sometimes Hazel got called Darkie too, because she was allowed in and others weren't. But she didn't care. She would have gone there every afternoon if she'd been allowed. It was the only blacksmith's shop in Leichhardt and Grandpa always had a couple of horses up the yard.

He gave lessons on smithing at the Fort Street College, and knew all about horses.

Hazel was intrigued by the strange rapport he had with them. Occasionally he let her hold a tail up while he shod the back hooves. She would watch him carefully, but when he caught her peering at him through long tail strands, or around a rump, or under a belly, she would look away, before sneaking a quick look back, in an effort to fathom how the horse and Grandpa seemed to talk. Unless of course, her grandpa really was a horse.

Whatever the mystery encircling Grandpa, the horses sensed and trusted it. Without as much as a sound or a touch, a horse would move this way or that at Grandpa's wish. Likewise, Grandpa would respond to a slight flick of the tail, or a gentle toss of the head and when black pools met, the big round eyes of the horse and the smaller eyes of Grandpa, they would stare deep into each other and blink, while strips of worn leather dangling from a rusty nail on the wall waited patiently for him to rein.

Hazel watched as Grandpa bridled another quiet horse and left in an echo of *clip clop*. Steam subsided and floated out the door and the new shoes of the ambling horse shimmered and disappeared into the mist, while inside she felt once more the warmth emanating.

How did Grandpa know things? How did he know when she was there? She'd tried to catch him out, sneaking up to the shop front and easing her head around the big wooden door. 'You're early today, Princess!'

She tried sneaking in the back, past the coals. 'Don't get too close to the heat!'

So she gave up.

At the end of each day Grandpa took off his huge leather apron and washed black dust from his arms and face before walking one block home to Seale Street, where, free from soot for another day, he would take a book from the shelves and sink down into his favourite chair.

He taught Hazel the correct way to hold a book, where to return it on the shelf and why, and how to mark a place. 'Always use a bookmark,' he reiterated, since the day he'd caught her turning down a page corner of *A Child's Garden of Verses*.

'All the kids at school do it,' she'd cried, as she tried to understand the look of shock and horror on her beloved grandpa's face.

He had a love of story and the natural flow of words. 'Don't ever take the story for granted, or you might miss something.' That's what he told her.

The story connected him to the past and present and offered hope. For Grandpa, to lose the story would be to lose the very purpose of life. It would mean falling into a moonless, everlasting night.

Joe Johnson took Hazel out to the back steps and they sat down together. She waited while he pressed tobacco into the palm of his hand and with a cigarette paper resting on his lower lip, he explained. 'Grandpa loves stories the way he loves horses. It comes natural. Like it does with ya mother.' He took the flimsy paper from his lip and rolled it carefully around the wad of tobacco. 'You see, good stories teach us who we are, to be good to one another, teach us the laws of nature an' that. But ya gotta understand the inside of the story, like the inside of a tree or the inside of a blade of grass, ya know…the inside of things…ya gotta listen to the sounds, feel the rain moving, see how everything fits in with everything else…ya know what I'm sayin'?' She watched as he ran his tongue down the side of the tightened Tally-Ho and struck a match on his shoe. 'Grandpa taught me about the importance of stories and he wants you to know too.' He lit the cigarette slowly. 'Knows all about horses cause it's in his blood.' He drew in his cheeks and blew out a long stream of smoke. 'That's the length and breadth of it.' And he flicked the dead match into the long grass.

Hazel knew that her father was right, as always. But she wandered down the yard muttering to herself, 'To hear him talk you'd think Grandpa was *his* daddy and he's not; he's Mum's!'

She swung round and round on the swing under the Moreton Bay fig, singing over and over 'God save our Gracious King', until Alice yelled from the window, 'Hazel, for goodness sake, don't you know any other song?'

'Yeah, Hazel! We're sick of it!' yelled Jimmy, as he ran into the yard with his mates.

Jonesy and Smitho carried an old square baby's chair, which they'd drilled holes into, while Jimmy cradled a mound of rope. Percy and Bluey followed, jittering about. They all wore long grey shorts: Jonesy and Smitho in grey shirts; the others blue.

'Giddy giddy gout ya shirt's hangin' out,' Hazel called. For her liking, there was too much sameness in boys. Grey. Blue. Shirts out. But she liked their show-off games.

Jimmy put the ladder against the tree trunk, climbed up and threw the ropes over the first branch. Then he climbed out onto the branch, positioned the ropes in the middle and let the ends freefall to the boys below. Percy yelled, 'I wanna go first, I wanna go first.' And with that he jumped into the chair, as Jimmy scurried down and the boys and Hazel began to tug on the ropes.

Percy, being a frail boy, shot up into the air like a rocket and smacked his head against a robust branch, while the children below, shocked by their combined strength, loosened their grip on the rope. Still holding the chair, Percy fell to the ground with a terrible thud.

Alice Johnson had been chatting to Joe in the living room, as Grandpa sat quietly, half reading, half listening, when they heard the yelling. Jimmy ran in as Alice, Joe and Grandpa ran out.

'We've killed Percy, we've killed Percy!'

Percy lay stretched out unconscious under the tree as Joe felt desperately for a pulse, but each time he felt what could have been a beat, Jimmy tugged at his arm, spluttering, 'We've killed him, we've killed him, haven't we, Dad?'

Hazel stood motionless, her face frozen in fear, while the Elswick Street boys moved about nervously. Percy had turned deathly white and wasn't stirring. Alice ran inside to fetch a blanket, while Joe gave the lifeless face two hard slaps.

'Nnnnnnnn.' Percy roused.

Joe didn't hang about. He ran flat out to Marion Street to fetch the doctor. Alice sent the children inside, while she cradled Percy in her arms, rocking him back and forth. Grandpa calmed the frightened children and then hurried to Elswick Street to fetch Percy's parents.

The following day they heard the outcome. Percy was fine except for one affliction: he had developed a stutter. Jimmy became even more afflicted—with guilt—for planning such a perilous game.

'Ya can't undo what's already done,' said Joe. 'If ya want Percy to know how sorry you are, then you'll have to watch over him. Be sure that nobody pokes fun at him, or laughs behind his back.'

'Well that's what I'm gunna do.'

'In future ya havta ask me about any games ya wanna play in the tree.'

Jimmy and Hazel gave a solemn nod. But the fright of nearly losing Percy centred Hazel's thoughts on war, and the vision of her father sailing away, the very day after her birthday. She decided right there and then what she wanted. Later she went searching for her father and found him asleep, spread-eagled under the tree.

'Dad, can I have a chair like Grandpa's for my birthday?'

He pulled himself up slowly onto one elbow. 'If ya promise not to put it in the tree.'

So with the hum of the cicadas, the sound of a saw droned back and forth as Joe worked away on the Lilliputian copy. Alice had found material similar to that covering Grandpa's chair in a haberdashery store on Broadway.

The whir of the sewing machine and the squeak of the saw commanded a respectful, if somewhat arrogant, smile from Hazel. She was pleased with herself, despite the disappointment and fear surrounding her father's imminent departure.

The chair had offered Alice and Joe a distraction too, and the joint project became more intuitive with less and less of the spoken word; Alice pushing her dread into the sewing machine, while Joe sawed away at his trepidation.

The birthday present received a silent nod from Grandpa before being presented to Hazel on the eve of Joe's departure. She positioned her small chair next to Grandpa's Brobdingnagian chair and then went to her bedroom to get a book from her shelves before rejoining him.

She sat up straight in the chair and dusted her hands before beginning the story. She glanced at Grandpa, as she placed her bookmark vertically down the page. He sensed the glance and smiled to himself without looking up. Joe smiled too, but with a twinge of pain. He left the contented scene and went outside to oil Jimmy's bike and tie the new tail onto Hazel's old kite.

And Hazel sat next to Grandpa and read quietly until she dropped off to sleep. Joe carried her to bed, acutely aware that it could be a while before he held his princess in his arms like this again. Alice turned the sheets back gently.

As the candles burnt low Joe went outside to sit on the back step for a bit. He stared into the leaves of the Moreton Bay fig and as images of his family flickered in the moonlight, he listened to the rustling leaves. This last night before war engulfed him.

TWO

SARI BAIR

With both thighs bayoneted, Joe Johnson was within sight of the hot, rugged ranges of Sari Bair. Bleeding profusely and weak from the heat, he lay twitching with pain and thirst. He could still smell the Aegean Sea as he stared vacantly out across the peninsula towards the Dardanelles, where great battles had been fought: Alexander the Great and King Darius fighting over the marriage of west and east, while the mountains hung in the distance, like the mountains back home that he couldn't reach. And as he drifted in and out of consciousness, he saw soldiers in robes, goats roaming and fishermen repairing nets. The hot sun pelted down. Shell fire. Moaning.

Rousing himself, he caught sight of a Digger off to his right, lying face down with his head in his arms.

'Water. Water, matey.'

The sun reflected off the lid of a water flask.

'Water…water,' Joe gasped.

Other cries followed, but the Digger didn't stir. And the injured's begging quickly changed to cursing.

'Get up, ya bastard!'

'Ya stinkin' coward!'

Joe couldn't stand the pitiful cries and, dragging his thighs hard against the hot earth to curb the bleeding, he pulled himself to the fearful soldier. 'C'mon, cobber,' he whispered, gently shoving him. But there was no response. Joe shoved him again and he rolled over. A bullet was lodged in his forehead and his jaw had been blown away. He was just a boy. A boy with an empty flask.

Joe put his head in his hands and passed out.

But the heartrending cries roused him and, as he knocked the boy and shook the empty flask once more, a can of condensed milk rolled out from under the Digger's body. He managed to spike a hole with his buckle and took a long sip before crawling back with it and tossing it to the remaining two Diggers.

But as the can was raised, a burst of fire rang out and left the two men writhing in agony.

Joe's wounds had forced him face down again and, sipping the can sideways, he'd escaped the sun's dangerous reflection.

Now he was alone. With the sun.

Eventually, Private Joe Johnson was picked up and shipped to a hospital. He was one of the lucky ones. But in his desperate attempt to stay alive he had contracted meningitis. Several reports had gone out that he'd died. He had been taken off one ship to a hospital in Egypt, and then off another at Malta. The last report came after his wrapped body had been shimmied down the wire from ship to shore, flying-fox style.

The ship's chaplain had prayed over him and prepared him for the worst, that he wouldn't make it home. But Sister Kenny, the army nurse, told him he would and the troops on the transport ships were more inclined to believe her. She was their own

Florence Nightingale, this Australian bush nurse, who'd found a cure for those kids back home with infantile paralysis. The Diggers were pleased that she had joined the army. And eight months after she told Joe he'd make it home, he did.

Alice had planned a hearty welcome, expecting him on Thursday with the docking of a troop ship in Sydney. But impatiently leaving the ship in Melbourne, Joe walked in, in the middle of Alice's hearty cleaning, on the Wednesday. With a broom shoved up the chimney she knelt upon the hearth, as black as the soot that showered on her.

'What are you doing here?' she cried.

Joe's face paled. 'Well, that's a fine welcome home!'

Celebrations quickly caught up, but Joe remained stony-faced and steely-eyed, as he watched his neighbours and relatives singing around him. Alice had made his favourite jam tarts, while thick beef sausages spat and sizzled on the wood stove.

Hazel kissed him on both cheeks and skited, 'I helped make the tarts!'

Alice closed her eyes to Jimmy wearing the slouch hat in the house as he tipped it and said, 'G'day cobber.' And as he wandered round with it cocked on the back of his head, he grinned each time he caught sight of Joe.

The family were relieved and overjoyed to have Joe back home. Even the normally reticent Grandpa was babbling, as he handed Joe another whisky. '*When's Daddy comin' home? When's Daddy comin' home from the war?* Thank goodness I don't have to answer those tired old questions again, eh Joe? The kids near drove me mad they did, while you were away. Good to have the same old songs though, eh?'

Somebody was singing 'For They Are Jolly Good Fellows'. Joe wasn't really listening, but the strands were catching on his sleeve and he tried to brush them off, while the excited chatter grew louder and louder, turning into a crescendo of one enormous cackle. He shook his head. A cymbal clanged and clanged again.

He hurried outside. Hazel ran squealing with a ragged, long-tailed kite and Jimmy pedalled by, twanging a bell, yelling and boasting that he'd fixed up his sparkling red bicycle. They turned and were tearing back down the street towards him, but he stood transfixed in the early night. All he could see were streaming white bandages and red spewing blood. All he could hear was the tinkling of an empty flask. And soldiers cursing. He rubbed his arm. A boy's arm. All he could feel was hot serge. And all he could smell was death.

Alice had come out onto the verandah to look for him. She had scarcely taken a breath of the early evening air when he flew at her from the front gate and shoved her sideways with such force that she went flying over the verandah wall, landing face down in the garden.

'Stay in ya bunker!' he yelled, running into the house and ramming bullets into his souvenir rifle.

'What's goin' on?' Grandpa called from the back step. But before anyone knew what was happening and Grandpa could get to Joe, he had begun firing.

'Get down!' Grandpa yelled.

Everyone dived to the floor, hiding behind couches and chairs, as Joe fired relentlessly over their heads. 'Stay low in ya bunkaaa!' he yelled. 'Stay lowwww!' And he fired and fired.

When the round ran out, Grandpa, Uncle Bert and Mr Sanders from next door tackled him and, while Aunt Daphne sat on him, Grandpa flung the rifle under the couch. A look of confusion swept Joe's face. Alice stood frozen in the doorway with a bewildered Hazel and Jimmy. 'It was the whisky,' Grandpa said, and gently ushered the visitors out.

Alice put Joe to bed, tucking white sheets around Turks and bunkers and death. And with Hazel and Jimmy safely tucked in for the night too, she and Grandpa sat silently warming themselves at the open fire, and toasted bread on blackened forks. The treacle tin, with a bullet dint in its side, stood on the floor between them and they quietly brushed the crumbs of war under the mat on the hearth.

While Gallipoli remained a hidden subject, Joe Johnson did reveal one thing. 'Those Turks were all right...lotta guts...suffered like the rest of us. Did their job as soldiers, that's all.' His bayoneted thighs were proof of that. He remained adamant. 'As a rule the Turks wouldn't fire on stretcher bearers, or the injured. Just sometimes they got a bit edgy.'

His brother had been injured in France and had turned up in Malta. Crammed into a hospital with dying soldiers and sheeted in despair, George Johnson swore he could hear Joe's voice calling to him in the depths of the night. But he'd heard Joe was dead. His hopes rose as he crawled through the blackened ward towards the unmistakable sound. However, relief at finding his only brother in this ghastly place turned to desolation.

Joe grabbed George's arm. 'Is that you, Alice?'

'It's me, Joe: George. It's George, your brother George!'

'Get that kid in the bunker, cobber. Get 'im into tha bunker!'

'It's me, Joe, George. It's *me!*'

'Alice, get Pa's horse. Get the horse, Alice!'

'Joe, listen to me. It's George. Help me, Joe. Joe, it's *me*, your brother!'

But Joe lapsed in and out of consciousness, hallucinating and oblivious of the fateful reunion.

When George Johnson arrived back in Melbourne, he collected his pay and disappeared. And nobody ever heard of him again.

While Joe was away at war, Alice had developed a habit of saving clippings from newspapers. Words that touched her. Comfort words. Now as she rummaged through the box of clippings, she came across the words of an unknown soldier.

Who made the law that men should die in meadows?
Who spake the word that blood should splash in lanes?
Who gave it forth that gardens should be boneyards?
Who spread the hill with flesh, and blood and brains?

Next day Grandpa hid the rifle in the roof and Joe never again asked where it was.

THREE

HARBOUR OUTING

It was a still, sunny day, just the sort of day Hazel had hoped for, but she was keen to get going. The sky could so quickly change.

'Hurry up, Grandpa! Can't you put May's bridle on faster than that?'

He stroked the docile draught horse, while Joe continued hitching the cart.

'Oh no! Look at all the dust and cobwebs!'

Grandpa ignored her, but Joe was in a playful mood and, swirling a rag from his back pocket, he dusted the seats. 'There ya go, Your Highness.'

She ran off laughing and collided with Alice at the front door. 'For goodness sakes, Hazel, watch where ya goin'!'

'Let me carry the basket, Mum.'

Alice slapped at the grappling hands. 'Not on your life! I don't want cutlery flying across the yard. Here, take the blanket. Grandpa can carry the basket.'

'What's Jimmy doin', Mum? We're never gunna get there!'

'We've got all day. Stop fussing about like a hen!'

'Just cause the sun's out now doesn't mean it's gunna hang round waiting for us, ya know. It could be rainin' this arvo. Could be pouring with hailstones as big as marbles by the time we get there!'

'Don't say "gunna", Hazel. I've told you a thousand times before, you sound like a little tramp.'

Hazel threw the blanket into the cart and Joe yanked her in after it, while Alice rested one foot on the tiny step and waited patiently for Joe's hand. Jimmy continued to bounce a tennis ball against the verandah wall. *Verump. Verump. Verump. Verump.* While Grandpa stood there, the reins loose in his hands.

'What's he doin'? For heaven's sakes, Mum! Make him get in the cart!'

'Jimmy, get in the cart before the sun drops out of the sky or Hazel has a heart attack!'

It was quite a distance from Leichhardt to Nielsen Park, but Hazel's fascination with Grandpa, as May capered and cantered to his turn of the wrist, in and out of traffic, along the busy Parramatta Road, managed to alter the 'we're never gunna get there' into something not nearly as tiresome. She mimicked Grandpa's hand movements and copied the strange sounds coming sideways out of his mouth, as he clicked and sucked his cheek in and out, May clopping faster, clopping slower, or coming to a gentle halt, while Alice sat back and enjoyed the quiet.

Broadway dazzled Hazel with its hustle and bustle: draught horses shifting wares, car-horns honking, trams turning, dressed-up pedestrians going every which way, all dwarfed by screaming billboards, BUY IT HERE, EAT IT THERE, and steam trains puffing in and out of Central Station, smoke twirling behind the towering post office of rugged stone that stretched six storeys into the sky.

When they finally turned east off Broadway, Hazel held the reins along the endless stretch of road, until the ambling cart reached Rose Bay and her attention was drawn down to the sparkling water. Grandpa took the cart the rest of the way, up the steep hill towards Vaucluse and down into Shark Bay, as he still referred to the newly named park.

In the shade of the trees, Hazel helped unload the cart, dumping the blanket and a cricket bat and ball into a huddle on the grass, as she peered through the trees. 'Can you hear that, Dad?'

'Hear what?'

'The water. Can you hear it?'

'What are you going on about now?'

'The sea's calling me! Can't you hear it lapping, *Hazel, Hazel*? See, it's calling me!' And she took off.

She ran to the edge of the water and peered down through the surface, watching tiny snake-like sand dunes slithering back and forth, a million grains dancing with the bubbles.

Back up the slope Grandpa tied a long rope from May's warm neck to a shady tree and Joe tipped water into a big rusty dish and scattered crisp hay over the soft, cool grass, while Alice made her way up a winding path to the clifftop with the picnic basket weighing her down, and called to Hazel below, her voice trailing off in the breeze. Jimmy dragged the blanket along the ground, saw Hazel too and cupped his mouth. 'Coo-eee! Coo-eee!'

Still balancing on the edge of the water, Hazel heard the shrill call and stretched her small neck towards the cliff. ‘Coo-eee!’ she called back.

And the call came again. ‘Coo-eee! Coo-eeee!’

She ran with the sound, along the sand and up the track to the clifftop, where she sank down onto the blanket, which Jimmy had half spread out.

‘Whatcha puffin’ for?’ he teased. ‘It’s only a hill.’

‘Why do ya have ta drag things along the ground, Jimmy? Ya got dirt and grass all over the blanket. It gets up ya nose. Ya shoulda shook it first! Help me shake it proply!’

‘For goodness sakes, Hazel, stop fussing! A bit of dirt won’t hurt you. Put the blanket down. I wanta put the basket on it,’ said Alice.

Hazel shook the blanket and squared it onto the ground.

Alice rolled her eyes. ‘Does Her Majesty think I could put the basket down now?’

Hazel laughed and ran along the edge of the cliff, hovering like a seagull, until she spied Joe on the beach rocks below. She ran down the winding path to her unsuspecting prey and scooped him up by the arm. ‘Take me down to the rocks on the other side, Dad. I want to see where we’ve come from!’

‘Crikey, Hazel, watch what ya doin?’ he quipped, as he was thrown off balance and loose rocks shifted under his feet. ‘Scare a bloke half to death, why don’tcha!’

But Hazel merely tugged him after her, towards the scrub that led to the cliff and inlet on the inner side of the park. Joe had no choice but to follow and slip, repeating breathlessly, ‘Alrighty, take it easy,’ as they slunk down the steep incline like donkeys, and finally reached the rocks below, where Joe calmed his pounding heart and rubbed his aching thighs.

Hazel was unaware that her father was trying to block out a

haunting cliff. The men had drifted in the dark, missing the wide beach and landing instead on a narrow stretch, with a sharp crag rearing up behind it. They'd struggled to the top, dragging their rifles and packs, only to find the Turks waiting for them. And men who'd been jokin' around moments before were swept screaming into hell, blood running like a waterfall. He shut out the rocks and looked across the water, pointing down past Shark Island to Sydney Cove. 'That's where they're going to build a bridge one day. From our side of the harbour, over to Milsons Point.'

'Who could build a bridge that big?'

'Tha government.'

'No one in the government could build a bridge that big!'

'Billy Hughes could have.'

'No he couldn't!' Hazel called, looking over her shoulder as she clambered back up the cliff face and enticed her father to chase her.

But, afraid to turn back, Joe continued to stare out across the harbour.

Hazel knew very well who Billy Hughes was. Grandpa had taken her to his shop in Balmain before he became Prime Minister of Australia. Billy this and Billy that. Her father and Grandpa were always talking about him. 'Billy Goat Gruff,' she yelled back at her father, stirring him to chase her. 'Turncoat, Billy Turncoat,' she yelled. That's what she'd heard them calling him.

Joe shielded his eyes from the sun as he turned towards the cliff. 'Hang on, Hazel!' But as the sun spun off the rocks he saw the flash of bayonets. He scurried up the cliff face, slipping on loose rocks and desperately trying to keep Hazel in sight. 'Hazel —wait!'

'Turncoat! Turncoat!' she called, slowing a bit towards the top.

Joe finally caught her and tackled her to the ground, a little more roughly than he should have.

'Ouch, Dad...I'm not a fullback!'

She always managed to make him laugh and he helped her up. 'Sorry. The sun was in me eyes.'

But she was off and away as free as the wind in the trees, even before he'd finished talking.

He rubbed his pounding head and sat down on a rock to catch his breath. 'If you stay where you belong you won't get hurt!' he called after her. 'Didn't know nothin', us volunteers.' He began to mumble. 'Ya used ta look after us workers, Billy. Backin' conscription? Ya knew what we'd been through. All them Diggers. All them boys.' He stood up, stared out over the harbour and wiped his eyes. 'Ya shoulda stayed in Balmain, Billy. Shoulda stayed where you belonged.' And he chucked a rock.

'Dad! Dad, whatcha doin'? Come on, I haven't got all day to wait for ya!'

This was Hazel's favourite picnic spot and now that she was almost in her teens she was allowed to explore on her own. She knew not to go too close to the edge of the main cliff that dropped sharply down into the water on the northern side of the park. But she loved to stand on its top and gaze across the vast expanse as it shimmered beneath her.

Nielsen Park managed to keep Jimmy and Hazel occupied for hours with its nooks and crannies, rocks, caves, trees, thick undergrowth, warm sands and cool waters. All tempting. And after leaving the others at the picnic spot, they climbed down through the thick underbrush to the beach on the inner side of the park. And, looking down the harbour, Hazel mimicked her father and gestured to where the gigantic bridge was to go, '...from our side of the harbour, over there to Milsons Point.' Then they climbed back up, picking wild flowers and making their way up to the top of the cliff. They plopped down on a flat rock and looked past Watsons Bay to where the open sea began. Hazel pointed towards the heads. 'That's where Captain Cook sailed. The Cadi clan lived here then.'

'How do you know?' Jimmy asked, sure that his sister would tell him.

'Aborigines were the only people here. They were standing right there where you're sitting, the men with fishing spears and the women with possum skin cloaks slung over their shoulders. They were watching the ship. Grandpa told me.'

'I wonder where they are now, then?' Jimmy asked, looking about. And he knocked a small stone over the edge and watched it sink down into the dark water.

'Once the harbour was all rivers and the land and swamps went right out further, that was thousands of years ago, before the ice melted and the sea rose up. There could be hundreds of dead people's bones out under the sea, even around at Bondi Beach. Because it used to be land once. I betcha didn't know that.'

'Land can't just disappear!'

'It didn't disappear! It flooded. I'm going to ask Grandpa if we can stay and watch the sunset and cook the fish over a fire, like last time.' And she raced off down the grassed embankment which led into Vaucluse Bay, while Jimmy tried to imagine the great harbour hole filled in with swampland and flowing rivers.

Grandpa and Joe were fishing off the rocks and Alice had

fallen asleep under the shade of a tree. But it wasn't long before Hazel's exuberance disturbed the tranquil scene and everyone was busy gathering firewood.

The orange sun sank low behind Bradley's Head and the apricot sky tinged the harbour yellow. Hazel went to the edge of the clifftop and looked out. The happy chatter seemed to sway the trees and send a soft breeze up behind her, along with the smoky aroma of smouldering fish. Streaks of sunlight danced across the water, enticing her to step onto the glittering catwalk. Mesmerised, she hummed. It was a hymn and she imagined she was on her way to heaven.

'Hazel, don't stand so close to the edge,' Alice called and the words dragged her back.

As Hazel joined her family around the fire, she watched Grandpa carefully turning the bream and mullet, checking the sun as it set lower in the sky. He answered her inquisitive stare. 'Fish should never be burnt and you must cook it before nightfall.'

Hazel nodded solemnly and refrained from asking why. The higher significance surrounding the cooking of fish seemed a responsibility she wasn't ready for and she was quite happy to leave it to Grandpa.

As the sun set, they all sang the pelican song and Alice began to tell stories, the story of kookaburra and how starfish came to be so flat.

Joe opened his tobacco tin, sniffed, and rolled a cigarette slowly, as he watched Alice's face become strangely animated and illuminated by the firelight. She seemed to drift away into another land, another time. Yet it was in these fleeting moments that his heart yearned for her most.

Tobacco smoke swirled upwards and Hazel watched it as she

listened, until the firelight faded and a story ended. 'And that's why we have to look after the harbour.'

Finally Hazel and Jimmy collected the rubbish and Grandpa deadened the ashes, while Joe and Alice packed the basket.

Hazel was unusually quiet as they wandered back down the track to the horse and cart. Grandpa let her be, but as he turned his attention to the horse, she finally spoke. 'Grandpa, next time we go out to La Perouse to shoe Billie's horse, I'm going to ask him why the Aborigines don't come to Nielsen Park anymore.'

He gave the horse a pat on the rump, holding the reins and turning it about.

He decided it was time. On the next visit to Shark Bay, he would take Hazel and Jimmy for a walk around the rocks and show them the mundoe, the footprint etched into a hidden rock. It was time to answer a child's inquisitiveness with respect. And next time, as Hazel handed over the reins, he would tell her about the place called Rose Bay, old Gingaculla, and the ritual site, and she would begin to understand nature's beauty, when it is intertwined with sacredness, spiritual endlessness and lore. Yes, it was time. But if it didn't feel right on the day, the children would have to wait.

As darkness set in down the long road home, gaslight blinked.

FOUR

THE FIERY COMMOTION

Joe's headaches were becoming worse, along with the pain in his thighs. He'd relinquished a small bootmaker's stall when he went away to war. The new owner had offered to take him on as a part-time offsider and Joe had gladly accepted. However, the hammering pounded away in his head and by Wednesdays, he just had to have a whisky.

He spent more and more time at the Petersham Inn and the Bald Faced Stag. And there was no chance of an invalid pension now, not since he jobbed the doctor. The regular doctor from Marion Street, who had rushed around to take care of Percy after the incident with the tree, was dead, a casualty of the war. This new doctor had stayed at home 'to look after the women and children'. Joe had his own opinion. But Alice persuaded Joe to see him anyway about the headaches, the pain in his legs and the possibility of a war pension.

'There's nothing wrong with you, cobber.'

'But me head pounds so bad, I start imagining things and I have ta take ta tha whisky!'

'Bit of whisky won't hurt.'

'What about me legs? I can't lift anything. Sometimes I can hardly stand up with the pain!'

'Not much we can do about bayonet wounds. The whisky's still ya best bet.'

'But I can't work with the pain! Coupla days at the most. Ya reckon ya could okay a pension for me, Doc?'

'Just give it time. It's bound to get better.'

'But it's only a piddly ten shillings a week!'

'Yes, but I can't give that to every Digger who walks in the door. It's my job to encourage you back to work. Just think yourself lucky that you came back at all.'

That's when Joe did it. And when he told Alice, she said, 'Good on ya. If I'd been there, I'd have hit him meself!'

He was too proud to go to another doctor and suffered in silence for as long as he could, before his pounding head and throbbing legs sent him reeling to the pub.

When he stuck to beer he was fine, but so much as a sniff of whisky sent him right off.

'The Turks are coming, the Turks are coming!' he yelled and tore down the street, cutting through Tomkin's paddock and making the chickens shriek. 'Get low in the bunker!' he screamed. And he ran like hell until he burst into the empty house.

Alice and the kids were out shopping. Grandpa was smithing.

'The Turks are comin',' he yelled, tossing newspapers across the kitchen floor and setting them alight, with ARMISTICE, WAR OVER and PEACE blazing, as he danced and threw bullets into the leaping flames. 'God Save Our Gracious King,' and there was an intermittent Indian call, the metal pellets ricocheting, reluctant to hit a drunk, and lodging themselves instead in pots and pans, while a ceramic sign, which had been hanging precariously above the wood stove, toppled to the floor and shattered the words 'Bless This House'.

The papers burnt so quickly that the flames had no time to spread and Joe finally collapsed exhausted onto the blackened floor. However, Mrs Sanders from next door had seen the smoke and she'd heard what sounded like a gun going off and had run around the corner to fetch the fire brigade.

Joe woke to the sound of the siren followed by a frantic knocking. He straightened his collar, picked up a saucepan from the floor, stuck it on his head and opened the door.

'We've come to put out the fire!' the fire chief roared.

Joe dipped the saucepan. 'Sorry, cobber. Bum steer. No fire here.'

'Mrs Sanders reported smoke,' the fire chief stalled, as he sniffed and tried to poke his head round the door.

'Sorry, bum steer!'

The fire chief burned red. 'There's a charge for calling: five bob.'

'See Mrs Sanders. Whoever calls pays!' And he shut the door in the fire chief's face.

Mrs Sanders waited on her verandah to warn Alice, when she passed by on her way home. 'He's mad, Alice. I had to get the fire brigade. He could have burnt your house down!'

Alice left the children with Mrs Sanders and with trepidation entered the house. She was relieved to find Joe asleep, but her heart sank when she saw the burnt floor and the dents in her pots and pans. The bullet box, another war relic, lay empty, offering her some solace as she examined the bullet holes in the walls.

The next morning Joe asked what had happened to the kitchen floor and he went off to work perplexed, believing for some strange reason that Alice was turning against him.

Grandpa went off in the cart to buy some timber and returned quickly, to replace the blackened boards.

Kegworth Primary

Miss Nobbs was a boring teacher. Hazel was reading a book hidden beneath her desk, as she usually did, and she got caught. 'Hazel Johnson! Do you think you're too good to join the class? Come up here to the front!' Hazel closed her book and reluctantly obliged. 'Now I want you to face the class and sing a nice little song for us.' And she smiled smugly, knowing that Hazel didn't have much of a voice.

But as Hazel gritted her teeth a tune came to mind. It was a jolly song her father had taught her after she'd heard him singing it with the men down at the Bald Faced Stag. And she soon lost her reluctance in the fun of it, singing with fake gusto as if she was half drunk:

Anzac boys are happy,
the Anzac boys are we.
The Anzac boys are happy
when they're out upon a spree.
They never never quarrel
and they never disagree,
and the password of the Anzac boys
is come and have a drink with me.

The whole class broke into a fit of laughter. Miss Nobbs turned redder and sterner than she normally did. So with arms waving in the air, she screamed at the children to stop laughing and when they couldn't, she turned her steely glare upon Hazel and hurtled a ruler through the air. It whizzed past Hazel and bounced off the blackboard with a loud crack.

In the playground Percy caught up with her. 'Don't ya kn... kn...know Miss Nobbs is a dr...drunk?'

'What?'

'She sneaks sh...sherry from her handbag. We s...seen her!'

'You mean, it wasn't my singing that sent her off?'

'Haven't you ever s...seen her swiggin' that little bottle? She calls it her medicine!'

Hazel had to admit that she hadn't. She had only noticed the way she caned kids when they got something wrong and the way she treated her with contempt whenever she got something right.

The following day, Percy seemed buoyed by the funny incident and scribbled on the blackboard, MISS NOBBS IS UGLY. But he got caught and without warning Miss Nobbs started whacking him. Before Hazel had a chance to grab the cane, Percy fell lifeless out of his seat and onto the floor. His heart just stopped.

A hush swept the room as Hazel stood riveted to the spot and the children backed out, huddled together in the corridor.

Jimmy heard Hazel screaming for him and he ran from his class to find the limp body of his little friend, cradled in his sister's arms. Miss Nobbs was sobbing.

He ran from the classroom, ran and ran, until he reached Percy's house.

When Percy's mum saw the shock etched onto Jimmy's face,

she shook him by the shoulders. 'What's wrong, Jimmy? What's wrong?'

'Miss Nobbs...Miss Nobbs,' he sobbed.

She grabbed his hand and ran with him to the school.

But when she saw Percy's little body and the broken cane lying on the floor, she went berserk. She grabbed Miss Nobbs' umbrella from the stand and whacked her over and over again, until the umbrella broke.

Any other occasion and the children might have yelled support, but they watched silently through the window, as Percy's mum collapsed on the floor and Miss Nobbs sobbed, 'I didn't mean to hurt him. I didn't mean to hurt him.'

She was charged with manslaughter and sent to a hospital.

And it all came out at the trial. She'd been orphaned when she was six years old and a childless uncle and aunt had taken her in. They'd believed in firm discipline and plain dress and while the girl's mind had developed, her heart had remained cold. She'd believed she was unworthy and discouraged people from looking at her, by keeping her facial muscles stony still and her eyes cast down. It seems it had worked throughout her life, until a Fred Weatherby came to teach at Kegworth Primary. He'd taught her how to laugh, and at thirty-five, she'd fallen in love. She'd wanted lots of children, but the engagement had coincided with the war. Fred didn't come back.

And class after class reminded her of the children she would never have and she began to sip sherry to help her forget. But she sipped too much, for too long. Now Percy was dead. She had wanted the children to learn, not love, so that they would never be hurt. Fred had said that it was love, not discipline, that made people feel worthwhile. But he'd left.

•

Miss Nobbs was replaced by a kindly teacher and the class at Kegworth Primary returned to normal.

Hazel loved Miss Morphett from her very first day at Kegworth and Miss Morphett respected Hazel's potential. Miss Morphett loved words the way Hazel loved food. And Miss Morphett didn't think Hazel or any child unworthy.

'*Murmuring*,' she said to the class. 'Isn't that a lovely sounding word?'

The class had called back words like *paradise*, *heaven* and *lollies* in answer to her request for lovely words. And Hazel had to confess that she was about to call out *custard* and *pancakes*!

Miss Morphett made her think more about the words themselves and she began to listen to the sound as much as the meaning. 'You could be a writer, or a teacher, or anything you want to be,' Miss Morphett told her. Hazel appreciated the encouragement, but things had deteriorated at home.

Joe had been fine working the odd hours on Mondays and Tuesdays, but by Wednesdays the hammering had become unbearable. Mr Hopping wouldn't fire him, but out of pride Joe quit.

He took a job helping in a furniture store, mending, shifting and delivering. The owner had come into the pub, in the usual fashion, and asked if anyone needed work.

But Joe's desperation and manly pride drove him to lift things that his shattered legs couldn't withstand. His boss didn't have the heart to sack him so he went to see Alice instead. 'He won't listen to me and I can't bear to watch him in agony. He's killing himself!'

Joe was ultimately left no choice in the matter, and Alice resigned on his behalf.

The next job offer in the pub seemed ideal. He was to drive

a small fruit and vegies cart around Surry Hills, and making a crust depended purely on how much he could sell.

He was fine for a while, but got into trouble again, when he gave fruit away to the poor kids in the neighbourhood. 'I can't stand to see the look on the faces of starvin' kids, when I have to drive right past,' he lamented to his new boss, who gave him one last chance. But when he tied up the cart outside the Surry Hills pub and nipped in for a quick drink, a little girl came by and bit the ends of all the carrots and that was the end of that! But Jimmy had work now and Hazel was looking for a job.

Joe's fits, as Alice referred to them, had worsened and he had turned to attacking Alice. She had hidden these attacks from the others and Joe could never remember what he had done, and vehemently denied everything whenever she tried to discuss it.

Saturday arvos weren't good for Joe. The locals congregated at the pub to listen to the races, the noise escalating. Alice was always happy to wave Grandpa and the children off to the pictures in Marlborough Street, but while Joe desperately tried to stick to beer, the noise and the pain in his thighs became unbearable.

The eagerness of Grandpa and the children to see the latest silent movie and to keep up with the ongoing perils of Pauline assisted Alice in her deception.

And with another Saturday afternoon coming around, they were off to see *The Hayseeds Come to Town*.

'You should be coming, Mum. You wouldn't be able to stop laughing if you did,' Hazel called over her shoulder as they left.

But she hadn't been in the pictures for five minutes when she felt sick in the stomach and wanted nothing but to go home.

'Must have been those peanuts you gulped down,' Grandpa muttered.

Hazel heard the yelling and rushed into the kitchen where her worst fears materialised. Joe was hitting out as Alice tried desperately to back away.

'Not the boys, Sarge, not the boys!' Joe yelled, hitting out in a blind stupor and boxing Alice into a corner.

Hazel grabbed the broom and whacked him from behind. Alice saw his eyes glaze. 'Run, Hazel! Run!' she screamed.

But Hazel stood and glared at him.

Joe glared back with a wild look in his eyes and, twisting, he searched desperately for a weapon.

'Run! Run!' Alice pleaded.

A pot of water simmered on the stove and Hazel felt the full force hitting her legs, before she had time to move or grasp the scalding shock.

She spent the rest of the weekend in bed, shaking, unable to walk or talk, and Alice nursed her.

And when she went to school on Monday, gloomy and wearing dark stockings on such a sunny day, Miss Morphett showed genuine concern, but Hazel clammed up.

Miss Morphett worked frantically to have her included in the special scholarship exam, which was due to take place that Thursday. This was Hazel's final year and the last chance she'd have to help. Kegworth only went up to the Qualifying Certificate and Hazel was sure to gain the top marks. But she was fourteen now and free to leave school. This state scholarship offered hope, with a free place at college and everything paid for.

Miss Morphett had been pleased when Hazel had agreed happily to sit the exam, but the thick stockings that covered her burns had caused an infection and by Thursday the wretched poison had set in.

Hazel and Alice lied at the hospital. 'I knocked the saucepan off the stove,' said Hazel, her head bowed, while Alice stared blankly out of the window. The doctor and nurse were kind, but looked at them both with a quiet air of knowing, which only made Hazel feel a whole lot worse.

The doctor from around in Marion Street had gossiped and now was his chance for revenge. He called on Alice, while Hazel listened, out of sight.

'I came to check if everything's all right. I heard about Hazel's accident.'

'The hospital doctor is treating her.' And Alice attempted to close the door.

'Your husband is suffering from shell-shock. If the whisky's only making things worse, you might have to consider putting him into the asylum for a while.'

'I don't need your advice.' Alice glared.

'His legs don't help. Once gangrene sets in they really should come off!'

But Alice too had been waiting a long time for this opportunity. Unaware that Joe had come in the back door, she drew back her broom and with all the force that she could muster she whacked the startled doctor. He fell backwards. 'Get off my verandah and don't come back!' she yelled, sweeping at him as he scurried down the steps. But when she turned to shut the door, she saw Joe standing there, ghostly white.

'They've locked other blokes up. I heard them talking about it down the pub. Fought for their country and now they're locked up in the asylum!'

'Don't take any notice of him, Joe. He's just a coward.'

'They locked Marty Fergus up, you know, Arthur's cousin.'

'I wouldn't let anyone do that to you. Now sit down, while I make a pot of tea.'

Joe followed her into the kitchen. 'They don't letcha out, ya know, not once you're in there!'

'Well, you don't have to worry. The war did this to you. I'm not about to forget that.'

He took the teapot from her hands and put it on the table. 'I don't want anyone taking me legs off either, Alice. I don't want me legs off! Don't let anyone do that, will ya?'

'Of course not. Now sit down and let me pour the tea.'

'I don't want to be just a trunk, stuck in some asylum.'

'Look, Joe, you suffered for all of us. I won't ever forget that. I know what the war has done to you. But you have to promise to stay off the whisky.'

'I'll stick to beer. I promise. It's beer from now on in. You'll see!'

Hazel leant back against the wall of her room. She had heard that before.

But he stuck to his promise, with a little help from his mates, and, with the odd job here and there, the fits subsided. The nightmares and terrible pain remained, but when Joe was just Joe, he was the same gentle man Alice had married.

Hazel forgave her father, but after missing the scholarship exam, she never felt quite the same way about him again. The words of her mother went round and round in her head. 'The war did it to him. The war did it to him. The war did it to him.' And she thought bitterly, *and how about what the war has done to us?*

FIVE

THE AFTERMATH

'I've got a job at the Nestle's factory!'

'But, Hazel, you finished the year as Dux of the school!'

Hazel babbled on over the top of her, understanding Miss Morphett's disappointment. 'It's good money and I'll be home in plenty of time to help Mum get tea.'

Miss Morphett sighed while she babbled on, frustrated by Hazel's sense of duty.

'It's right by the water. All I have to do is catch the Abbotsford tram.'

'But all you'll be doing is packing chocolates all day!'

'Everyone says it's like one big happy family down there. Volleyball, ferry rides, even an annual ball. And you're allowed to eat as many chocolates as you like!'

Miss Morphett tried to laugh, but all that she could manage was a wan smile.

She was only partly listening, because something wonderful was about to be lost to the world. Hazel had sensibility and intuition, beyond that of most fourteen-year-olds, but Miss Morphett tried to look on the bright side.

The following week she gave Hazel a book of Australian verse, with glossy illustrations of billabongs, gum trees, kookaburras and possums. The inscription simply read:

To Hazel
Good Luck at Nestle's
From Miss Morphett, Kegworth Primary.

Hazel bitterly resented her lost opportunity. A door had blinked open and closed. A glimpse. And she had let Miss Morphett down. 'No good crying over spilt milk, Hazel!' Her mother's response had sunk deep. She did cry, inside. Spilt milk? How could she explain?

She climbed slowly each morning onto the Abbotsford tram and stuck her head into a continuous story, losing herself in its pages, oblivious of the regular passengers, the guard and the driver. They could have been a million miles away. But each time the guard stood beside her and gave a polite cough, everyone laughed as she jumped from her seat and almost dropped her book, while the guard held her stop.

However, despite the disappointment, a whole new world opened up. Floor supervisors, conveyer belts, mass efficiency, mass production and mass lunches, in perfectly kept, palatial grounds.

Red and white flags flapped from a private wharf and green lawns greeted chugging ferries, while cabbage palms with trunks as majestic as giraffe necks fanned the lunching workers, and rose gardens perfumed the air from the stone gate entrance to the far sea wall. A place of beauty, where efficiency brought reward.

The supervisor approached Hazel with his clipboard, and placed a pencilled tick next to her name with the letters 'FP'—fast packer—and "FR", ferry ride.

Nothing was ever sure with her father's fits, so to save any further disappointment, she decided not to mention the ferry ride at home, until the day actually arrived.

'Ferry ride? What ferry ride?' Alice called, as Hazel hurried out the door with her sun hat tucked under her arm.

'I'll tell you all about it when I get home!'

As she waited by the wharf with the other fast packers, the supervisor introduced the Nestle's photographer and they were all asked to lie down on the embankment, on giant letters marked out in white chalk. A human word evolved, as crisp white uniforms stood out on the green grass. NESTLE. There was a click and a flash, then the word fell apart as the fast packers ran onto the waiting ferry.

Hazel had made friends at Nestle's easily and enjoyed a sense of security that she hadn't felt since the days before the war.

The following day, as she returned from a timed toilet break, she took a moment to scan the factory floor. The supervisor glanced up, checking, yet somehow reassuring. But as Hazel looked away, a deep sense of loss swept up the spiralling stairwell, snap-freezing her fingers to the metal rail. The schism between herself and her father had bared itself, across the whirring security of conveyer belts. A large chocolate family had appeared before her and she watched as babies were wrapped in shimmering blankets and placed in paper cradles; tiny children packed into boxed cots, for transfer into treys, zacs, deeners, and quids, while the supervisor with his pencil and clipboard smiled approval and ticked the snuggest cots.

The strong smell of chocolate wafted up and reminded her of swirling tobacco smoke. She peered over the rail into the sea of workers moving in waves and she longed for a past which had surreptitiously sailed away.

She had teamed up with Peggy and Josephine, who were a lot of fun, but not in a silly way like some of the boys and girls at Nestle's. Peggy and Josephine were respectively a year and two years older than her.

Peggy was as vivacious as she was curvaceous, with wide eyes that ran after life. She found it difficult to keep still and the conveyer belt had a hard time keeping up with her. But she was as caring as she was fun-loving, with auburn hair that spun off in all directions and green eyes that pried into and absorbed everything. She wanted to understand everything and everyone, not in a gossipy fashion, but so that she could help life roll along its merry way. 'Flux. That's what I believe in,' she would say, whenever a subject got too serious. Peggy wanted to keep moving and, although her feet were planted firmly on the ground, her head moved so rapidly from side to side that Hazel and Josephine would joke. 'One day, Peggy, your head is going to spin right off!' And she would nod in all directions and laugh. Clothes fell free and easy on her, because her face held the attention, it seemed, so that her body could just float on by.

Josephine had a figure that was nicely rounded in relation to her height, making her neither willowy nor squat. And whichever way she turned she appeared refined, and spoke with a gentle lilt to her voice. Soft curls of mousy brown played around her ears, while tender hazel eyes shone like gemstones. Unlike Peggy, Josephine had a steady gaze and she preferred to sit and listen, wandering off in her mind and coming back when she felt like it. 'Are you listening, Josephine?' Hazel and Peggy would prod her, if they thought she hadn't come back when they needed a response. 'I'm always with you,' she would answer and look away into the distance before surprising them with infinite knowledge of what had just been discussed, and an added comment thrown in for good measure. No matter what Josephine wore, she always managed to look dignified, yet somehow sensuous.

Hazel bristled with all the intensity of a poet, hiding disappointment and pain with a certain cheekiness, while enjoying the blessed side of life. To her, life was a story and there was always somebody at the factory who reminded her of some character or other in a book, walking straight out of a Henry Lawson, or a Steele Rudd story, and there were times when she'd slip up and call them by their fictional name.

Nature held a similar fascination for her, causing Josephine and Peggy to laugh when she cried, 'Watch out for that ant,' while the thankful insect scurried past, waving its back leg. And they would shake their heads in disbelief as ladybirds, bees and grasshoppers always seemed to land on her and not them, while they ate their lunch in the Nestle's garden. 'Ladybird, ladybird, fly away home. Your house is on fire and your children are gone.' This never failed to send the tiny spotted orange creatures on their way after they had crawled the full length of Hazel's arm or leg and criss-crossed her sandwiches. Hazel explained that although the words sounded cruel, a ladybird would visit all day if you let it. Josephine and Peggy respected her fascination with crawling insects, relieved that the bees in the garden respected it too, and left them to enjoy their lunch, while they buzzed over Hazel. But her stories of bull-ants and spiders left them brushing at their hair and constantly checking between their legs and on the grass, to Hazel's mischievous delight.

Hazel was petite with piercing black eyes and black curls that fell over her brow. The ability to slip in and out of the world, bursting forth and disappearing, never failed to intrigue Josephine and Peggy. She was inward and shy, yet fiery and bold; quiet, but vivacious. 'She's in flux!' Peggy explained, when Hazel suddenly reappeared after floating off, while Josephine called her 'the magician'.

The three girls became good friends and spent Saturdays together. They would take a ferry ride, swirling their parasols, and pretend they were rich girls snubbing rich boys from the north side of the harbour, or they would take the tram to Bondi Beach and splash about like tomboys. It was a penny from Leichhardt to the city and a penny from the city to Bondi. They called themselves *the trio* and went everywhere together.

Hazel, like Jimmy, gave a substantial proportion of her wage to Alice, but she still had enough left over to enjoy herself. It only cost the tram fare to visit the Art Gallery, or the ferry fare to sit on the cliff at Watsons Bay and watch for dolphins, sharks, or a possible whale.

Hazel talked a lot about her brother Jimmy and she laughed about the time he had put a halfpenny on the tramtrack so that it would be flattened out and made as big as a penny. Peggy and Josephine laughed too, but more from an interest in meeting Jimmy than from listening to the stories.

Although Jimmy and Hazel had always played separately there remained a strong bond between them and Jimmy became more and more protective of her, especially since the unspeakable burns. He was gentle, yet athletic and strong, with the quietness of Grandpa.

She began to take Peggy and Josephine to watch him play football at Leichhardt oval, but soon turned away from this escapade. She wasn't as comfortable around boys as she had been. Some of this was due to her teenage years, but most to a deep disappointment in her father.

She hated violence but, even more, she hated the way it was accepted in boys and suppressed in girls. She wouldn't accept Peggy's explanation that boys were somehow more prone to cruel acts. 'Snips and snails and puppy dog tails, that's what little boys are made of,' she chanted.

Why then had Hazel felt an overbearing desire to hit her father after she missed the scholarship exam and why had she used such force to whack him with the broom, when she had found him hurting her mother? 'Girls are taught *not* to hit, while boys are taught *how to*,' she said. 'That's why Jimmy's got boxing gloves and I haven't. It's got nothing to do with snips and snails!'

Hazel came from a strong boxing line. Grandpa had boxed, while even obese Uncle Bert had served his time in the ring. Joe used to box and Jimmy did too, so the rules of the ring were well known in her house. 'Never hit a man while he's down; no hitting below the belt; good, clean punches; wait for the bell…' Hazel could say it all in her sleep.

'Well I think it's nice that girls aren't as cruel as boys, wherever it comes from,' Josephine laughed, as she put her arm through Hazel's and tugged her teasingly in the direction of the boys, who were standing on the corner waiting for them to pass, George Cousins, as usual, standing out.

Although Alice had become an expert at covering up for Joe, Hazel sensed the telltale tension and guilt of her father. She wished that her mother didn't love her father quite so much and that she could turn around and hit him back, or at least let *her* do it. And she never felt wicked for thinking that way. But Alice continued to cling desperately to the past and blame the war for their sad predicament.

'It's not his fault, Hazel. It was the war! He did his duty: God save the King and all that. Now, for better or worse, richer or poorer, I have to do mine!'

Despite her tone, Hazel wondered why her mother seemed eternally grateful to her father for marrying her and she mumbled to herself, 'That's all a woman can do: accept things, when she hasn't been taught how to box.'

Her mother was beautiful and Grandpa still called her his pretty princess. Her hair was greying but her black eyes shone and her face still lit up when she told stories. And her laugh still had that funny lilt to it.

Hazel found some things hard to understand, but despite this difficulty, she had enjoyed the attention of George Cousins and other boys at the local dances in the Petersham Town Hall, even if she did shy away from anything more than friendly flirtation. That is, until Eddy Palmer happened to cross her path.

Peggy had run off and married the Nestle's supervisor and Jimmy had started up a little farm out at Chipping Norton. The Charleston had arrived and Hazel and Josephine were caught up in the craze.

Hazel had set a gramophone near the back door, allowing plenty of room to dance in the yard and, with the music blaring, they practised the Charleston over and over, hoping to perfect it for the next local dance and especially for the upcoming Nestle's Ball.

Along with the dance came the image. Cropped hair shorter than any girl had dared before, with mothers sewing fancy dresses copied from slick American magazines. Daring hemlines hugging knees. Flowing scarves. And long strings of shiny beads.

Hazel and Josephine sashayed about the yard; hips, heels and spangles swinging in all directions, to the silent amusement of Grandpa. Hazel's twentieth birthday was coming up and it was time to swing!

The girls failed to see Jimmy and Eddy Palmer arrive. Jim winked to his friend and they stood watching quietly, while Hazel and Josephine shook their beaded dresses faster and faster, prancing and dancing, laughing and posing. Jim watched Josephine as intently as Eddy watched Hazel.

Eddy had brown curly hair, larrikin eyes and a sportsman's physique, more wiry than muscular because he was six feet tall. He was one of those lifesavers from down at Coogee Beach, a good footballer and cricketer, an all-round Aussie sportsman. But he had a boyish shyness around females. He was used to muckin' around with the blokes and the sight of Hazel in all this strange finery, giggling and wiggling, left him completely dumbstruck.

Jim had met Eddy through the cricket club. He was jovial and honest and a bloody good cricketer and Jim had wasted no time talking him into a joint farm venture.

He had managed to check Alice's wellbeing by dropping round each week with a little extra money for her, but he'd found it increasingly hard to speak to his father.

Grandpa worked hard, but there wasn't much money around and he accepted barters more often than not. He would come home loaded up with fruit and vegetables, or fresh bread and cakes. 'Tell them no more cakes, Grandpa!' Alice pleaded, knowing it was to no avail, as the bread bin spewed cream buns across the table.

Hazel had sensed somebody watching, but spinning around too fast she tripped on her dangling scarf, and sprawling forward a good few feet, her hands twisted in beads, she landed hard on her knees, right at Eddy Palmer's feet.

Instinctively he bent down and with one clean sweep, unceremoniously hoisted her to her feet, causing Josie and Jimmy to break into laughter.

Hazel snatched her scarf from Eddy's clumsy hand and turned on Jimmy. 'Don't you know how to knock?'

This only made Jimmy laugh all the more. 'But we're in the backyard!'

Hazel pranced off to her room without waiting to be introduced and she stayed there until Eddy left. She could hear Josephine and Jimmy laughing in the living room and she was intrigued by the stranger's voice. It was somehow carefree and drawling with fun. 'Very sure of himself,' she scoffed into her book of English verse.

Jimmy knocked on her door before walking in to kiss her goodbye. Hazel was too ashamed to look him in the eye. Her unusual burst of rudeness had surprised her, but Jimmy seemed to understand. 'You looked smashing in that get-up.' And as he turned to walk out the door, he whispered with a twinkle in his eye, 'I think Eddy fancies you.'

Hazel knelt on her bed and watched them head for the gate. Josie was chatting gaily but it was Eddy who had her eye. He had a sort of lanky walk, swaying as if he was on the ready for something, about to clean bowl someone, or run onto a footy field with that head-down confidence football players have and she watched him saunter ahead of Jimmy and Josie and hoist himself easily into the driver's seat of the cart. Jimmy kissed Josie on the cheek, but Hazel barely noticed.

Eddy took the reins and with a click of his mouth the horses turned towards Elswick Street and just when she thought it was safe to lean further out the window to watch the cart, he looked back.

Josie jumped onto Hazel's bed. 'Jimmy kissed me! Didya see? You should've come out, Hazel! Eddy's nice, don't you think?'

Hazel didn't answer at once, but she promised herself that she wouldn't behave so rudely next time.

And a few weeks later on a warm Friday evening, she hurried home from work, excited at the prospect of seeing Eddy again at the local dance the following night. But as she skipped down the side path and rounded the corner into the backyard, she stopped in her tracks.

'Get down! Get down in that bunker!' Joe was pushing Alice backwards, towards the Moreton Bay fig.

'Dad!' she yelled. 'What are you doing?'

At the sound of her voice, he gave Alice one almighty shove and pushed her flying over the garden seat, which upturned on top of her.

'Stay in that bunker!' he yelled, before rushing at Hazel and tackling her to the ground, her nose whacking against a rock. 'Got 'im, Sarge!'

Alice scrambled to her feet.

'Stay in that bunkerrr!' he yelled, running towards her. But as he glanced back at Hazel, Alice hid behind the tree.

Losing sight of her, he swirled about and fell against the chook pen. The gate flew open and chooks shrieked into the yard. He gave chase and caught one by the neck. 'Shoosh!' he whispered into its startled eyes, as he watched the others squawking and running out onto the street. 'Get back into ya bunkers! Get back here, ya mugs!' he yelled after them.

But his desperate shouting only made the chooks squawk louder and run faster down the street. 'We gotta get water, cobber,' he whispered into the grappling chook's head, but it slipped from his hands and slithered to his feet. Horrified, he turned the dead bird over in the dirt. 'C'mon, matey, wake up. Please, wake up!'

Hazel had remained still, half in shock and half in an effort not to antagonise her father. But as she brushed tears from her eyes, he came towards her.

'It's all right, Dad. I'm not dead,' she whispered in fright, as he bent over her and patted her arm.

He shrugged towards the limp bird. 'But our cobber is! Our little cobber's dead!' And he broke down and cried.

Alice came from behind the tree and righted the garden seat. 'Hazel, help me get him over here.' And they sat him down on it.

Then, half dazed, Hazel rounded up the chooks and put the dead bird on a little heap of hay behind the shed, while Alice calmed Joe, holding him to her breast until he fell asleep.

Mrs Sanders, who had heard the commotion, climbed back down from the fence.

With gentle persuasion, Josephine had managed to coerce Jimmy into bringing Eddy along to the next local dance. And Eddy had agreed to come, but jokingly told Jim to tell Josie he wasn't really interested in sissy things and apart from body-surfing, that included anything that didn't involve a bat or a ball. He knew that she would relay this to Hazel.

Hazel had been looking forward to the dance. She was curious to see the extent of his defensive teasing. But now she would remain in the dark. On Saturday she woke with two black eyes. Grandpa had risen early and taken off to do some work at La Perouse. Alice woke late, feeling drained by the previous evening's experience. She thought it odd that Hazel's bedroom door was closed and there was no sign of life. She knocked softly and went in. Hazel was sitting up in bed, gazing out the window, but when Alice caught sight of her daughter's face, she reeled back.

'I can't remember, but I think I hit my nose on a rock,' Hazel said mechanically.

Alice was silent.

'I'll just stay in my room over the weekend. Tell everyone I'm sick.'

Alice didn't answer.

'With a bit of luck I'll be right for work on Monday.'

Alice walked to the window and stared out. Hazel's eyes were black and purple.

She saw the look on her mother's face. 'If anyone finds out, I'll just say I fell on a rock.'

'I'll bring you a nice breakfast,' Alice answered softly. And she returned with a tray lined with her best white lace cloth. A pale pink hibiscus rested on a voile serviette, while steam drifted upwards from fried eggs. Hot toast melted wads of butter and the teapot offered a coy arm, as Alice handed her the tray. 'I'm sorry about the dance,' she muttered. And left.

Hazel rested the tray on her knees and savoured the comfort of a hot breakfast. But her head hurt and, as she wriggled about, trying to get comfortable, the hibiscus gaped at her like a sick throat with a raging tonsil.

Later in the morning Joe knocked on Hazel's door and waited. She put her head into the pillow and pretended to be asleep. The door opened slowly and she heard him put something heavy down on the dressing table. He picked up the tray and closed the door quietly behind him.

It was the gramophone and the Charleston record. Alice had told him Hazel was feeling pretty sick and once more he had no recollection of the previous night's fit.

And once more Hazel had pangs of deep disappointment, and once more there was no one to hate. All there was was war; a war that refused to go away.

SIX

THE CHARLESTON

'I'm sorry, Josie. Hazel has come down with something.'

'But she was all right yesterday!'

Alice lowered her eyes.

'Is she asleep?' Josie persisted.

'Yes,' Alice lied.

'She did say it was all right for me to ask Jim to bring Eddy along. Maybe I shouldn't have fussed so much.'

'It's not your fault she's sick, Josie!'

'But I've mucked things up good and proper! Eddy will think she's just snubbing him again and Jimmy's goin' ta feel like a ratbag, and it's all my doin'!'

'You're worrying too much. Jim and Eddy will understand. It's bad enough that Hazel can't go to the dance without you letting it muck up *your* night!'

'It just doesn't feel right to go, with Hazel lying there sick.'

'But you're all ready and you look beautiful.'

Alice was beginning to think she'd never get the dear girl out of the house. 'Hazel will feel terrible if you miss the dance because of her. And what about Eddy? It will look worse if you're both missing, and you can't let Jimmy down: he's expecting you.'

'I suppose if I don't go and explain, Jimmy will be worried and Eddy will think Hazel isn't interested at all. Then I'll never be able to get Jimmy to talk him into coming to the Nestle's Ball!'

Alice heaved a sigh of relief. 'So that's your plan, is it?'

'Well he is nice, don't you think? And he's Jimmy's best friend. You do like him, don't you?' Alice smiled and nodded. 'I think Hazel likes him, although she did get sick. You don't think that she got sick because of my meddling, do you?'

Alice clasped Josie's hand. 'Hazel didn't get sick because of you. It's not your fault. She was looking forward to the dance, but it can't be helped and it's no good crying over spilt milk, now, is it? I want you to go to the dance and I want you to have a bonzer time.'

Josie was like another daughter to Alice. An only child, with her father a casualty of the war, she'd spent a lot of time at the Johnson house. To have both girls hurt by Joe's warring filled Alice with deep regret. She tried not to show it. 'When Hazel's better, you'll be able to mag all about Eddy and the dance. And you can mag to me about it too!'

Josie sat in her limp lemon dress, the night lights swimming in her hazel-eyed sadness. How could she Charleston without her best friend? Joe felt her disappointment, as he guided the horse and cart, the *clip clop* settling into a steady pace, the big horse, with its ambling rump, hypnotising the two into silence.

She arrived at the Town Hall before Jim and Eddy, entered

with dread to wait, and hoped that Eddy would cop the excuse and that Jimmy would cop the embarrassment. A sensitive apology without dwelling too much, that would be the best way to gain Eddy's trust. She glanced towards the door and felt like a dill, standing all alone, twisting her long string of beads, as she'd twisted Jimmy's arm.

Despondent, she accepted a dance and waltzed away on the indifference of the one, two, three, one, two, three and failed to see Jim and Eddy arrive.

Jim stood transfixed in the doorway. He'd never seen Josie look more beautiful. It wasn't the colour of her dress, or the cuteness of her new bob cut; it was the way she floated in some other realm, where nobody could touch her. His Adam's apple slid slowly to the top of his neck.

Eddy had seen her, too, but only fleetingly. He moved into the hall casually, searched the sea of swirling faces, while Jim headed for the dance floor and politely cut in on Josie's partner. Eddy grinned as he saw them embrace and sway and whirl with the music, deep in conversation. But his grin faded when the music stopped and Jim approached him.

'Look after Josie for me, mate. I just have to check on something!' And he hurried off.

Eddy listened good-naturedly as Josie attempted to explain Hazel's absence. 'She was really looking forward to tonight. She loves dancing, especially the Charleston, and she was really looking forward to meeting *you* again!'

He looked away and said nothing, while Josie struggled for words. 'She, umm, asked me to apologise to you, that is, if you were here, because she didn't mean to be rude you know, the day you came to the house, she, umm, she just felt silly, falling over like that, in front of a stranger.'

Josie wouldn't normally infringe on Hazel's privacy this way, but she knew her friend well enough to be sure that in this predicament she would understand. And, given Jimmy's strange burst of anxiety, she tried to distract Eddy from his hurried exit, while dissuading him, in the light of Hazel's previous snub, from thinking that Hazel wasn't interested at all.

He didn't answer, but as the music blared, he gave an awkward grin and whisked her onto the dance floor. She was bowled over. Eddy Palmer could Charleston!

Joe and Alice were in the kitchen enjoying hot cocoa and poker. Grandpa had walked around to the billiard parlour on Parramatta Road to play dominoes, while behind the closed door of her room, Hazel sipped from the tin mug of cocoa that Alice had taken in to her, the warm liquid running down her cold throat as she watched the steam rise. The warmth was the deciding factor. She would read the story to the end, before going to sleep.

She became lost in the pages. She could do that: step right into a story, move about with the characters and chat to them while smelling flowers in vases and manure in paddocks. Not to intervene in the story was the most difficult part and she thought of a way to write Eddy in. She imagined words to suit a larrikin and she put herself in too, a petite-fleur type trying to keep up with a gangling gait and she started to chuckle, right in the middle of a sad part.

But there was another male voice outside the book, and outside her door. It was Jimmy. She stuck her head under the pillow and feigned sleep. 'Ya there, Haze?' And she heard the door creak open.

She was lying on top of the eiderdown and instinctively he looked for any telltale bruises or marks. 'You awake, Haze?'

She didn't answer. He was about to leave, when he noticed the steam rising from the mug. He listened to her breathing. It was more of a hollow gasp, too rapid for deep sleep, and he watched the pillow rise and fall in a sequence more suggestive of concealment than contentment. 'You awake?' he asked again and bent over her. She didn't reply, so he yanked the pillow from her to a startled gasp and flailing arms as she tried to snatch it back, two eyes confronting him, black as coal.

'I fell on a rock. It was an accident.'

She'd said it too quickly. 'An accident my foot! I'm not leavin' till you tell me what happened.'

'I fell on a rock! I told ya!'

'What rock? And what were you doing, Miss dainty shoes, Miss Charleston, to fall like that?'

'I just tripped, like when Eddy was here.'

'What? On a scarf?'

'No! I fell on a rock!'

'Where? What rock?'

Hazel was becoming flustered. She knew Jimmy was suspicious, and it was almost impossible to lie to him. 'All *right*! But I did fall on a rock. I was trying to help Mum. Dad was having one of his fits and I tripped, that's all. It's just a couple of black eyes. It was an accident. It doesn't really matter, Jimmy! It's no good crying about it.'

Alice sat nervously in the kitchen. She could hear the voices. Jim had insisted on seeing Hazel and there was very little she could do to stop him. She looked across at Joe. His hearing had never been the same since the war. He sipped his cocoa and stared at the cards in his hands, moved one from the centre of the fan to the outer, and looked up triumphantly as Jim appeared. 'Three kings and a pair of aces. How 'bout that, son! First full hand all night, eh, Alice?'

A deliberate swipe with the back of Jim's hand sent the cards flying. 'I'll give ya a full hand!'

Joe's brow creased in anger. 'What didya do that for?'

'Why don't you pick on someone your own size!'

'What are you talkin' about?'

'He doesn't remember anything. It was an accident!' Alice pleaded.

'What are you goin' on about?'

'What did you do to Hazel?'

'What's he talkin' about, Alice? You said Hazel was sick.'

'It was an accident, Joe.'

'What? What was an accident?'

'Hazel's in there with two black eyes and missed the dance because of your lousy fit!'

'I don't remember no fit.'

'It was just an accident, Joe. It's done now!'

Jimmy tapped a bruise on the back of his mother's neck. 'Was that an accident too?'

Alice touched her neck and felt the pain. She struggled for the right words, but Jimmy was already thrusting a pair of boxing gloves at Joe and pulling a second pair on himself. Hazel almost fell into the room. 'What's all the shouting?' she demanded, her swollen eyes bulging at them.

'I'm sick of it, Hazel! I'm sick of the fits, I'm sick of the excuses and I'm sick of the war. Only cowards hurt women!'

'Coward?' yelled Joe, his confusion turning to fury. 'Coward? I'm an ANZAC!'

'You hit women: your own wife and daughter!' Jimmy yelled.

The stench of death began to seep up Joe's nostrils and he felt the sun belting on his neck, as he tugged at the gloves and clambered down the back steps. And over by the paspalum, the dust spewed up years of hate and grief.

Alice shuffled in between the two of them. 'Stop it! Stop this nonsense this minute! Do you hear me? Stop it!'

Hazel tried to pull her from the flying punches. 'Dad! Jimmy! Watch out for Mum!'

But the rules of the ring took over in the slam of each punch, in each cold glare, jabbing and sniping, war erupting and exploding, men fighting until one of them went down.

Hazel ran after Jimmy, only to see him gallop away on the big, red stallion. She watched him ride bareback like Grandpa, leaning forward, close to the horse's neck, as he disappeared into Elswick Street. She longed to run after him. She wanted to join in the dance. But a deep pang tore her back. Alice was kneeling over Joe.

Jim had found it unbearable, living at Seale Street, since the scalding of Hazel's legs. Like his sister, he had come to accept his father's warring, the shell-shock, the fits. And living in Grandpa's house had made it difficult to intervene. It was only a shack at Chipping Norton, but it had given him just the right space. He hugged the warm neck of the stallion tight, his tears mingling with horse sweat. He had finally taken a stand. But he felt like dung.

Alice put Joe to bed and the hum of the cicadas grew louder. It had started up with the fight. Now the deafening drone sounded like a fight crowd yelling for more. Hazel pushed her face deep into the pillow, into soft feathers, searching for a time before war, and she fell into a dream. She saw a Sacred Kingfisher in flight and high up in a tree she saw a black crow.

Jim searched the dance floor for Josie. The war had to end.

He caught sight of Eddy chatting with some of the blokes down the back of the hall. And then he saw Josie making her way towards him. 'Is Hazel all right?' she asked anxiously. He nodded and led her onto the dance floor.

As the dance ended, they joined Eddy at the long, wooden table, where tea and fresh scones were being served. Hot tea was poured from the huge metal teapot into large tin mugs, while a porcelain plate was piled with the soft white scones. Josie took one from the centre and watched the crumbs fall onto the delicate, yellow posies that looped a lacy gilt edge. Eddy broke the silence.

'A beer ud be nice!'

Jim laughed.

'Is Hazel all right then?' he ventured.

Jim nodded. 'Just a pain in the gut, that's all.'

'She'll be fine tomorrow, then,' said Josie, before she realised how it must have sounded to a man who might still suspect that he'd been stood up.

Eddy disappeared into the night, moonlight on the pale grey mane of his horse, his dark shirt billowing out into nowhere. He patted the mare's neck and sucked in his cheek 'Giddyup, girl!'

Jim's stallion became restless. He eased the reins and the horse gave a slight rear back. 'Easy, cobber.' Josie clung to Jim's waist as he pressed his heels into the horse's round belly.

Taking Josie home had made him happy in more ways than one. Most importantly, there was the kiss after he lifted her down from the horse, her inquisitive eyes meeting his and the smell of freshly cut grass in the air, as natural as the girl he was holding.

'Yes!' he had answered when she asked him about the Nestle's Ball. 'Yes again,' when she made him promise to bring Eddy.

'And no, Eddy doesn't like to dance. Lots of crushed chalk for a slippery floor, my persistence and his interest in Hazel got him to Charleston, so don't go letting Hazel think he's a tap dancer, or somethin'!' Secondly, Jim was happy to ride back to Chipping Norton alone, without having to explain to Eddy his need to check on Hazel.

Eddy kept his distance from Hazel after that, but to please Jim he agreed to partner her to the Nestle's Ball.

When the night of the ball arrived, Grandpa couldn't hide his fascination as the girls paraded, swirling and shaking cheeky fringes on sequined dresses, candlelight catching the sparkles and pushing dull secrets and dull furniture back against the wall.

Alice came in from the kitchen. The sparkles reminded her of the harbour, the sunlight tossed onto its glittering surface, and she saw once more that diamond catwalk.

'You look like a princess!' Grandpa whispered, the tears welling in his eyes.

'A princess?' Hazel laughed.

'Hooroo,' called Joe, pulling Grandpa towards the door.

Alice had wanted them out of the house before Jim arrived. Joe knew it, but Grandpa didn't.

'Where are they off to?' Josie asked.

'Let's put the gramophone on,' Hazel interrupted.

'Just down to the billiard parlour, for a game of cards,' Alice answered quietly.

BILLIARDS. The yellow letters faded into the old blue timber of the hall facing Parramatta Road. Inside, rusty tin signs—ZAC A GAME OR TREY A BET—dangled over two worn billiard tables. Men leant against the walls, smoked and watched players aiming cues, while at the far end of the hazy room two young scallywags, no more than twelve, leant on the bacca counter, blew smoke rings into the air and coaxed the bacca man to judge the twirling rings. A blue-speckled dog belonging to the red-freckled boy cocked his head and watched too. Old packs of cards and beer-stained dominoes were neatly stacked on small tables.

Sanders was shuffling cards and he looked up as the two men approached. 'Hey, Joe, Jack, wanna game?'

Back at Seale Street, Hazel and Josie were teaching Alice the Charleston. The record spun round and round on the turntable, while Hazel glanced at the door, half expecting her father to burst in and spoil things.

But by the time Jim and Eddy arrived, the three women were singing at the top of their voices. It was an attack of nervous excitement in the girls and a much needed release for Alice.

Jim smiled at the sight of the three most important women in his life enjoying themselves. He had developed a strong, manly demeanour and it caught Alice off guard, as she greeted him with a motherly hug. Eddy impressed her too. He had a rough edge, but a genuine warmth. And as she watched Jim and Hazel wandering down the path with Josie and Eddy, her heart swelled with happiness and pride, and she withdrew, contented, into the empty house.

The Nestle's auditorium buzzed with excitement. Factory workers dressed up to the nines sang in nasal chorus, 'Every Little Breeze Seems to Whisper Louise' with such terrible mock French accents that Horrie Dawes, the bandleader, burst into muffled laughter, and, putting his hands over his ears, yelled out his familiar call, 'What is it we've all been waiting for?'

'The Charleston!' the cry went up, and almost brought the roof down.

Trumpets and saxophones blasted the revellers and the energy fairly bounced off the walls. Swinging his sax, Horrie began to Charleston on stage and with the trumpeters tapping and jigging, the excitement spilt onto the floor, swirling the fringes on flappers' dresses and causing men's jackets to twist and tail out; all the colours of the rainbow kaleidoscoping around the room, the ladies twirling long beads, glorying in the complex moves of legs and knees; the men rejoicing, while conveyer belts, left idle, shook and waited.

Hazel thought Eddy was heaps of fun, while Eddy began to think that girls were all right, after all. Jim and Josie smiled, pleased with themselves. 'Glad you came, cobber?' said Jim, tapping Eddy on the shoulder.

'Beats dominoes!'

The Ball finally ended and the weary stars spilled out into the night. Eddy and Jim escorted the girls back to Leichhardt and then caught the last tram to Coogee, where they were staying. The following day Josie and Hazel were to join them, for lunch and a swim at the beach.

SEVEN

SWIMMING AT COOGEE

The Palmer house was in Long Bay Road, on the way to the gaol, about halfway between Coogee and Maroubra. It was small and neat with a narrow front and back yard, but a wide side yard that looked down over the ocean at Lurline Bay.

When Hazel and Josie arrived, Eddy proudly introduced them to his parents and the excitement of the previous evening carried on over lunch. Mr and Mrs Palmer enjoyed the happy chatter and were curious about this new dance craze.

'My goodness, fancy that,' Mrs Palmer smiled. 'Short dresses at a ball!'

'And men with two-toned shoes,' laughed Mr Palmer. 'What is the world coming to?'

'Josie and Hazel looked smashing, didn't they, Eddy?' Jim said with a twinkle in his eye.

Josie blushed and dropped her fork and Hazel bumped her head on the table as she tried to retrieve it.

Eddy laughed. 'What do ya reckon about those long bead things, Jim, flingin' about? Thought I was gunna lose me head. Had to keep duckin'!'

Everyone laughed. And nobody refused when Mrs Palmer brought out the homemade apple pie, with its decorative pastry leaves, smaller ones set around the outside and two larger ones in the middle. It had come straight from the oven and a jug of hot custard sat steaming on the table.

After the noisy lunch Hazel helped Mrs Palmer wash the dishes, while the others laughed and chatted on the verandah.

Hazel liked Mrs Palmer and felt comfortable with her. She particularly liked her pride in her family. And Mrs Palmer liked Hazel because she'd never seen her son so talkative and happy.

'An ancestor of Mr Palmer's was a purser with the First Fleet.'

'Really?' answered Hazel, her interest rising. 'What happened to him?'

'He became a commissar for the government. His property stretched from the water's edge at Woolloomooloo practically back to Surry Hills. There's a street named after him!'

'Oh, whereabouts?'

'It runs along the back of the Art Gallery. You know the one?'

Hazel's mind drifted. Before shopping at Broadway, her mother would often take her and Jimmy down through the park to the Art Gallery, arriving as the tall doors were swung open. And having the gallery practically to themselves, they would rush to their favourite painting. It was always there, until one Saturday they ran on ahead of their mother and found it missing. Hazel smiled at the memory. Frantically, she and Jimmy had run about the gallery, searching up and down the long corridors, and, rounding a corner, they had run smack-bang into Jock, their favourite guard. 'Oh, it's you two scallywags again!'

'Our picture's gone, Jock!' And they waved their arms towards the wall, both talking at once.

He knew which one they meant. 'It's been taken away for a good dust,' he assured them, and smiled to himself as Hazel walked off in a huff, calling back over her shoulder.

'Well it had better be clean by the next time we come!'

'Yeah!' added Jimmy.

'I'll get onto it right away,' he called after them.

'I don't like the other one. It's ordinary, got no story!' Hazel scoffed, before she disappeared around a corner, with Jimmy swaggering after her.

Silently Jock agreed. Compared to George Lambert's *Across the Black Soil Plains* with its thirteen draught horses tugging a leaning wagon through thick, sucking mud, the replacement was *ordinary*. He understood the children's fascination with the bold browns sliding around the piled-up goods wagon, as it listed precariously, the wagon master trying desperately to right it. He'd often felt like getting into the picture to help.

He'd witnessed many times a child's eye seeing things that adults didn't. Hazel and Jimmy had never failed to capture his attention as they played happily alongside the long painting and brought it to life. Acting out stories was second nature to them and they seemed less inhibited than most children. Hazel talked mainly to the big grey draught horse that led the team as it tugged steadfastly, refusing to be sidetracked.

She would canter on the spot and click her cheeks in and out, in a sort of horse talk. 'Sh…sh…show me, sh…sh…show me, how to be so strong.' And sometimes she'd sing, 'If you tell me, please if you tell me, I won't tell anyone where you've come from.'

Jimmy would stand alongside the horses, just like the wagon

master, guiding them out of the thick mud 'Steady, Spartacus... You're the strong one, Zenna. Don't you others go fallin' asleep!' And the names that he and Hazel had chosen laboriously for each and every horse were always the same, while the tiny dog that peered from round the back of the wagon was always Careful, and the lone spare horse was always Straggler.

Jock would watch them from round the corner, so as not to interrupt their play. Sometimes Jimmy could be heard offering the wagon master assistance, while on other occasions he offered advice. Hazel called the wagon master Pa and Jock smiled as she cantered on the spot, sucking her cheek in and out, and calling, 'Keep 'em goin', Pa! Keep 'em goin'!'

Taking a closer look, Jock saw that the children were right. Each horse was different, while the little dog at the back did look nervous.

Hazel's dark complexion had caused a passing curiosity in Mrs Palmer, but was overridden by her sheer delight in the girl and, instead of enquiring, she had offered her some womanly advice. 'Eddy's like his father: typical Aussie, sports mad. They both grew up thinking it's somehow sissy not to play sport, or even worse, to take the advice of a woman!' And later, she steered the conversation to some old swimming stories.

Eddy suspected that his mate's family had an Aboriginal side, but it was of no real concern to him, one way or the other. He liked them. He was too polite to ask outright anyway, and, besides, it was not in his typical blokey nature to steer towards anything remotely sensitive. If Jim and Hazel gave it no mention, he wasn't going to bring it up. Working class Sydney was pretty much the same, no matter what. A fair-dinkum bloke looked out for his cobbers and stuck up for the underdog. Josie gave Hazel's background no thought at all: Hazel was just Hazel.

So, inadvertently, by not mentioning it, Eddy and Josie left Hazel even further in the dark.

'It's all a matter of reverse psychology with those two,' said Mrs Palmer. 'If you want Eddy to do something, tell him he can't and if you don't want him to do something, tell him you do. If you stick to that you can't go wrong.' And with that golden rule imparted, she winked at Hazel and pulled out the plug. The water gurgled as it disappeared down the plughole and the ladies rejoined the gentlemen, Hazel happy that Eddy's mum had taken her into her confidence.

Later in the day the excitement rose up again and splashed over the foursome as they played among the waves. Hazel loved the sea and she was fascinated by Eddy's ability to bodysurf, as he chose a wave and rode it right up to the sand with only his head poking out, the rush of the sea herding him along.

Although he'd been a lifesaver at Coogee, he preferred the rougher surf of Maroubra. He was well known to the locals. They'd seen him bodysurfing off the southern reef at Coogee and around by the Malabar wreck at Maroubra and training with the footy team, or playing cricket in his whites at Coogee oval.

Coogee was renowned for its sea baths, Wylie's mixed, Giles, the ladies' baths and the closed-in men's nude baths, and the Coogee Aquarium, where Eddy had gone as a Randwick schoolboy, leaping off the tram, tearing off his uniform and jumping straight in, without having to mess about with swimming trunks. One day the severed arm of a shark victim had been sucked into the baths, where he was swimming. Eddy had never forgotten that day, but it hadn't interfered with his bravado and love of surfing and he still ventured out into the open sea, in the hope of catching a better wave.

Growing up in Coogee, he knew all about swimming. He'd heard all the stories.

'My grandfather told us that Aussies used to swim like ducks,' laughed Mr Palmer.

'But *your* dad swam in races back in the late 1800s, didn't he, dear?'

'Yeah, he ended up doing the sidestroke, with a trudgeon kick.'

Mrs Palmer smiled. 'But *you* learnt the crawl.'

And Mr Palmer nodded proudly.

'Where did you learn that?' Hazel asked.

'Over Cavill's Baths at Lavender Bay. One of the Cavills taught me. Can't remember which one 'cause there were about seven of 'em, all champion swimmers, they were!'

'Is that where you raced in them days?' Hazel asked.

'Sometimes. Dad raced at the old Figtree Baths, near where the Domain Baths are now. Sydney's first baths, they were, just sitting in the harbour, a gentlemen's baths and a separate baths for the ladies. The gentlemen flirted with the sharks, while the ladies were kept well hidden!' And he and Mrs Palmer laughed.

Hazel thought it odd that even though Grandpa had been a good swimmer, he had never spoken of baths or races. It seemed he'd always swum in rivers or the sea. He'd taught her to swim in the Parramatta River, the Georges River, at the La Perouse end and around at Nielsen Park.

'By the turn of the century and the new crawl stroke, people came from everywhere to watch the races,' Mr Palmer enthused.

'And when the tram came right up to Coogee, it was like Broadway round here, wasn't it, dear?'

Mr Palmer looked over the top of his glasses. 'Only the daring had a dip in the surf. Considered immoral to show yourself like that! But down at Wylie's Baths they had underwater competitions and diving exhibitions. Eddy's aunt was a champion diver, ya know!'

'My sister Valma. State champion, she was. And the women started going into the surf too, with the men! Like that rebellious girl, Fanny Durack.'

Mr Palmer laughed. 'Some old fuddy-duddies thought she would singlehandedly bring about the moral decline of the nation!'

'Then she turned round and became the first woman to win a gold medal, swimming in the Olympics.'

Hazel wanted to join in. 'We were at the Domain Baths the day Boy Charlton beat that world champion, weren't we, Josie?'

'I was there that day,' Eddy interrupted. 'Arne Borg, the Swedish bloke. Boy ended up beatin' him by a mile.'

'We were lucky,' said Josie. 'Lot of people couldn't get in.'

Mr Palmer smiled. 'No wonder! Thousands turned up to watch *that* race.'

Eddy laughed. 'Too right. We had ta cancel the cricket! Only match that day was over at the SCG. The locals waiting for Alan Kippax to make a double century against Victoria.'

Jim piped up. "That's where *I* was. And when it come up on the scoreboard, *Charlton beats Borg*, the place went wild!'

'And he was only sixteen,' Mrs Palmer added. 'Just dived in and swam. Such a sweet boy, and he won the world championship!'

'Too right. One in a million. Manly legend!' said Eddy.

'They called him "Boy" because of his age, but I never seen a boy so big,' laughed Mrs Palmer.

Eddy grinned. 'Manly all right.'

'His coach was a champion swimmer, too,' said Mr Palmer. 'Forgotten his name.'

'Tom Adrian,' Hazel answered, surprising even herself.

Joe and Grandpa had turned Tom Adrian into a household name. He'd come back from the war, like her father, suffering shell-shock, but went on to coach Boy Charlton to victory. He was a ray of hope in their house, even more than Boy. But they'd stopped talking about him after he jumped into the sea while sailing with Boy to the Paris Olympics.

Hazel had a natural love of the water, and Eddy, since he had been knee-high to a grasshopper, had accepted it as a normal part of life too. His Aunt Valma had jumped off the Coogee Baths tower with him in her arms, when he was barely two years old. But Hazel still swam sidestroke, as Grandpa had taught her.

Down at the beach, Eddy took her by the hand and she ran with him into the waves. 'Show me how to catch one,' she pleaded, as the waves washed over her.

He picked her up and tossed her onto a breaker. 'Kick!' he yelled. 'Kick!'

She felt the full force of the ocean's edge, the rushing water lift her body up onto its shoulders, race her towards the shore, until she fell off, tumbling into the foam, bumping along the beach bottom, tiny grains of sand running into her mouth and nostrils.

Eddy breezed up on a wave. 'Not bad for a girl!'

She dug her cupped hand into the wet sand and threw the dripping ball at him, laughing as it slid down his wet back. He swept her up in his arms and raced with her to the shore, dropping her struggling body into the dry, grittle sand and laughing at the unseemly sight. 'Ya look like a lost mermaid,' and he pointed down the beach. 'That's Wylie's Baths, named after

Harry Wylie, the manager. Boy could he swim! Champion distance diver he was!'

'Distance diver? That was banned, wasn't it?'

'Wanted to reckon underwater swimming was dangerous. But we still do it!' And he kicked back a wave.

'Is that swimmer Mina Wylie related to him?'

'Harry's daughter. She was a distance diver too. Still sneaks a go at it! I've seen her.'

'She must have been good, to get to the Olympic Games.'

'Silver medal, Stockholm 1912. First time women were allowed to compete. Mina and Fanny, they showed everyone a thing or two! Selector bludgers, lot of hoo-haa about girls swimming in races. But when everyone screamed blue murder they let 'em go. Had ta make their own way there, took 'em forever and they come back with silver and gold!' Eddy gave a cocky grin. 'Well known round here, they were.'

Hazel felt the strength of his body against her as he turned about. But a strong wave broke right where they were standing, caught her behind the knees and flipped her sideways into the water. Eddy laughed as he helped her up. Then he raced off to catch a breaker.

Hazel watched as he swam further and further out. Then he stopped and turned, bobbing in the ocean. She could see the huge wave forming behind him but he seemed unaware as he glanced off towards Josie and Jim. Then just as the gigantic wave was upon him, he flicked his legs, shot his arms out in front and rose to its top and as it came crashing down he stayed with it, like a torpedo racing forward and sucking its firing wake behind, his body hidden by the wave. He twisted and turned his shoulders this way and then that, manoeuvring himself right up to Jimmy's and Josie's side. The wave had reached its destination too, and after dropping him off, rolled its cloth of glittering jewels onto the sand.

By late afternoon, tired out by the sun and the surf, the happy foursome made their way home, stopping at Sydney Cove just long enough to watch the sun set over the harbour, a perfect ending, with its last rays kissing the surface of the water.

When Hazel arrived home the sunset had faded. Books were scattered across the living room floor and the house was in darkness. Her heart sank. 'Mum? Grandpa?' But there was no reply. She smelt the whisky and found Joe slumped on his bed. She shook him wildly by the shoulders. 'Where's Mum? Where's Grandpa?' But he just slumped back onto the foul smelling pillow.

'Hazel!' There was yelling and a bang on the front door. 'Hazel! It's Mrs Sanders!'

Mrs Sanders' face had bad news all over it. 'Where's Mum? Where's Grandpa?' Hazel demanded.

'Your mother's all right, Hazel. Grandpa had a slight turn. Mr Sanders has taken them to Lewisham Hospital.'

Hazel didn't wait for the rest of the story. She took off up the street and ran all the way to the hospital.

Grandpa lay there sleeping, pale and lifeless. A clinical smell hung in the air and seeped around and out of the sparseness of the hospital ward, where things were so still that Hazel could hear the echo of her footsteps following her along the endless corridor.

Alice sat on the far side of the bed and held Grandpa's hand. She barely looked up. And the two women stayed until a nurse came and told them to go home.

Reluctant to face what Joe had done, Alice turned the key

slowly in the lock, while Hazel hung back and checked the letterbox before silently following her inside. There were the books still strewn from wall to wall, some open on their backs, others balancing on their sides, the chaos around Grandpa's chair almost too much for Hazel to bear as she sat there straightening pages and handing each book to Alice as if it were made of Venetian glass; Alice dusting the covers, front and back with a lace handkerchief before she returned each book to its rightful place.

Jim had received the urgent message and, after visiting Grandpa, he and Hazel caught a tram to Broadway and walked in silence down through the park to the Art Gallery.

It was still there. Their painting. And they stood gazing into it. 'When Grandpa's well again, we're movin' out. Mum's asked Uncle Bert and Aunt Daphne to move in with Grandpa.'

'Where are you goin'?'

'Mum organised it all down at the RSL. They found someone to rent us a house at Cabramatta.'

'Cabramatta? That's not far from Chipping Norton. I've told Mum before that yous could come and live with me!'

'You know she won't leave Dad. He's got no one. Where would he go, Jimmy?'

Silence fell over them. They continued to gaze into the picture, but they no longer saw what they'd once seen.

On Wednesday, Hazel broke the news to Josie.

EIGHT

LEAVING LEICHHARDT

Hazel would spend many weekends with Grandpa, but as she determined this, another responsibility became clear. She had developed a knack for calming her father whenever war was about to break.

Everything Alice did on the home front exploded in her face. Hazel cringed as she watched her mother draw on every one of her emotions, warm gentleness to guilt and ire, and it was only when all else failed that she turned to Hazel.

They worked as a team, Alice disappearing into the kitchen to prepare something Joe fancied, while Hazel distracted him with ditties and silly jokes. 'Ya heard the one about the elephant and the flea?'

'Ya bonkers, Hazel.' And he'd yell into the kitchen, 'Ay, Alice, she been on tha piss again? She's a ravin' ratbag!'

Alice wouldn't answer and inevitably he'd say, 'See? She thinks ya bonkers too!'

'Yeah, but what happened to the flea?'

And they'd muck about, while Alice unobtrusively set the table.

After tea, Hazel played the spoons while Joe sang, 'The Anzac boys are happy'. And they propped each other up, singing and swaggering along the hall, voices trailing, Alice praying and waiting for the silence when Joe passed out.

After the most recent drunken jaunt, she sighed, 'You're a genius, Haze!'

'No, Mum. I'm just mad and you're not!'

'Well, not too many kids can defuse bombs in chops!'

'Do you think it's contagious?'

'Madness? Na, I just brought you up right. War's madness. It's violence that's contagious.'

'Maybe we should call ourselves lieutenants or majors.'

'No, we're firing line, love. Like your poor drunken father.'

But as they sat on the back steps and looked up into the moonless sky, it became harder to see the funny side.

For Hazel to leave the streets of Leichhardt, the sunsets on the harbour, Grandpa, Josephine, the ferry rides, the trips to La Perouse, Bondi, Coogee, the Art Gallery, and her beloved Nielsen Park was nothing, she realised, to her mother's leaving.

Alice sat under the Moreton Bay fig and imagined the thick forest of trees lining the banks of the Georges River, and she thought about the little farm at Chipping Norton and being close to Jimmy. But she couldn't escape the sadness of leaving Leichhardt.

Cabramatta had once been called the Moonshine Run, the forest foliage so high and thick that the silvery slivers of moonshine barely penetrated the trees, the wide river offering the only clear run of moonwash. Grandpa had told her the

Cabramatta story. And she clung now to the image of the tall trees, standing shoulder to shoulder, protecting the earth, the oldest of them whispering secrets to the moon, bursting it over and over again with laughter.

Yet, despite this, she felt lost as she sat in the profound silence of the tree. It was like losing her mother all over again. 'I'll be back,' she whispered.

There was no way to describe Joe's leaving. He hid from it at the Bald Faced Stag.

Josie came to help Alice and Hazel pack. 'Maybe if I come to visit I could stay overnight and we could all go swimming and take a picnic lunch down to the river bank and Jimmy and Eddy could come too and we could visit the farm at Chipping Norton and feed the chickens and the horses, the possums and that little pet joey.'

Alice and Hazel nodded, while she rattled on. 'And we could go to the flicks in town when Valentino's on, or see Mo McCackie at the Tiv. You could stay here with Grandpa, or at my place, and we could all go!'

The van came. Hazel went to fetch Joe from the Bald Faced Stag to help with the loading, but as she stood at her usual beckoning window, she saw him sitting alone in the corner, staring vacantly at the floor. Normally it was a rowdy scene, Hazel taking it all in before she yelled from the window, watching as her father happily played cards, or laughed and sang with the locals. Today it was different.

Joe made his way home, dragging his feet, while Hazel raced on ahead, skipping and turning, turning and skipping, in a vain attempt to hurry him along as he dug his hands deeper and deeper into his empty pockets.

Uncle Bert was bringing Grandpa home from hospital the

following day. Joe couldn't bear to face him. Hazel and Alice had been to the hospital to say the difficult goodbyes. They didn't want Grandpa to feel deserted, when he wasn't to blame. And they didn't want him to feel sad for them.

Grandpa saw only goodness in their leaving and his heart ached. 'It's got nothin' to do with the way Joe feels about us, ya gotta know that. Just doesn't know what he's doin'. It don't alter me feelings for him. It's a separate war thing and that's how I'm gunna keep it.' He trusted Jimmy to look after Hazel and Alice. And that faith balanced his loss.

There were presents for Grandpa, books wrapped in pretty paper and tied with ribbon and left for him on his favourite chair. Alice left a copy of *Bush Ballads and Galloping Rhymes* by Adam Lindsay Gordon who, like Grandpa, was a lover of horses, while Hazel had left a book of quotes, which had been a prize from school. She had placed a bookmark carefully at 'The Home Life' by L. Larcom and she'd pencilled an asterisk next to the part which read:

If the world's a vale of tears,
Smile till the rainbows span it;
Breathe the love that life endears
Clear of clouds to fan it.
Of your gladness lend a gleam
Unto souls that shiver,
Show them that dark sorrow's stream
Blends with Hope's bright river.

And as the cart pulled away, Hazel stared back, back at Seale Street, back at Myrtle Street, back at Elswick, Fort Street, back at Kegworth Street. Back. Back. Back. Until she could see no more of Leichhardt.

They trundled along the Parramatta Road for miles, until the turn into the Dog Trap Road led them towards the Southern Road and further and further into thick scrub. The metal wheels of the cart rattled over the dirt road and disturbed the bush birds. Alice watched a flock of sulphur-crested cockatoos flying across the clear, blue sky; a trail of white and yellow, leading the cart to a sacred site.

Hazel was learning to hate. But the hate, like the resentment, had nowhere to go. She wished she could leave it by the side of the road before they reached Cabramatta, but the heavy wheels turned round and round and churned her up with the dirt.

Alice's clever manipulation of the move and all it entailed had brought Joe and Jimmy together for the first time since the fight. Eddy, oblivious of the tension, had done much to help, just by being there and while helping to unload, his easygoing, jovial nature made him the perfect buffer and Hazel and Alice loved him for it.

'Mr Johnson! Catch!' And he pretended to pass Joe a kitchen chair from the van, like a football.

The day passed and the new home was settled without too much fuss. It was a small house and the tall gums surrounding it made it appear even smaller, but it had a large yard with a paddock at the back and the river was close by.

Counting the Johnsons, there were four families in Doris Road, with the houses on one side and the bush leading to the river on the other. On the residential side, wild grasses backed up from the road to a narrow dirt track, which ran along in front of fences and vacant lots, like an arrow without a point. Birds pecked at the track unperturbed by the occasional pedestrian and at the road unperturbed by the odd horse and cart.

The following Sunday, Grandpa turned his cart into Doris

Road, with Josie sitting happily beside him. Hazel had waited impatiently by the gate and she ran along beside them as they approached. 'Hurry up, you two, or it will be time to go home!'

They'd planned a day at the river and Jim and Eddy had been invited, while Mr Morris, the new neighbour, had offered Joe the loan of his rowing boat for the day.

Hazel was happy to have her family and friends together once more, and for the first time, Alice could see hope in this new beginning. Joe had been his old self for the past week and he'd promised to steer clear of the pub.

Mr Morris had a kindly freckled face and a big red nose, which broadened when he grinned. He handed Joe the oars. 'There ya go, cobber!'

Joe put the oars on his shoulder. 'Good on ya!'

'Haven't used the boat for a while. Might be an idea ta check for leaks before ya take the family out.'

'Okey doke!'

'Might 'ave ta take a bucket with ya, eh?'

'Oh, I'm used to bailing meself out,' Joe laughed.

And as he sauntered down towards the river, he imagined he was a woodchopper, with axes over his shoulder instead of oars, and he began whistling 'They were only playing leapfrog', remembering how cobbers from the war had sung so heartily on the ship as they'd sailed back home.

But the oars began to feel more like rifles and he was relieved to finally reach the tree where the old rowboat was tied. He placed them carefully across the wooden seats and rolled up his pants. There didn't appear to be any serious leaks, but he untied the rope and slid the boat through the wet mud and into the water, singing 'You'll get no promotion unless you're on the ocean', in an effort to forget rifles.

He rowed to the first bend of the long winding river before letting the boat drift, and soaked up the silence. It was so good to be in Australia, floating along on the Georges River, with the water lapping, gently rocking the boat and lulling him into a long-forgotten sense of peace. But just as the war was drifting away, a noise in the scrub disturbed him. He sat bolt upright and scanned the trees. When the noise came again he slid to the bottom of the boat, then peeked out over the rim. A grey kangaroo peered back and, as he reached for the oars, it leapt away.

He rowed back uneasily, remembering the men who hadn't returned, and the deep, even strokes he had used to row up the river turned into shallow flicks, skimming the surface and splashing water up into his face and, anxious to have his feet back on dry land, he flicked faster and faster until the boat slid back into the mud. He quickly tied it to the tree and hurried home, but the guilt of survival kept overtaking him.

He was no sooner home than the others were ready to leave, their laughter filling the air as they wandered off ahead of him, towards the river; jostling, tripping and swapping, trying to decide who should carry what; Eddy teasing and tossing things backwards and forwards to hide his discomfort around the women.

'Whatever you do, don't spill the water in the billy!' Alice called.

Joe caught up and when they finally arrived at the swimming spot, he spread the rug out under the huge gum tree and watched the youngsters chuck towels every which way as they stripped down to their latest Speedos, while Grandpa and Alice disrobed a little more demurely, down to their old woollen cossies. A willie wagtail, who'd spent the whole morning collecting spiders' webs for a nest, ducked for cover behind the picnic basket and watched open-beaked as the strange creatures ran into the water, fell over each other and sank.

Grandpa and Alice decided to row the boat to the other side of the river and Joe gave them a push off, before propping himself against the tree.

Taking an oar each, they were trying to row in unison, the boat tilting this way and that along with the laughter, until they finally synchronised their strokes and headed towards the far bank. Joe watched them veer off towards Grandpa's side and chuckled at the sight of the old boat refusing to go in a straight line. He didn't have to worry about them toppling out, because they always enjoyed a swim.

Eddy and Jimmy had taken off after them and Eddy, with his strong stroke, swam ahead of Jimmy in what looked like an attempt to beat the boat to the other side. Jimmy stopped halfway and swam back to Josie and Hazel, who were having their own swimming race to a fallen log.

Jimmy got to the log first and clambered onto it, before taking Josie's outstretched hand. Hazel held on, splashing water into his face, until her laughter was swamped by her drenched hair and his retaliation.

They stayed all day, swimming, boating, fishing and exploring the river bank. Cabramatta was a good spot and as the sun sank low in the sky, Grandpa made a campfire, while Joe tipped the water from the boat and tied it up to a paperbark tree.

Grandpa took some of the bark and wrapped it around the eel and mullet they'd caught before placing it on the fire to cook. Carefully, Jimmy stood the billy in the hot ashes and Eddy threw some spuds in beside it. The women watched and sucked on blackberries, which they'd collected along the bank in an old river bucket.

And as the last morsels were eaten, Grandpa told a moon story and Alice told the story of how eel came to be. And the perfect day slipped away.

For Joe it was a long walk home. His head hurt and his thighs ached. Watching his family play happily by the river had intensified his guilt. The crimes were left unmentioned, but he felt them tugging at his groin. How could he hurt Alice, or Grandpa, or Jimmy or Hazel? If only the pain would leave him.

He found the pub the next day. He referred to it as the Cabra pub. Hazel was indifferent to its proper name.

A little wooden fire station stood next to the stone town hall, while Cabramatta station with the stationmaster's office stood opposite. Further down the road was the sawmill, paper shop, produce store, barber's, and turning into the crossroad, the pub, the haberdashery and the billiard parlour. Apart from this junction, there was a church, Cabra-Vale Park and Hartley's Oval. That was Cabramatta. 'Cabra'—white grub; 'Matta'—place of water. Where the Cabrogal clan once chased possums and danced.

NINE

THE POTATO BOX

The house reeked of whisky and, at the sight of Joe, Alice hightailed it into the kitchen to toss sausages and chips into a pan, while Hazel began to sing ditties at the top of her voice.

Joe finally collapsed into bed without warring, and, heaving a sigh of relief, Alice lit a candle and Hazel joined her in the kitchen. The house was blessedly quiet, and, anxious to keep it that way, they silently shared a jug of hot cocoa.

But before they had time to refill their mugs, a bloodcurdling scream tore through the house. They tried to get up, but the war was already rushing in, the table tipping, the jug smashing, hot cocoa splashing across the floor.

Alice pushed Hazel towards the door. 'Run, Hazel! Run!' And she tried to follow, but Joe grabbed her arm, spun her hard and bashed her against the pantry cupboard. Hazel tried to grab her mother's free arm, but her foot slid in the cocoa and she fell hard on the floor, while Joe spun Alice round and round the kitchen, yelling. 'Butchers! Friggin' butchers!'

Hazel scrambled to her feet and tried to grab Alice from Joe, but as he lost hold he shoved Hazel with all his might and she fell back, smacked her head on the doorknob, and slid unconscious to the floor.

Alice shook Joe by the shoulders, 'Joe, you've hurt Hazel!' But his eyes were glazed. 'Look what you've done to Hazel, Joe!' She shook him so hard the pantry door swung open and he gazed into the empty space where the potatoes were usually stored and, rubbing his pounding head, he whispered, 'We gotta get 'im into the bunker!' Alice tried to pull away, but she slipped and whacked her head on the table.

Frustrated, Joe pushed Hazel into the potato space, a wooden shelf barely skimming her face, and shut her in, before crawling the full length of the hall on his belly and slithering under his bed like a snake. Safe in his bunker.

Slowly Hazel regained consciousness. Her eyes tried to focus, while her mind tried to fathom. She seemed to be in a box. A wooden box. Darkness all around her. She tried to think. Her limbs were numb and all she could see was black. Fear swept over her. She was in a coffin. She tried desperately to keep her eyes open, but death stroked her brow.

The candle above the stove had gone out and Alice woke to the clang of tin cups knocking together on their hooks. The open window had let in a strong breeze, flapping the curtains at her.

She found Joe asleep, his feet sticking out from under the bed, but she couldn't find Hazel. She lit the candle and went outside.

'Hazel,' she whispered into the dark, 'Hazel, where are you?' But there was no answer. Alice remembered Joe's last words, 'We gotta get 'im into the bunker!'

She hurried to the kitchen and in the disarray her eyes fixed on the closed pantry door and, clambering over an upturned chair, she pulled it open. She was shocked by the sight of Hazel's lifeless body stretched out in the potato box. 'Hazel!' she gasped, patting frantically at her blank face as she carefully edged her out. 'Hazel!'

Hazel's eyes opened slowly. 'Oh, Mum…I thought I was dead…I thought I was in a coffin.' And she threw her arms around Alice's neck.

Alice tried to laugh. 'Well, you weren't Snow White encased in glass. You were in the potato box!'

Hazel turned her head towards the cupboard and laughed thinly into the hollow. But as she looked up at her mother, she saw blood mingling with tears and felt a terrible foreboding. 'The candle's burning out!' she gasped.

Alice quickly lit another.

'Do you think we could get the electric light put on, Mum?'

'Well, I don't know about that. Mrs Morris said that every time somebody pulls the light cord, it costs a penny!'

Hazel closed her eyes.

'But we'll see,' Alice added quickly. 'We'll see.'

'What happened, Mum? How did I get here?'

'You slipped in the cocoa and knocked yourself out.'

'Cocoa? I don't remember any cocoa.'

The following day Alice searched for an answer. It frightened her that Hazel couldn't remember, but she was torn by a mother's love and a wife's duty. Joe was just another forgotten

Digger and even if he had received a proper pension, how far would that go? Where were the specialists for his legs? Where was the help for his shell-shock? All she could hear was his yelling, 'I'm not gunna be just a trunk!'

And panic swept over her. The sight of Hazel, stretched out unconscious in the potato box, was distressing enough, but the mention of a coffin had shocked her out of her blind tolerance.

She told Joe what he'd done and once again he denied it. 'You say that every time, Joe! You know I don't lie! You're sick, Joe. You're sick in the head.'

Alice knew that she was frightening him, but she had no choice. She knew all about his remorse and once more she saw tears welling in his eyes. But this time she had to keep going. 'You could have killed me and you stuffed Hazel in the potato box! She thought she was in a coffin. It's bad enough you hurting Hazel, Joe, without terrifying her to death!'

'Yous can't send me to the asylum, Alice. They'll never let me out. And they'll take me legs! I never meant to hurt yous. I love yous. Ya *gotta* know that.'

She walked to the back door and stared out. 'You promised to stay off the whisky when we moved out here!'

'I know. I tried. I tried! But whisky's the only thing that stops the friggin' pain.'

'What about Aspro? Couldn't you take more Aspro?'

'They're lollies, Alice. Lollies can't help!'

Alice turned back into the room, feeling helpless and unable to muster the final strength to turf him out. Hazel saw what was happening. It had happened so many times before. But she was sick with fear for her mother and now there was Eddy. What would happen to her mother if she were to marry? They were trapped, the two of them, like caged rabbits.

'Dad, look, me and Mum are going to spend a few days at Grandpa's. That will give you time to sort out where you're gunna go, until you can give up the grog. Ya can't stay here; me and Mum have had enough!'

Hazel tugged at Alice to get her into the bedroom, knowing she would change her mind again if she was left too long in the same room as Joe.

This was the stand. Hazel was acutely aware of the suffering in this moment. But just a little longer and she would have her mother out of the house and on the way to Grandpa's. She opened a small case and helped her pack a few essentials. She heard the front door close. Alice heard it too.

Joe had to get out of the house. He wouldn't have been able to bear their leaving. With his head bent low, he walked slowly along the track towards the pub. He knew that one day he'd have to go. What would he say if Jim called by, looking for Alice and Hazel? He didn't want to fight with his son again. And it frightened him to think that he was hurting them both. He didn't want to end up in the asylum! His mind drifted back to the fun-filled days at Nielsen Park. Maybe he could find a cave to crawl into. His head started to ache and he wandered across to a tree stump and sat down.

Hazel closed the door and, holding Alice by the arm, hurried her down the path. The gate squeaked behind them, but they didn't look back. The worn track seemed to stretch for miles in front of them, but it was only a ten-minute walk to the station. When they rounded the bend they saw him. He was sitting on a tree stump and gazed into the long grass. He didn't look up and they tried to walk past. But Alice looked back.

'What are you doing sitting there, Joe?'

Hazel was losing again.

He looked at Alice vacantly. 'I was goin' to the pub, but I've changed me mind.' He stood up and started to wander back down the track.

'Where are you going, then?' she asked anxiously.

'Down to the river.'

Now Hazel knew that she'd lost.

TEN

JUMPIN' THE RATTLERS

Alice stopped darning. 'What do you want for your twenty-first, love?'

'Do you think we could have the electric light put on?'

'Electric light! Well that's the funniest birthday present I ever heard of! There must be something else?'

Hazel put her head back in her book.

'I was thinking of making you a frock. I saw the most gorgeous lilac silk down at Broadway, and black patent shoes,' Alice leant forward, 'with the daintiest pattern you ever saw.'

Hazel shrugged and went on reading.

'It's no good you changing your mind later. I can't make a silk frock like that overnight, you know.' She began to darn, glancing at her stubborn daughter, until she stuck herself with the needle. She sucked on the pricked thumb and sighed. 'Well, if that's what you really want. Seems silly to me, giving my only daughter electricity for her twenty-first.'

Suddenly, hugging replaced the wall of silence. 'Love ya, Mum. Love ya, love youuuuu!'

'All right, Hazel! Stop slobbering over me and I'll tell you what I'll do. I'll go down town tomorrow and I'll find out about it.' She shook her head. 'I never heard of a girl wanting electric light instead of a gorgeous lilac frock and black patent shoes.' And she pushed the wooden block back down inside the sock and continued darning.

It was a diabolical situation. Her mother calmly mending her father's socks, when it was only last week that he'd ripped everything in the house apart. Yet this strange ritual brought a sense of normality back into the house and Hazel sat watching as her mother held the sock tight over the block and criss-crossed the hole with the thick wool thread. And in that moment Hazel vowed, *Nothing is going to spoil my twenty-first.*

She was planning to stay at Grandpa's for the weekend of her birthday. Eddy, Jimmy and Josie were taking her to the Tivoli, and on the Sunday they were all going to Coogee, while Alice was planning a quiet dinner for the Friday evening, before she was to leave for Grandpa's.

Alice spent the Friday afternoon preparing Hazel's favourites: roast leg of lamb, rice custard with nutmeg and a rainbow cake with chocolate icing. And, with a bowl held firmly against her aproned hip, she paddled cake mixture with a wooden spoon and implored Joe to stay away from the pub. 'You can get the candles and balloons from the paper shop, Joe. And don't forget: I need you back here by four o'clock to help me move the table! There's two nice cold bottles of beer waiting for you in the ice-chest. Now don't forget: four o'clock!'

But when Hazel arrived home from work, the house was in darkness. She made her way gingerly down the hall towards the closed door of the living room and as she turned the cold knob, the darkness rushed out at her. But through it she heard an angel's voice.

'Pull the cord, Hazel.'

It was her mother and she almost cried with relief as her father added, 'Come on, Haze, we haven't got all night!'

A gleaming white cord hung before her. She reached for it and tugged. There was a click and a flash and the room lit up, lightbeams picking out the silvery threads of Alice's best damask tablecloth, lightbeams spilling into the kitchen, hallway and out the window and across the grass.

'Pull the cord again, Haze!' Joe called.

She pulled the cord and the lightbeams vanished. A candlelit iced cake stood on a platinum stand like something holy, a gold key propped upright, like the cross of Jesus. And her mother and father began to chant, 'Happy birthday to you, happy birthday to you—'. And she watched the shadows dance, before pulling the cord and flooding the room with light again.

'Ya supposed to blow the candles out first!' laughed Joe.

'And make a wish,' chirped Alice.

She took a deep breath and blew. 'We're still in the light!' And she ran through the house, ringing church bells with the pull of every cord, surreptitiously exorcising devils from the potato box.

Alice called after her. 'I think everyone in Cabra has been in today: the bako, the milko, the prop man, all pulling the cords on and off, on and off.'

'Goodness gracious!' Hazel yelled. 'All those pennies!'

She was transported back to a time before war, as they played cards and laughed like they always did and at midnight Hazel retired, no longer a child, and with power over darkness at last.

The next morning she could hardly keep up with her joy as it raced her into Leichhardt, down Elswick and into Seale Street, where she could just see Grandpa's head over the verandah wall as he sat in the big cane chair waiting for her. 'Grandpa!' she called. And he waved, his joy meeting hers. 'We've got the electric light!' And she ran up the steps to hug him, while he coaxed her into an idle rocker.

'What's all this about electric light?'

'That's what I got for my twenty-first!' And she squeaked the rocker back and forth.

'What on earth are you talking about?'

'The electric light!'

'Didn't your mother buy you a present?'

'That *was* my present, Grandpa! A magic cord! You pull it and the room lights up and you pull it again and the room goes dark. And you can sit anywhere you like and still read your book.'

'Can you turn this magic light up and down?'

'Don't be silly, Grandpa. You pull the cord, and it comes on; you pull the cord, and it goes off.'

'Light's meant to go up and down slowly,' he sniffed. 'Like sunlight, or gaslight.'

'But electric light is instantaneous. It's modern. It's modern light.'

'Eyes were made to adjust. All ya hear these days: modern this and modern that!' And he sauntered inside. 'World's in too much of a hurry.' And he carefully tied string around a brown paper parcel.

'A person could die from suspense out here, Grandpa.'

He reappeared and handed her the flat parcel. 'Now *that's* a present,' he said proudly.

It was a beautifully bound copy of Lord Byron's verse and as she turned the soft delicate pages, Grandpa smiled. 'Instantaneous silence, eh?' And he began to recite in that mellow voice that Hazel so loved.

She walks in beauty, like the night
Of cloudless climes and starry skies;
And all that's best of dark and bright
Meet in her aspect and her eyes:
Thus mellowed to that tender light
Which heaven to gaudy day denies.

His intuitive nature and timing proved a priceless gift, as Hazel's thoughts turned to Eddy and a love she had long been denying.

That night at the Tivoli, the foyer buzzed with excitement: men unswerving, dressed in brown, black, blue or grey; the women swaying, turning and curving, in red, yellow, blue, pink and lilac.

Jim and Josephine entered the theatre ahead of Eddy and Hazel. Eddy was awkward in such situations, but when Hazel slipped her arm casually through his, his gait quickened and he cheekily overtook. 'Crikey, watcha doin' you two? Ya wanta miss the start?'

Eddy had no idea about presents for girls, so he had entrusted his mother with his wages and intention, but he took full credit as he clipped the clasp of the gold locket around Hazel's soft neck, grateful that she kissed his cheek after this amazing feat and not before.

Hazel fingered the heart-shaped locket and gave a coy smile.

The curtain went up, but he didn't notice. He kissed her, right there and then, in front of a full house and the master of ceremonies.

After the show, Eddy and Hazel sat on the garden seat beneath the huge fig tree, moonlight filtering through the branches. 'Can you hear the crickets?' she whispered. Eddy had fought against the very idea of marriage. He was an Aussie sportsman. A man's man. A bloke. He didn't need a woman telling him how to bat, or run his life. But now, with his arm around Hazel's tiny waist, he desperately wanted her to tell him what he should do.

Silently she bathed in the moonlight and the happiness of the past two days and as she looked upwards into the huge, overhanging tree, her leg brushed against Eddy and he kissed her soft, warm mouth and, before he knew what he was saying, he blurted out, 'Haze, will ya marry me?'

She stared into earnest eyes and could feel them throbbing. She had held him away for so long and now the longing engulfed her. But how could she marry Eddy with the situation at home? She kissed him tenderly and lay with him in the grass.

The next day Eddy was happy in the surety that she would marry him, but he was confused. Why hadn't she answered outright, or talked wedding stuff? He decided to play it safe by not mentioning it to Jim or the others, unless Hazel did. But she didn't.

Jimmy had refrained from asking Josephine to marry him. He was unsure that the farm could sustain them. First he had bided his time, to build the farm up, and now with the depression hovering, the crop was bringing in less and less at the markets. Eddy had taken a job with the railways and he moved back to Coogee.

The following year, Jim's crop of peas brought only a halfpenny a pound at the markets. Josie had been laid off at Nestle's and Hazel was hanging on by the skin of her teeth. Jim knew that he had to leave. He had heard there was work in the country, shearing.

The thought of leaving Josie tugged at his heart. He would come back, of course, whenever he could, to check on his mother and Hazel and he would put aside part of his wages for them. But Josie, what could he do for his dear Josie?

She knew what he was going through. 'Jimmy, can we get married when you come back?' she asked boldly as they stood together and looked out over the barren garden beds of the little farm.

'How can I ask you to wait for me, Josie?'

'Things will improve, you'll see. You'll be back soon. I just know it!'

He picked her up in his arms and spun her around, shouting to the mountain ranges and far off Katoomba in the distance, 'Mrs Johnson!' And a low drifting cloud picked up the sound and carried it away.

The next day he jumped a rattler and headed west and as the local houses disappeared from view, he gave an intangible wave, to Josie, Hazel, Eddy, his mother and one final wave to his father.

The wooden box was bare and draughty and smelt of manure and stale hay. He leant back against his matilda pack, feeling more like an animal on its way to slaughter than an honest man looking for a job.

Then he jumped from the box at Lithgow and asked around for work. There wasn't any, so he jumped the next rattler to the next town and then another to the next and another, moving on down the line, getting a couple of weeks' work fruit-picking here and a couple of weeks' fence-mending there, staying in any one place only until the work ran out. And as the year rattled by, he travelled the western track until he finally landed some droving work at Condoblin with board. Others weren't so lucky.

Hazel lost her job at Nestle's and as she stood at the exit, the conveyer belts sadly whirred, *tatah... tatah... tatah*. And she felt like a little girl once more, saying goodbye to her father. She let the trams pass, one after the other, and trudged up the hill towards the station.

Another letter had arrived from Condoblin. It was good news. Jimmy was coming home for a few days. Alice, Hazel and Josie could hardly wait. And Joe was looking forward to seeing his son again.

He jumped off a rattler at Cabramatta and passed by the pub to check on his father. There was always someone who'd buy a Digger a drink, if he hung about long enough, and Joe was good at that.

There was no mistaking the men from the rattlers as they climbed up embankments shaking loose dust from cowboy hats, their unkempt hair that had long since seen a barber falling down over furrowed brows.

The publican saw Jimmy first and wasted no time on welcome-backs. 'Ya ole man's been at it again, Jim, scullin' whisky all mornin'. Had to send 'im packin'. Thought I'd betta warn ya!'

The word 'whisky' shot through him like a bullet and he took off, running towards the short-cut track, his matilda swaying and bouncing while his tin billy belted into his back.

Hazel was returning from a walk by the river when she saw Mrs Morris running down the road. Mrs Morris didn't even hurry to the clothesline when it spat rain and, although she appeared to be waving and yelling, Hazel wanted to ignore her and linger in the thoughts of her river walk. But as the breathless woman drew closer, her words became clear. 'I'm goin' for the sergeant, Hazel. I think he's killed ya mother!'

Blood streaked the hallway and trailed into the bedroom and Hazel strained to hear her mother's voice, but all she heard was, 'Get dowwwwn —'

She picked her way through the horror and found her mother slumped between a chair and the wall, Joe's hands clasped around her neck and her eyes bulging.

She grabbed the hat stand and crashed it down on her father's head and, as he toppled, she clambered over him to get to her mother.

'Butcherrr, stinkin' butcherrr!' he screamed and flung himself at her.

Hazel smacked his face hard. 'It's me, Dad! It's Hazel! Mum's hurt!' But she was left to fight as she had never fought before, the rules of the ring going out the door as she punched her father below the belt and kicked him hard in his injured thighs, while he punched and kicked back, blind with rage. She pushed and he pushed, until they stumbled outside. 'Stand up and fight, until you hear the bell, stand up and fight…' The tune went round and round in Hazel's swimming head and she clung like grim death to the verandah post.

'Get down!' he yelled.

'I'm not goin' down,' she cackled and laughed, gripping the post.

'Ya mad! Ya bloody mad!' He was slowly coming round. 'Ya mad, Hazel! Ya bloody bonkers you are!'

'Just like you,' she laughed. 'No hittin' below the belt! Come out clean now!'

Joe plopped down onto the verandah steps as Hazel continued to heckle, her head spinning and her legs wobbling like jelly.

Then she saw Jimmy and she blinked. He cleared the fence with one leap and ran towards her. Joe took off, but ran smack bang into the burly new sergeant, who was hurrying towards the house.

Shocked by Hazel's state, Jim ran after Joe and, ignoring the sergeant, gave his drunken father one almighty punch that sent him reeling. The sergeant grabbed Jim's arm to save Joe from being hit again, while Joe babbled, 'Lock 'im up, officer, before he kills his poor old father!'

Mrs Morris had caught up to them and she screamed breathlessly, 'No, sergeant! Let Jim go.' And she pointed her finger at Joe. '*He's* the basher! *He's* the one that bashed his wife.'

'Shut up, ya ole cow!' Joe yelled.

'Gawd struth! What is this? A domestic? Who the blazes are you?' the sergeant barked at Mrs Morris.

'I'm Mrs Morris. I live next door to poor Mrs Johnson.'

'And who the blazes are you?' he barked at Joe.

'I'm the man of the house.'

'Well get home and sober up, before I knock ya head orf.'

'He's not goin' home. If you don't run him out of town, I'll pull his balls off,' Jim yelled, as Joe struggled to free himself of the sergeant.

Mrs Morris persisted, pointing at Joe. 'He's the murderer, he's the culprit!'

Mr Morris caught up. 'Jean, let the sergeant look after it now.'

'Yeah. Get home, ya ole cow. Mind ya own business!' Joe yelled.

'Who are you?' the sergeant bellowed.

'I'm Morris, the neighbour. Let Jim go. Ya gotta check on Mrs Johnson, officer. She's in a bad way.'

Jim had broken away from the sergeant and was racing back towards the house, cursing 'How could I have forgotten Mum?'

'The doctor's there already,' Mr Morris called to the sergeant. 'There's an ambulance on the way.'

'The message I got to get round here must 'ave come from the doc,' he muttered to himself, as he hurried after Jim, and dragged Joe behind him.

Jim couldn't believe the carnage inside the house: upturned furniture, a blood-splattered floor and away in a corner, his mother. The doctor was attempting to revive her and a blanket of guilt and fear swept over him. If only he had got to her sooner. 'Oh God, dear, dear God, please save my mother.' And he held onto Hazel.

Joe, in his drunken stupor, sat on the step and watched bull-ants running over his shoe.

When the doctor finally nodded that Alice would make it, Jim thanked God, before carrying Hazel to the waiting ambulance. The ambulance officers followed with Alice, while Joe hung his head and watched the ants, as his wife and daughter were carried past.

'What do you want me to do with him?' the sergeant growled, as Jim climbed into the ambulance.

'Run him out of town and never let him back!'

The sergeant hoicked Joe down to the railway station and chucked him onto a train. 'If I ever see you anywhere near Cabramatta, I'll blow ya brains out,' he yelled, and as the train pulled out from the station, the sergeant kicked at the platform and sent tiny bits of gravel flying after the scurrying train. 'Can't stomach cowards who blame the grog,' he sneered to the station-master, before spitting a golly that cleared the fence a second before he did.

Jim stayed in town for a few weeks and Hazel and Eddy decided to marry, before he had to leave again for Condoblin.

When they all stood under the tree at Leichhardt, Alice's wish was finally granted. Hazel would be safe with Eddy. And, as she stood beside Grandpa with Josie at Jimmy's side, tears of joy and sadness rolled down her still black and purple face.

ELEVEN

A PENNY A HAND

Josie and Jim walked to the railroad crossing. A steam train shunted towards them, its pistons slowing, the driver leaning from the cabin in a bid to escape the heat. Enough men had been seen jumping these rattlers in search of work to warrant respect and a blind eye, as the trains puffed across the winding tracks of New South Wales, leading men into and out of hope.

'When I come back we'll get married,' Jim whispered, with a longing to stay that comes with an unbearable leaving.

The driver pulled the whistle and Jim climbed into a box car.

'Come back soon,' Josie called, over the *hoot, hoot, hoot* of the whistle, her voice drifting off in a puff of smoke as the black humped engine crossed her path.

Eddy moved into the house at Cabra. Hazel had decided against renting a place of their own. People were still losing jobs and she'd witnessed an eviction.

Angry locals had congregated in front of an Elswick house as the evictors carried out their unspeakable duty. She had gone to visit Grandpa and found him right in the thick of heckling neighbours.

'Friggin' mongrels!'

'Yella bellies!'

'Rotten bastards!'

'Bludgers!'

There was a moment's silence, until the evictors appeared again.

Little Jeffrey Henderson stared in disbelief as his clothes were thrown onto the footpath, the crowd booing and yelling louder.

'How can yous just chuck a man's family out on the street?'

'Lousy mongrels!'

'Ya rotten bludgers!'

Jeffrey couldn't fathom why they kept chucking things, when all the neighbours were yelling at them to stop. He was no bigger than a grasshopper, but he rushed a burly evictor and pummelled into him. 'Friggin' mongrel! Friggin' mongrel!' While his little brothers ran round and round the rubble.

'Jeffrey, come 'ere!' Grandpa called. 'Come over 'ere, cobber!'

Tears ran down his face and he spat at the evictor, 'Friggin' mongrel!'

Grandpa grabbed a hold of him. 'It'll be all right,' he whispered, although he knew that it wouldn't.

Jeffrey could see the EVICTED sign, the huge letters covering his house. And the burly evictor was coming out again. 'He's got me cricket bat! He's takin' me cricket bat!' he cried. And he rushed at him and kicked him in the shins. 'Friggin' mongrel! Friggin' mongrel! Friggin' mongrel!'

EVICTED. The huge word burnt itself into Hazel's mind.

Eddy was among the few to still have a job and soup kitchens were opening up all over Sydney, the queues longer and longer. 'Give us this day our daily bread' took on a whole new meaning, with thousands of heads bowed in dependency, rather than reverence. Decent men and women, lined up with decent neighbours, holding out plates and bowls. SOUP KITCHEN ,the sign said. But it spelt much more.

Mr Palmer was struck down by a fatal bout of influenza.

Mrs Palmer was devastated. 'I told him, Eddy, over and over again, not to go near the water on terrible bleak days. But he wouldn't listen. I told him over and over, but down to the beach he'd go. Oh, Eddy, why wouldn't he listen? Why wouldn't he listen?' And Eddy held her and tried not to cry, in front of his mother and Aunt Valma.

Later, he walked along the beach that his dad loved so, and he remembered the day his dad had called out to him, *That's my boy!* It was the day he'd jumped off the diving board all by himself.

Valma lived at Woy Woy now, and Mrs Palmer was moving to her sister's house. She was leaving Coogee. The thought of staying was too painful. She couldn't look at the beach, and the rent was getting too much anyway.

Eddy helped her pack up the house, and he fought back tears as he packed a part of his life away.

He managed to hold on to his job, and by the following year a baby kicked and turned in the warmth of Hazel's body. It was still hard times, but Eddy was bursting with pride, while Hazel rubbed her round belly and vowed, '*Nobody better harm this child!*'

Eddy stopped in at the billiard parlour from time to time and shared his bacca, but he rarely went to the pub. The beer shouts had got out of hand and, anyway, he had promised Hazel before they married that he would give up the grog. He hadn't, of course, and he would start up again when things got better. 'The missus will come round,' he told the blokes at the pub. 'A working man's gotta 'ave his beer. Goes without saying, eh?'

At night you could see Eddy and the Cabra blokes sitting under the street lights playing cards, a common but funny sight: grown men congregating under telegraph poles, their houses immersed in semi-dark, with electricity a luxury or cut off. But a card game still offered that all important community tie, that strictly male ethos, which softened the blow of their inability to provide; blokes sticking together through strife, at a penny a hand.

Eddy came home counting the copper coins and rubbing his cold knuckles. 'Did ya win?' Hazel asked, more from habit than interest. And he dropped the pennies on the open page of her book, more to attack the book than from generosity. 'Cold as charity out there tonight, Haze!'

He still felt uncomfortable around women and needed his mates to talk sport to and be crass with. But Hazel continued to fascinate him with her books and air of haughtiness, as she knocked his hand away and fussed when he teased her apron strings undone. 'Don't be silly, Edward!' she would say, with that strong lilt in her voice that still buckled his knees.

Josie had received a telegram from Jim. *Dearest Josie, I'm home soon, please marry me. Make whatever plans. Be there in three weeks, to hold forever. Love Jim.* She read the words again and again and, brimming over with happiness, ran to her mother, who was bending low in the garden to pick strawberries.

'Mum, look!'

'Good heavens, Josie, you nearly knocked me over! Don't thrust things at me when you can see my hands are full.'

'But read it, Mum. Read it!'

And joy soon replaced the succulence of strawberries. 'Oh Josie, what lovely news!'

'I have to tell Hazel.'

In her haste, a hat went on backwards and flowers which normally sat sedately at the back of her head bobbed over the brim as she ran to Petersham station, her heart pounding as she leapt onto a train, that had already begun to pull away.

The train seemed to take forever as it stopped at each station and people drifted slowly on and off, and the view from the window became a blur, as it sped along, with Josie peering ahead, while trees and houses flickered past, until at long last it pulled into Cabramatta station. Josie waited impatiently at the door and jumped off before she should have.

From the station she cut through the paddock and, as she came along the shrubby track, she saw Hazel about to lower the clothes prop, white sheets dancing like angels over her head.

'Hazel! Jimmy's coming home,' she yelled, waving the strawberry stained telegram, as she ran through the long, sticky paspalum. 'We're getting married!'

Hazel looked up to see her rushing straight towards a grazing horse. 'Josie! Watch out for the horse!'

But she kept running and yelling, 'Jimmy's coming come! Jimmy's coming home!'

The horse bucked and there was a sickening thud.

At the sound of Hazel's scream, Alice rushed from the laundry. 'Hazel! What's wrong?' But Hazel was already running towards the scrub.

Alice ran after her. 'Hazel! What's happened?' she yelled.

Hazel disappeared into the long paspalum, and reappeared cradling Josie and rocking back and forth and back and forth and back and forth.

Eddy had heard the scream too, but by the time he reached them, Alice was hysterical. 'She's dead, Eddy, she's dead. Josie's dead!' Hazel had passed out and was lying lifeless in the grass beside her friend.

'Fetch the doctor, Alice!' Eddy pleaded, and forced her away from the terrible scene as he picked Hazel up in his arms and carried her inside the house. And, laying her on the settee, he gently removed her bloodied smock and wiped Josie's blood from her swollen belly. But as his hands washed over the firm, new life, the thought of Josie lying alone in the swaying paspalum brought on a wave of helplessness he could hardly bear.

Pulling a sheet from the line, he went to the spot where Josie lay and, kneeling beside her, he brushed grass seeds and blood from her cold face, before the crisp white sheet shut the sun out.

The doctor arrived and when Hazel woke, frantic, he sedated her and, while she slept, Eddy carried Josie's lifeless body to a waiting ambulance.

Standing on the verandah with Alice, he watched the white van disappear. 'You and me, Alice, we have to be strong for Jim—and there's Hazel and the baby to think of.'

But Alice could only stare blankly down the road.

He had to go to Josie's mother.

Jim stayed for the funeral and left. The rattler took him as far as it could into the desolate country before spitting him out. From then on, each town he rolled into merely resembled the one he'd just left, as he drifted and bucked about, jumped on wild bulls and stallions that others wouldn't, grateful only that he didn't have to stay too long in any one place and drinking a bit more than he should have.

Hazel missed Josie terribly, but she gave birth to a dark-haired boy with brown eyes that followed her everywhere, earnest eyes that allowed no time for grief.

One day as Daniel slept soundly, she answered a knock at the back door. The man would have been in his thirties; a local. She'd seen him downtown with a pregnant wife and three or four kids, ranging from about ten down. His hair was parted neatly in the middle and combed down flat, still wet, while the smell of fresh boot polish led her eyes down into two shiny, black pools.

'Need any odd jobs done, missus, for a bit of tucker?'

She stared up the yard at the paspalum, which had crept in from the paddock where Josie had died. 'The grass badly needs cutting up the back there, and if you could fix that wire on the back fence.' She couldn't tell him how much the paspalum hurt her, and she knew that if he was offered food without work, his world would crumble too. 'I would be really pleased if you could do that.'

The young man gave a polite nod as he took a step back. Hazel watched him walk towards the chook pen, where the sickle and the old push mower were propped against a wall, and she watched as he took off his shoes and placed them carefully on the rickety fence-post. He sensed her gawking and turned towards the house, but she ducked in the nick of time.

Holding the knife high over the bread, she let the thick treacle run into its centre. Sometimes she spread dripping on bread and sprinkled it with salt, capturing the flavour of meat cooked the night before and devouring it all over again. And she thought how lucky she was.

She had been one of the last to be laid off at Nestle's and Eddy still had his job, even if it was only the basic wage of three pounds ten. It was a big drop from the four pounds two and six that his wage used to be, but at least he had a job. Jim still sent Alice a bit of money whenever he could, from wherever he happened to be. And Grandpa still managed to survive on his communal bartering.

Hazel collected a couple of eggs from the chook pen, chokoes off the vine and some freshly dug potatoes and placed them carefully into brown paper bags. She had been saving a bunch of bursting green grapes for after tonight's tea, but as she looked at the neat man in the yard finally free of paspalum, she added them to the bag of wrapped sandwiches.

He pushed the mower back against the chook pen, rolled his cuffs down and took his shoes from the post before making his way to the back door. 'All done, missus,' he called.

He was tying his shoelaces when Hazel appeared with the parcel. 'Watch the eggs,' she said politely.

He raised his head and tried not to sound too pleased. 'Good, missus!' And as he disappeared around the corner of the house, he took a piece of red chalk from his pocket and marked the gatepost with it.

It puzzled Hazel why men looking for odd jobs began to walk straight into her yard. Until she found the red chalked cross.

TWELVE

TURNING BACK

Jim was now in the south-west region, and as he climbed the sharp embankment by the railway track he noticed a small boy staring after the train. The boy had his back to a stallion, that was galloping wildly towards him and snorting at the billowing smoke.

'Hey kid, get outa the way!' Jim yelled.

But the boy didn't budge.

'Hey kid, get out of the way!'

In desperation, he yelled at the stallion and waved his hands in an attempt to distract it from the boy's path. But it thundered on. He ran between the boy and the galloping horse and waved wildly. 'Whoa, boy! Whoa!'

The boy turned as the horse reared up and Jim tried desperately to calm it. 'Whoa there, boy! Whoa, boy! Whoa!'

A horseman rode frantically towards them as the stallion quietened. He stopped at some distance, careful not to spook the horse and he called out to Jim. 'Point the boy in my direction, matey.'

Jim did so, while the man on the horse gestured to the boy to back up slowly towards him. He fingered a lasso nervously and when the boy was at a safe distance from the stallion he called to Jim, 'Now you back up, matey.' Jim did so, as the lasso landed around the horse's neck.

The man dismounted and tied the rope to a tree. Then he knelt down in front of the boy. 'You okay?' he asked, tousling the boy's hair. The boy nodded.

The man shook Jim's hand warmly. 'I'm Ted Adamson. You crazy, or God come back?'

'Jim Johnson.'

Ted called to another rider. 'Marty, take Jim up to the house. We'll get the stallion later.' And he hoisted the boy up onto his horse. 'Ya won't say no to a beer, will ya, Jim?' And before he had time to answer, Ted had galloped off.

Marty offered his arm and Jim leapt up onto the horse behind him and they soon caught up with Ted. He offered an explanation. 'My boy's deaf. If you hadn't come along, that crazy stallion would have trampled him.'

The horses separated again. 'The boy's mother died giving birth,' Marty said over his shoulder. 'Ted owns the biggest sheep property round here, but the boy's the most important thing in his life.'

'What's his name?'

'When Linden was dyin' she took one last look out over the valley and she called him Dale. She really loved this place. Property's called Lindendale now.'

Green pastures stretched away from the homestead, while in the distance weeping willows hugged the Murrumbidgee River, whose receding waters had left a golden blanket of everlasting daisies and, spotted across the landscape as far as the eye could see, the indescribable green of gum trees mingled with the blue sky.

Ted welcomed Jim to Lindendale with open arms and the understanding of loss between the two men seemed to offer Jim a safe haven and he listened to Ted speak proudly of Linden, finding at long last that he could speak of Josie.

But it was while swimming in the Murrumbidgee with Ted and Dale that Jim began to long for home. It had been two long years since he'd left Cabra.

'What's "Murrumbidgee" mean, Ted?'

'Big water,' he called, before floating away on his back.

'Me grandpa was telling me "bidgee" on the end of a river's name means flat place.'

But Ted was already out of earshot.

A flock of sulphur-crested cockatoos flew over the river and a kookaburra's laugh took Jim back to the river at Cabramatta.

He worked every morning with the wild stallion, trying to forgive the mistrust of a grazing horse. And every morning, just as he was about to give up, a gentle breeze would spring up out of nowhere.

The Lindendale welcome had reeled Jim slowly back into life, softening the gulf between him and Cabra and making it easier to venture home, when he had some time off.

Jim always brightened at the sight of Daniel and the sight of Jim never ceased to brighten Hazel. The depression that had plagued Sydney for years seemed to be lifting.

And with Jim home once more they were all on their way to the river. Grandpa hung back, taking everything in, while Jim piggy-backed Daniel and Hazel ran backwards in front of them, singing 'To market, to market, to buy a fat pig', Daniel giggling, Alice swinging the picnic basket trying to keep up and Eddy running along in front, doing mock overarm bowls.

When they arrived at the picnic spot, Eddy coaxed Jim into swimming across to the other side of the river to get some grapes from the orchard. Fruit was scarce and even Hazel had been across there with Eddy, feeling like Ned Kelly with her handful of grapes as she sneaked back, sidestroke. But it was more the adventure that had lured Eddy when he had swum across in the night and brought back a sugar bag of fruit. That was until a young girl, further down where the rivers met at the junction of the Georges River and Milperra Creek, had her arms taken off by a shark that had somehow found its way up past Cabramatta to Lansvale. There had been a massive hunt and the shark had been caught. Still, Eddy never again ventured across the river at night.

But the river continued to be the pivotal point of Cabra family life, even with the occasional jellyblubber stings, which were rubbed with riverbank mud, while the blubbers themselves were unceremoniously caught and left to burn and shrivel up in the sun.

Cabra-ites loved to watch Eddy dive from the high branch that hung out across the river. With his arms stretched out and his body perfectly straight, he would fly through the air and plunge down into the deep water hole, leaving barely a splash behind him. He knew the river and its currents well, but he stuck his chest out when Hazel swam beneath the surface, checking for any fallen logs or snags, while he waited and peered down from the branch.

She would surface, her neck stretching towards the sky and

she would lift one arm and wave to him. 'All clear, Eddy!' And he'd watch her as she'd lean back and give her legs a little flick to propel herself out of the way. He always knew just where he was going to land and he would swim up under her. And she always knew that he was going to pull her leg.

The river also offered a special Christmas spirit, for around its banks pine trees grew, replenishing themselves from one Christmas to the next, and families came with their axes to choose a tree.

One year, Eddy dragged home a tree that swept the ceiling and stretched from wall to wall, as if it was having a gigantic yawn. The decorating remained a family ritual. And this year Jimmy would be back.

He'd found another farm that offered space for him to be alone with Josie, while the gardens would serve as a link back to his mate, with discussions, as they'd had so many times before, of soil and sowing.

And just as he had promised, he strode through the door, tanned and tall with his arms full of Christmas bush and presents.

He had grown up under Alice's roof and nothing had really changed, despite the aftermath of Gallipoli. The family photo with Joe in his army uniform still had pride of place on the mantelpiece. The Australian flag stood in a jar next to it and the picture of the larrikin Prince of Wales on his 1920 visit to Australia stood next to that.

Jim remembered how his mother had taken a liking to the Prince, because he had failed to appear at a government function in the Sydney Town Hall, going instead to an RSL club, where he was found drinking with Diggers. The officials had panicked, thinking they'd lost him, and Alice had laughed her head off at the thought of them trying to explain to Buckingham Palace that they'd lost the Prince, while he was off having a beer with ordinary Aussie blokes.

Jim would always be Hazel's knight-in-shining-armour, even over Eddy, yet she longed for Josie to be by his side with all the innocence of their youth. But that was a time gone by.

Calming her father had tired her out and all the cover-ups had left her feeling drained, deceitful and lonely.

With her father now gone, the stark reality of the difference between her pre-war family and post-war family had overwhelmed any relief that she was supposed to feel. She had gradually built a wall, neatly cementing each brick into place, to shut herself in with the safety of her childhood.

Now as Jimmy stood once more beside her, she linked her arm through his and tenderly brushed fragments of Christmas bush from his shoulder.

'Gawd struth, I'm gunna have ta behave meself now you're back,' said Eddy, grinning broadly and shaking Jim's hand vigorously.

Daniel stood looking quizzical before he recognised his Uncle Jim. Then he ran head down and full pelt at his uncle's knees, and knocked him off balance. Alice laughed, while Jim scooped him up and onto his shoulders.

'Giggyup, Unca Jimmy!' Daniel cried gleefully. And he bumped up and down on Jim's shoulders.

Hazel soon lifted him down and slapped his bottom gently. 'Let Uncle Jimmy have a cup of tea first, Daniel.'

'But Unca Jimmy is my horse.'

There was a moment of silence, until Jimmy laughed. And Hazel silently thanked God for the innocence of children and their ability to bridge unspeakable pain.

Alice returned to the kitchen to check on the roasting leg of lamb and finish preparing the vegetables from Eddy's garden, while Hazel checked the pudding, which was wrapped in cloth and hanging from a rafter. Hazel wanted to make sure the silver threepences and sixpences she had hidden inside it hadn't made their way out and, happy with that, she stirred the custard round and round, while Alice peeled the potatoes and sang 'Good King Wenceslas', as she rocked her wide hips back and forth.

Daniel led Jim with Eddy in tow out the back to see the rabbits Santa Claus had brought him. The little grey rabbits had taken precedence over the wooden boat, football and bucket and spade, which lay forgotten for the moment beside the Christmas tree.

Grandpa arrived in time for dinner with an armful of presents. They were eyed suspiciously by Daniel, but the others all knew what was in the flat, square parcels.

Eddy was happiest when digging in his vegetable garden, regenerating the old plants with new in a never-ending cycle, each crop improving with each turn of the soil.

Daniel knew never to touch the plants or to walk on the garden. 'If you touch them, they'll rot,' Eddy explained, with an air of knowing that left Daniel in awe. And if Alice or Hazel bent to pick a tomato or a few peas in Eddy's absence, Daniel would pull at their skirts and scold them wide-eyed. 'Dey wot, dey wot.'

And Eddy's manly pride surfaced during dinner. 'You grow the sweetest vegetables, Eddy,' said Alice.

'Best vegetables I've ever tasted,' said Grandpa.

'Do you think the way they're cooked has anything to do with it?' Alice laughed.

Hazel had arranged the Christmas bush that Jim had picked on his way and as she gazed into the delicate red flowers, she asked Eddy pensively if he would make a garden for her to grow some flowers along the front of the house.

He turned to the men and scoffed, 'Flowers! What good is growing anything you can't eat?' And he laughed a deep belly laugh.

Hazel knew that, to Eddy, nothing in the whole world could be more sissy than flowers. And she knew that even if she had used the reverse psychology, as Eddy's mother had suggested so long ago, it would not change his contempt for even the idea of it.

After mashing up Daniel's pudding and letting him find his threepence, Hazel watched to see where the other coins turned up. Alice had found one and Eddy and Grandpa had found two each. Unfortunately, she had put them too close together and she and Jim had missed out. However, Eddy thought that putting silver in puddings for luck, connecting us somehow to the powerful metals of the earth, was a bit silly, so he quietly slipped his silver treys into Jim's bowl to please Hazel. He knew she wouldn't mind missing out, if it meant Jim finding two.

After dinner the presents were opened and happy chatter filled the house, while Daniel played happily with the discarded wrapping paper.

Still bubbling with the Christmas spirit, the contented family made their way to the river, where one after the other they dozed off in the shade of the huge gum tree. But not before Eddy had jumped from a branch into the water hole, with Daniel in his arms.

After tea Hazel went to the little church with its mystical steeple and as she stared into the mosaics of the stained glass window she spoke to Josephine, as she always did, and as she thanked her for sending Jimmy back a stream of light came down from the window high up in the loft.

Eddy did make a garden bed for Hazel, but he left the flower choices and the planting to her. She arranged squat plants along the border, slender in the middle row and tall plants at the back. While ordering them, she'd thought carefully about colour. Purple and velvety black pansies, pale pink carnations and a mixed selection of stock.

As the flowers bloomed, Hazel became pregnant again.

Although she looked longingly to the birth, it was tinged with trepidation. Somehow it had crept into her head that there had to be a death to make way for a new life. The trauma of Josephine's death while she was carrying Daniel hung like a dark cloud over her. She tried to push the thought from her mind and busied herself in readiness for this new baby.

Daniel kept looking for it under the cabbages in his daddy's garden. Eddy had told him that's where you find new babies and Daniel would never doubt anything his father said. He looked every day for months, determined to prove his father right, as his mother laughed and said, 'Don't believe everything your daddy says!'

Daniel had spent many hours watching the vegetables grow and he expected to see a baby's head pop up from under the soil between the cabbages and beans, sprouting arms, little fingers and toes. His care with the cabbage leaves turned to concern, as he remembered what his father had told him.

'Danwel not touch bubby, or bubby wot,' he repeated to Hazel, shaking his head from side to side.

Hazel didn't have the heart to shatter a little boy's trust, so after the birth she allowed Eddy to place the newborn baby among the cabbages, just long enough for Daniel to find it.

'Well, will you look at that!' Eddy said in faked surprise. 'It's a little boy!'

Daniel stood very still and stared down into the garden bed. Then he reached out for his father's hand and looked up into his eyes. 'Danwel touch?'

Eddy laughed and bent down to pick the baby up, and, crouching low, with his new son now resting upon his lap, he took Daniel's hand. 'Daniel, meet Simon,' he said proudly, as he put a tiny hand inside one even tinier.

Daniel stared in disbelief. His daddy even knew the baby's name! And he looked down into Simon's hands with their fingers folding in and reaching out. 'Show mummy,' he beamed, in his haste not to leave her out.

'Look wot daddy gwow,' he said, running into the kitchen, and pointing excitedly at Simon, who was curled up in Eddy's arms.

Hazel wiped her hands on her apron, and with that haughty expression, she gave Eddy a long sideways glance. His eyes twinkled back.

The afterbirth had arrived before the baby and the difficult Caesarean section had ensured Simon's safe passage, but had very nearly cost Hazel her life.

THIRTEEN

UNLOCKING THE ALBUM

Alice was a big help with the baby while Hazel recovered, and when Eddy wasn't at the Chullora railway yards he was happy to mind Daniel, playing cricket and football for hours on end and leaving no doubt about who enjoyed games the most.

However, this Friday evening Daniel was busy waiting for his Uncle Jimmy to arrive. He ignored his father while Simon slept peacefully dreaming of milk.

'Bit of a nip in the air, Daniel. Wanna help Daddy fetch some firewood?' Eddy coaxed.

He toddled off after his father, while Hazel knelt on the hearth and crunched newspaper into the grate and scattered coal dust over yesterday's news.

The men returned, big arms and little arms laden with logs and branches, which they dropped with a clatter onto the hearth. Daniel watched as his father placed the smallest branches, criss-crossed over the paper and coal and then the next biggest, with the biggest of all on top, leaning the bits of wood into and against each other, as if he was setting up fiddle sticks without tossing them first. A match was struck and the flames flickered and danced, but when Eddy waved a folded newspaper over them, Daniel jumped back. 'Look out, Daddy!'

Eddy sat back in his chair and patted the rug beside him. 'Sit back here, cobber.'

Alice carried in a steaming teapot and Hazel a tray laden with bread, butter, tin mugs, sugar, milk, plates and knives.

Hazel switched on the wireless, while Eddy took a blackened long-handled fork from the hearth and spiked a thick slice of bread. He pointed it towards the flames, while Hazel spiked a slice on another long fork and handed it to Daniel, who delighted in watching the bread change colour. Alice poured hot tea into the mugs and nobody spoke as deep, slow voices came out of the wireless. Daniel stuck his finger into the hot buttered toast. 'Why dis, Mummy? Why dis?' He wanted to know where the butter went.

'Sh!'

'Why dis, Daddy?'

'Sh!'

'Eat your toast,' smiled Alice.

Frustrated by the shushing, he refused to show the slightest interest in silly voices coming out of a box and he curled up on the rug and went to sleep.

This wireless was so much better than their first crystal set, which could only be heard by one person at a time attached to an earpiece. Hazel remembered the night when her mother had insisted that the attachment be placed in a bowl on the table, so that they could all lean over and listen to 'Ghosts in the

Kitchen' because it was everyone's favourite. Their next wireless had run on batteries and had to be wheeled in a pram to the garage to be charged up. One night it ran out just before the end of a murder mystery and her mother and Eddy had driven her mad, arguing over who the murderer was.

'It had to be the gardener!'

'The gardener? What makes you say that?'

'He was always hanging around.'

'It was the brother.'

'The brother? How did ya come to that, Mum?'

'He was a sneak.'

'Yeah, but the gardener was more likely to cut somebody up.'

'What—for no reason?'

'Well, what good reason did the brother have?'

'He was mad. Mad people don't *have* any good reason. They just do things!'

'What makes ya think he was mad?'

'He was the one who started all the arguments. Didn't ya notice that? Got a kick out of upsetting people. Sadistic streak.'

'He was just a troublemaker, a tease, a bit silly.'

'A bit silly? Coming from a worldly family like that?'

'What made him sadistic, then? There was nothin' in the story!'

'It was just about to come out when the bloody battery went dead!'

'I still reckon it was the gardener.'

'The gardener was just a stickybeak. He couldn't kill an ant.'

'Still reckon he did it.'

'Why? Why would he cut somebody up?'

'Because he was sick of getting picked on for never being right.'

Alice laughed. 'He was a stickybeak.'

'Well, if he was a stickybeak and the brother was a tease, who else could have done it?'

'Don't look at me,' laughed Hazel, as she came back into the room. 'I wouldn't want to upset you both!'

'Why, who do *you* reckon it was?' asked Eddy.

'It could only have been the brother, Hazel,' Alice interrupted.

'It was the priest.'

'The priest? What makes you say that?' Alice demanded.

'It's always the most unlikely, isn't it?'

'So ya just guessing,' said Eddy smugly.

'No, I called over the fence. Next doors told me.'

Jim finally arrived and Daniel woke to another strange sound. His uncle Jimmy was warming his back at the fire, while pulling something noisy out of a sugarbag. Daniel instinctively tried to move away, but before he could stand up, a yapping puppy had jumped into his lap and shook its fluffy tail in his face and licked his nose. The yapping and squealing woke Simon and he let out an enormous cry, while Hazel gave Jimmy one of her looks. 'Now look what you've done!'

'I thought a puppy might soften the blow of Daniel havin' ta share yous now,' said Jim, smiling defensively.

Hazel sat by the fire with Simon sucking, Daniel squealing, the pup yapping, Jim and Eddy laughing and Gran calling over the hubbub, 'Who wants a cuppa?'

There was only one name for the pup, with its black patch over one eye and black and white patches all over and, as Gran placed a warm saucer of milk on the floor, she called, 'Spot, here Spot!'

•

The weekend went all too fast and Jim was gone once more.

The following week Hazel felt stronger and eager to see Grandpa. She dressed Daniel and Simon in their Sunday best and set off.

It was a warm, crisp day, but as the train chugged closer and closer to Leichhardt, she became colder and colder and as she hurried down Elswick Street, a foreboding slowed her turn into Seale Street, where she saw the doctor's sulky outside Grandpa's house.

Daniel pulled at her skirt. 'Wot wong, Mummy?' And he tried to tug her forward.

She took a deep breath and hurried down the street with Daniel running beside her while she cradled Simon.

The doctor was clipping his bag shut when she entered the house. 'I can't find anything wrong with him!'

'Can I talk to him?'

He smiled. 'No reason why not.'

Uncle Bert and Aunt Daphne took Simon and Daniel out into the sunshine on the verandah.

Grandpa appeared to be asleep as Hazel moved quietly to his side, but as she bent to kiss him he opened his eyes. 'Can I see the boys?'

Aunt Daphne passed Daniel and then Simon through the window that overlooked the verandah and Hazel perched Daniel up next to Grandpa, while Simon twisted his tiny head on her arm and studied the old man's face.

'They look like Isabella, with their black curls and dark eyes.'

'What was Grandma like?'

He looked at her so intently that she felt his eyes pass through her and into another time.

'Can you reach the album?' he whispered. 'The key is in that drawer.'

Hazel unlocked the album and turned the pages slowly until Grandpa's hand rested upon hers. 'That's your grandma.'

It was the same photograph that she and Jimmy had laughed at the day she'd sneaked the key to the album. 'But she's a dark lady, Grandpa.' And she looked at his brown skin and saw it for the first time.

He sank back on the pillow and pressed the open album against his chest. 'Isabella was my mermaid.'

And his story tumbled out.

Hazel couldn't believe that she'd missed such a story, a secret story, sitting right under her nose. Her head was swimming and swaying and she listened in silence, until Grandpa's voice faded. 'I never saw my little sister Essie again. Said she died in an accident.'

The shock of this lost link and anger at the injustices suffered by her beloved grandpa caused her to blurt out, 'You don't know who your real father was?'

'Big secret them days. Me and Essie and Isabella, they called us half-castes. That's why they took us away from our people.'

Hazel was becoming exasperated. 'Isabella could have been your sister for all you know. Eddy could be my long lost cousin. How would anyone *know*?'

His voice was barely audible. 'Isabella was from Botany way...saltwater people...short tails...my waianya, my mother, was a river woman...long tails.

'How do you know your mother was a river person?'

'I remember swimming in the warm river waters, chasing possums up trees and watching waianya digging up wild yams. I remember her telling stories, sitting round a crackling fire on a starry night. And she used to sneak up to the fence and tell us things. She told me about our grandfather. He was Duck River: Watagora clan. He fought with Pemulwuy, the spirit bird warrior. They fought to save the rivers and the animals and birds and they fought to stop the new people from moving further up the big sacred river…she meant the Hawkesbury. The other rivers were my rivers, the ones I swam in as a boy: Duck River, Parramatta River, Georges River. That's where I swam.'

Grandpa rarely talked about himself and Hazel was shocked by the difference.

He stared into her confused, angry eyes and then out across the verandah to the children. 'What you have to remember, Hazel, what I been trying to teach you, is that ignorance kills things. It's why I read so many books and I want you to read. Good stories teach things: morals, humanity, survival.'

'What do you mean, Grandpa?'

Grandpa drifted back to the orphanage, the sandstone buildings barely visible behind the thick hedges and tall fences. Old Andy Jones was there, pruning the rose bushes that led up to Mrs Biggs' heavy wood door, the sweet perfume of red and pink roses tickling his nose. Beyond the fence he saw waianya, disappearing into the scrub that stretched away from the back of the orphanage to the river, and in full sunshine, between the two dormitories, Andy's vegetable patch.

Then the cold classroom loomed into view and Daisy was helping him and Essie with proper English. Essie was clutching the delicate pink rose that Andy had sneaked to her after the whipping. Grandpa flinched at the sight of the chook pen in the far corner of the yard where Essie had dropped the feed dish, while Mrs Biggs laid into her for speaking language to the chooks. She was cowering in the scattered seed as he ran towards her. She was yelling, 'Yerrabana,' and getting whacked again for not calling him 'Jack'.

Grandpa sniffed, as he turned towards Hazel.

'I might speak good English and read good English books, but I've still got Duck River inside, till the day I die and after. You can't change that by stopping language, or covering up rocks.' He took a deep breath and closed his eyes. An overwhelming sadness swept over her, as Grandpa reached for her hand.

'I want you to be happy, Hazel, you and the boys, for me and Isabella and Essie and waianya. This city's got strong spirits, deep foundations, that's what this city's got! Everyone's free to share them. But remember your ancestors and one day your children will be able to put their hands up with pride, you'll see. One day everyone will respect the spirit of this place: the river spirits, the mountain spirits and the sea spirits, the marks in the rocks.'

Hazel was speechless as she tried to grasp what Grandpa was saying. She listened as the floodgates opened and his life poured and tumbled out, his eyes sunken with a sadness deeper than the river, than the harbour, deeper than the sadness in her father's eyes or her mother's when the war came and went. Deeper even than the sadness in Jimmy's eyes when Josie left.

And he in turn saw the anguish in her eyes and tried to lighten the situation. 'If them new ones hadn't treated us as savages and pagans, they might have found that their God was here thousands of years before the Bible. They only had to listen to the celebrations. But people only trust sameness. Everyone gotta look the same, think the same, talk the same, walk the same, dance the same, worship the same and natives, well, a little too close to nature for the gentry,' he laughed. 'They spend most of their time running away from the natural state!'

'Have they changed anything, Grandpa?'

'Only their clothes.'

'But it's a modern world now. What am I supposed to do?'

'Take ya time, that's the secret. See where ya fit. Everything goes round and round. We're all connected, all part of the same universe. You belong everywhere, Hazel; everyone does. Listen to what nature's tellin' ya, trust ya instincts, ya emotions. That's what makes us human; not modern light, modern talk and modern clothes. Rushin' about…can't see what good can come from it.' Grandpa closed his weary eyes. 'It's what's in the earth, what's in the heart and mind that count.'

She gazed into his stillness and saw Josie rushing towards her through the swaying paspalum. 'How do I belong, Grandpa?'

'The river has always held you, Hazel. And the sea.'

'But what about now?'

'Sun and moon still balance day.'

She glanced back at him and the album still open in his lap. 'Why is Grandma dressed like that?'

'Gentry dressed her up like that to take pictures, just like an English lady, to show how they could civilise blacks. But they only saw the hat and the dress. Isabella's eyes tell the story.'

'Why are you telling me all this, now?'

'Because I want you to know that despite my English manners and book learning, I'm still Darug and Isabella will always be a woman of the sea. She came from the sands and she went back. I want you to know nobody can change that. The heart of Sydney can't be changed, no matter how much they dress black girls up.'

'Is that what I feel, deep down? Isabella, tugging my soul towards the water?'

'You're the river and the sea, Hazel.'

'The truth never hurt anyone,' Hazel said indignantly.

'Truth kills people every day!'

Isabella had lived in fear of losing Alice. There had been all those before her, floating dead in the harbour from smallpox. No more singing. No more ceremony.

And she became crazy with fear after each loud knock on the door that brought inspectors into the house to check that Alice was being brought up right. 'Don't tell them the truth, Jack. We gotta keep pretending!'

Isabella and Jack had become good at keeping the truth to themselves as the inspectors came and went, patting Isabella and Alice on the head. But by the time Alice turned three, the truth had killed Isabella.

Hazel stared into Grandpa's sun-wrinkled face and couldn't think of anything more to say. She held his hand in hers and pressed it gently to her cheek.

'See, Hazel, sometimes it's best to keep truth to yourself and sometimes it's not.'

'Hiding things killed Isabella.'

'Hiding the truth saved Alice and you. The end of a time killed Isabella.'

'There's no reason why anyone would want to take Daniel and Simon from me, is there?'

'People believe what they want to believe. Easier to see us as nomads and pagans.'

'But why don't you hate anyone, Grandpa?'

'Hate withers things. It's love that keeps them alive.'

'The doctor said I can't have any more children so I'd die if I lost Daniel or Simon.'

'You'll have more little ones, Princess. I can see a little girl and you won't lose the boys if you keep truth to yourself.'

'But what will I teach them?'

'Patience.' And he handed Hazel the key.

She locked the album, took it into the living room and replaced it carefully on the top shelf. When she went back in to Grandpa, he was fast asleep. She kissed his weary brow and shuddered at the thought of losing her boys.

On the train, Hazel hugged Simon close and grasped Daniel's hand and when she arrived home she didn't say anything to her mother about what Grandpa had said. Eddy had never brought the subject up, so she wasn't going to; now or ever. But as she bent to tuck Daniel into his cot, she heard the low-pitched sound of the boobook owl. *Boobook, boobook* it called into the darkness. The deep-throated curlew followed, *karr-er, karr-er*.

Moonlight washed in over Grandpa, taking him back.

FOURTEEN

THE MERMAID

Jack Smith was strolling across the clifftop at Shark Bay, his long fishing spear propped casually against his shoulder. It was a fine summer morning and he was taking his time. A sacred kingfisher peered at him from a low, bare branch and he laughed at the majestic coloured bird pretending to peck at a grasshopper, while waiting for him to return with succulent shellfish.

Turquoise, cream, black and ochre. The colours of the kingfisher stood out against the backdrop of bursting yellow wattle. Seagulls circled above as Jack Smith made his way down to the rocks where the cliff phased away. Down through the lantana that had quickly spread its roots into nooks and crannies and cradled orange and yellow faced flowers. Pelicans gliding in, Jack waded slowly into the water with his spear raised, while the seagulls hovered. The sea was calm, the sky was clear and there were plenty of fish about. It was what he called a perfect morning.

And after spiking mullet, he left his spear on a rock and swam about under the crystal clear water, catching shellfish in his hands, then he squatted on his haunches to sort out what he'd throw to the pelicans and seagulls, while the kingfisher waited. He put his catch into a sea-soaked sugar bag, then sank into a cool rock pool and lay face up to take in the sky.

And as he sauntered back along the clifftop, the sandy beach on the western side of the rocky escarpment spread out before him. It was still early morning and as he fed the kingfisher, he was surprised to see a woman and a child walking along the water's edge below. The girl began to run ahead, her light reddish brown curls bobbing and glistening in the sun, while the young woman seemed happy to lag behind. She looked like a mermaid, with her long fishtail skirt swishing about her ankles and her wild black hair hanging down over her shoulders. She turned and looked up to where Jack was, as if she knew someone was watching her. He ducked behind a tree before he had a chance to see her face. And when he peered out again he saw her paddling, dress held clear and shoes in hand, kicking the water up as she continued on her way to the far end of the inlet. She moved freely yet with grace, and Jack was drawn by the gentle morning sun down the embankment to the soft sands.

The girl was running towards him. The woman had turned too and when she saw Jack she called to the girl to wait. But the girl ran on, while he stood gazing at the young woman moving his way.

'What's up there?' the little girl asked him, pointing to the spot he had clambered down from.

But Jack couldn't answer as the young woman approached

and he found himself looking into the black pearly eyes of a sun-soaked mermaid.

'Can we go to the top of the rocks?' the girl pleaded. 'You never take me up there, Isabella!'

But the mermaid didn't answer. She lowered her head and looked at Jack inquisitively from under her sea-splashed eyelids.

'What's up there?' the girl persisted.

'Bird's nests, wild flowers and a view down into the sea,' Jack said mechanically, his mind reluctant to leave the mermaid.

'Will you take us up there?'

But before Jack could answer, the mermaid spoke. 'Not today, Edith, we're not properly dressed.'

'I'll be here tomorrow,' Jack offered quickly.

'I'm not allowed to take Edith near the cliffs.'

'Mother won't mind if you and this kind gentleman keep a good watch over me. Please, Isabella. She'll let us come tomorrow because she is busy packing up for our trip to England and she wants me out of the way.' The girl turned to Jack and screwed up her face. 'She says I'm more of a hindrance than a help, whatever that means.' Then she turned back quickly to Isabella. 'And if I don't see what's up there, I might never know. We might stay in England and never come back to Vaucluse House again.'

The mermaid's voice dropped. 'Course you'll be back, Edie.'

'Where do you live?' the child enquired, anxious to know if the man really would come back.

'Leichhardt,' Jack said, more to Isabella than to her.

'Leichhardt! That's on the other side of Sydneytown. Father lived near there once. At Petersham. What do you do there?' she asked cheekily and kicked her feet at the water.

'I'm a blacksmith. I work with horses,' he answered again in Isabella's direction.

'Ooh, did you hear that, Isabella? A blacksmith. Just like my grandfather. Mother's father is a blacksmith at the quay. Do you know him?' But she ran off towards the water before he could answer. She was too young and innocent to understand. Her mother's parents were the lowly side of her family tree, meant to be hushed up—not boasted about. So her mother was taking her elder sisters to England, in the hope of finding them suitable husbands.

This precocious child had taken a liking to Isabella, and because she was the youngest and the most boisterous of the girls, Mrs Wentworth had made Isabella directly responsible for her. Edie's innocence and vitality were comforting to the young Isabella. But now, after three years of caring for her in the beautiful gardens surrounding the big house and free access to the children's wing with its sitting room full of books and games and noise, Isabella would be left alone, a mere domestic at the mercy of the head housekeeper. She fought back tears at the thought of being separated from Edie, who had been five when she'd arrived. She was now eight but still tugging on Isabella's skirt, just as she had so many times before.

'That's my father's property anyway,' Edith said, pointing towards the cliff. 'And my sister owns Greycliffe, that big house up there. You have to have permission to be here. And what's that you've got in your bag?'

Jack smiled at the child's desperate attempt at authority. 'Your father gave me permission to fish off the rocks because I'm breaking in one of his horses. And I've already been introduced up at Greycliffe.'

'Oh!'

'I'm coming back tomorrow to dive for some coralline in the bay. Your mother wants to take some to England with her.'

The mention of her mother in practically the same breath as her father and Greycliffe was just too defeating for words. So she tried another tack. 'How lucky you are to be able to dive for coralline! What colours are down there under the sea?'

Jack smiled at Edith's polite persistence. 'From the deepest scarlet to pale rose and brilliant yellow. Which would you like, my lady?'

'Well I shall have to come back tomorrow to tell you. It is too difficult to choose on the spur of the moment.' And she flashed a demure smile, which couldn't help but creep up at the sides, stopping just short of a victory sign.

Isabella smiled broadly and nodded a polite goodday.

We'll see you tomorrow, then!' Edith called over her tiny shoulder.

Jack watched Isabella disappear into the morning mist between the Moreton Bay figs, and as he watched her spirit fade away, he reached out for her.

It rained the day Jack Smith was buried. The wind blew and blew as his coffin was lowered into the earth at the foot of the Blue Mountains, which rose high over the Hawkesbury and Georges Rivers, dwarfing Duck River and the bidgee place of his Darug past. No birth date on the tombstone. Just a going date, a going to his Isabella, to his waianya, a going back into his ancestry.

Alice went home to Leichhardt with Bert and Daphne. Her wish was feasible, with the Palmers' growing family and need of more space.

The fresh smell of rain was still in the air when she took the book from Grandpa's old bookshelf and ventured out into the garden. And as she sat on the worn wooden bench beneath the old fig tree, a soft breeze joined her and played with the pages. Grandpa's bookmark with the river ducks fell to the ground and as she bent to pick it up, she saw a horseshoe sunk in the mud. 'Oh, Grandpa, where's Josie?' And out rushed her grief.

FIFTEEN

ACCIDENT PRONE

The years passed quickly, yet Hazel, like Alice, continued to suffer the loss of Grandpa and Josie. But when Daniel and Simon cantered about in the yard with their mouths caught in that twist to the side, sucking air, hissing in and clicking out, that strange Grandpa noise, followed by 'Giddyup, giddyup, giddyup,' she would laugh and remember the happy times, when Grandpa had brought Josie to Cabra in the horse and cart.

But an overprotectiveness had crept into her mothering and whenever she watched the boys play cricket with Eddy, her heart would leap into her mouth if he hit the ball too hard, as Daniel or Simon ran straight for it and stepped obliviously into its zooming path. But she kept her fears silent, because Eddy would call the boys sissy if they jumped out of the way of a ball.

They could both sing 'God Save The King' and they waved their Union Jacks on Daniel's birthday, that May day when King George VI was crowned. And they were well aware of manners.

They tumbled about in the yard but were spick and span when Hazel took them out. On the outside, Hazel was Cabramatta's perfect English mum; nobody was going to catch her out. And her boys were good little Aussie boys, full of patriotism and sport.

But she was shocked to find that she was pregnant again. The doctor had said Simon would be the last. She was caught completely off guard and Eddy panicked when he heard he would have another mouth to feed.

Jim couldn't have been happier and he offered to help out, but Eddy was too much of a bloke to take it. 'Thanks anyway, but I can look after things!' And Jim nodded and left it at that.

Alice shared her apprehension but it soon turned to joy as she and Hazel began sorting through the box of baby clothes, the oldest among them reeking of mothballs.

Daniel became vigilant at the cabbage patch once more, explaining the origins of life to Simon and Spot with an air of superior knowing that only an older brother can carry off.

Expectation filled the air and Hazel felt an awful pressure to hurry things along. But she was content in this pregnancy and wanted to hang onto it and savour what she wasn't really supposed to have.

At the river Eddy watched the boys while she floated on her back and let the water take her weight and her baby as she drifted down the river. With the clear blue sky domed above her, she felt safe and secure in the earth's womb. Then she wanted her baby back and sank into the clear water, swirling her hands and kicking her feet just enough to keep her afloat and in touch with her swollen belly.

•

Eddy piggybacked the boys in turn all the way home. But he bounced them into excitement and they fought to swing up onto him together, their tiny hands grasping at and clinging to his throbbing neck. Spot yapped and Hazel turned back to look for the cheeky kookaburra who laughed, *koo-koo-koo-koo-kaa-kaa-kaa-kaa*, at their skylarking, while perched a safe distance away in a tall gum tree.

In the afternoon she surrendered herself to a soft breeze that swept back and forth in gentle foreplay over her full body, and she almost dropped off to sleep on the settee. But just as she was dozing off, Daniel shook her face roughly.

'Simon's swallowed a penny, Mummy, Simon's swallowed a penny!'

Simon had found a halfpenny that had fallen between the cushions of his father's chair and before Daniel could stop him, he had put it into his mouth. In the midst of a chuckle he had swallowed it and it had lodged sideways in his throat.

Hazel started as Simon turned blue. Eddy had heard Daniel's cry and was frantically trying to remove the coin. Simon coughed and spluttered and just when Eddy thought he had it, it slipped back. Daniel watched anxiously, white faced and silent, as his father struggled and just as Daniel was about to cry, Simon coughed up the penny.

He lay quietly, and then began to convulse from the panic and loss of breath, while Hazel worried that the copper from the coin would seep into the well of his tiny body.

Eddy picked him up and ran with him towards the doctor's house. Spot raced ahead, while Hazel and Daniel ran behind, trying desperately to keep up.

The Palmers cut across the back paddock, down the track and through the paspalum, which now grew taller than Daniel. Eddy lost sight of his eldest son, as the tiny figure pushed back the sticky grass that flicked in his face. Hazel kept Daniel in sight, but at the sound of her squeal Eddy glanced back to see her fall head-first over a lazing cow. Quickly she picked herself up and waved to him to keep going while she caught Daniel once more by the hand. The cow scrambled to its feet and, stretching its neck after her, gave a long *moooooo*…

The doctor stabilised Simon, but suggested he be transferred to the hospital for observation.

When they got there, Eddy stepped outside for a smoke while the nurse tucked Simon into the cot and Hazel waited anxiously for the duty doctor.

He finally arrived, checked Simon and checked the nurse's report. Then he looked hard and long at Hazel. 'Having another baby, I see!'

Daniel held onto his mother's skirt. 'You people have to take care of your children if you don't want to lose them.'

Hazel went cold, but just at that moment Eddy returned and the doctor changed his tone. Shock had welled up in Hazel and a new unspeakable mistrust of men in white cotton coats. It wasn't until Simon smiled up at her that her fear of recrimination subsided.

'Mummy fell over the cow,' Daniel giggled to the nurse.

Hazel's relief that Simon was all right turned the embarrassment of the cow incident into a deep belly laugh that went on a little longer than maybe it should have.

Eddy added his own relief. 'I didn't know whether to keep running, or go back and apologise to the cow!'

'Mummy didn't say sorry to the cow.'

Hazel picked Daniel up and gave him a hug, while the nurse gave him a red and white striped bullseye from the lolly jar.

'So the cow said moo to Mummy,' he added excitedly as he sucked the stripes off.

The young nurse glanced at Hazel's bulging belly and couldn't hold back her laugh. She tried to apologise for her rudeness, but the laughter wouldn't stop and that just made Hazel laugh all the more. The white coat came back and told Eddy politely it was time for them all to go home and that he could pick Simon up in the morning. The nurse quickly left, and Hazel was glad to escape from the coat's sight, before he changed his mind.

She hurried to catch the nurse and made her promise she would keep an eye on Simon, until they returned first thing in the morning. The nurse gave Hazel a cheeky wink and patted Daniel on the head, 'You can pick your baby brother up, safe and well in the morning.'

Although Daniel's big brother attitude made him serious and sensible, it still allowed Simon the freedom to explore. But this first incident would soon lead to Simon's lifelong tag of 'accident-prone'. And there was nothing Hazel could do about it.

SIXTEEN

THE WAR COMES BACK

Hazel loved poetry and recited poems by heart with a love of expression that never ceased to enthral the boys. Alice's gift for storytelling had clearly been passed down, along with Grandpa's sensitivity to language.

Daniel's favourite was 'The Man From Snowy River' and Simon's was 'Mulga Bill's Bicycle'. Her storytelling fascinated Daniel speechless, her voice going up and down over hill and dale, stockwhip cracking, rounding the horses, cantering along, her face contorting, eyes widening and narrowing at the twist and turn of every word. And as Simon listened open-mouthed, she would fly with Mulga Bill's bicycle as it 'made a leap of twenty feet into the Dead Man's Creek'.

No sooner had Daniel reached school age and marched off with pencils and marbles rattling around inside his shiny schoolcase than a miraculous baby sprouted from the cabbage patch. Yet, as the months hurried on, this John Stanley baby was more fascinated by his brothers' interest in him than by his mother's stories.

He had arrived without much fuss and had joined the family as a matter of course. This easy transition from cabbage patch to family had encouraged him to mimic his brothers, and Hazel watched helplessly as her dear baby became more and more like Simon. If there was a chair to topple off, he'd find it and in the race to knock over anything that brimmed with milk, he jockeyed for position but couldn't quite match his brother in that. If Simon or John Stanley was found within arm's length of a cup, bowl, glass, billycan or jug, it was systematically moved.

On Saturdays, Daniel gloried in his role of elder brother and rode his scooter to the bookmaker's house with his daddy's bets in his pocket. Some Saturdays he was asked to go back to collect the winnings. He didn't know what 'winnings' meant, or why there weren't 'winnings' every Saturday, but he loved going back to collect, because it made his daddy very happy. He felt so grown up, parking his scooter at the gate and walking into the back room of the bookmaker's house, the noisy blokes stopping to watch as he reached his hand up to the counter for the flat brown envelope.

'So what didja back t'day? Have a big win?' they'd call out. And he'd nod, take the winnings and stride back to his scooter. On a recent visit, the bookmaker had handed him a fat envelope and the blokes joshed and laughed, 'Big win t'day! Don't go spending all them quids at once!' And he'd ridden home so fast that when he rounded Doris Road, he'd fallen off his scooter.

Hazel used home remedies to treat the boys, so she could save on visits to the doctor, but her constant worry over John Stanley, as well as Simon, caused her distress. She dreaded the prospect of accidents that might leave her vulnerable to the white coats. But the rarity of Daniel's accidents and his sensible nature did much to strengthen her hope, as he watched over his younger brothers with repeated grown-up retorts, like 'Watch where yous goin', ya idiots!' or 'Screw ya heads back on, why dontchas?'

Hazel's last visit to a doctor, or quack, as Eddy referred to them, was when Simon broke his thumb after sticking it down a plughole and knocking a full packet of Rinso onto it as he tugged to get it out. This visit had caused her a sudden attack of palpitations, sweat dripping from her brow onto the sterile floor, as the white coat stood over her and his eyes scanned the brown and white patches of skin that covered her face and arms. 'Rather extensive, isn't it?'

She moved away, her eyes asking him to keep his voice down, but he ignored her and went on, 'Just a pigmentation disorder. Only affects Aborigines. I'm from the country and doctors here wouldn't have a clue, let alone the rest of Sydney. So if anyone asks what it is, just mention corpuscles—that'll baffle 'em.' And he laughed.

Hazel wanted to get home. Nobody had drawn attention to this before. When she'd first noticed the change, Alice had assured her it was harmless. And anyway, Eddy wasn't interested in the appearance of things; wouldn't know what she had on from one day to the next, and the difference between polka dot and floral stumped him. He was only concerned with numbers and preferred to say nothing than to take the gamble on upsetting a woman.

Simon's thumb reappeared, cast in blinding white plaster and Hazel bundled him out of the hospital grounds without turning back, and stopped for nothing until she turned the corner into Doris Road again, where she was safe at last. Simon ran on ahead, while she held onto a telegraph pole and vomited.

The same palpitations began to occur whenever she left the house. But she kept this malady to herself and merely tried to stay at home more often. She insisted to Eddy that she had to be there for the boys when they got back or in case of an accident, which could necessitate an early departure from school. Of course the speed with which the boys flew in through the back door, chucking schoolbags into their bedroom, grabbing a football and tearing out through the front, made a mockery of Hazel's excuse. The boys would rather have died from injury than be sent home like sissies to their mother.

But Hazel became an expert at covering her fear and developed a multitude of excuses for not leaving the house. 'The prop man comes today and I need a new prop' or 'I'm not well' or 'It's washing day' or 'It's ironing day' or 'Where could I possibly find the time to go out?' or 'It's too hot' or 'It's too cold' or 'It looks like rain' or 'If I don't clean the stove today, how can I cook tea tonight?' She started to believe them all herself. And she came to feel quite noble as she raised the importance of her role as housewife and mother to a level she felt it deserved. She was no longer just 'the missus'. She was Mrs Martyr, keeping herself hidden from the white coats and the welfare.

So nobody questioned her when she cauterised her finger to save a trip to the doctor. It was a waste of time mentioning the 'D' word, or the 'Q' word. The mere mention of either brought scorn. Eddy continued to use the 'Q' word anyway, in an attempt to reduce the fear of the other.

And Hazel continued to rely on home science, bush remedies passed down from Alice and Grandpa. The closest she came to professional help was consulting a medical handbook, or collecting health articles from the newspaper. She did her own extracting and mixing and if anyone was silly enough to mention the 'D' word or the 'Q' word, she would quickly retort, 'What would they know?'

Her fears were compounded, though, when a teacher called by to enquire why the boys hadn't been to school for three days.

She pulled out the old pram and flick-dusted it and headed towards Cabra oval with John Stanley. The culprits saw her coming and ducked into the footy change-rooms. But when they peered round the door to see if it was safe to come out, they saw the parked pram.

Panic stricken, they looked for another way out and saw light streaming in from an opening above the change-bench. Simon climbed up first and was halfway out, when Daniel grabbed his feet. 'We're gunna get killed for waggin' it, Simon, but we're gunna get even worse killed if we run away from Mum!'

Simon dangled between a belting and the grassy freedom below, but the fear of never seeing home again finally beat him. Reluctantly he wriggled his bottom until his feet landed safely back down on the slatted bench.

They came out, pretending to button their flies and Hazel turned the pram for home, with the boys waddling behind her, without a word.

Her trust was kept in a tin of Zam Buk and with her brood safely back home, she rubbed the antiseptic cream, roughly, into Simon's grazed knee. It was the thick green of the forest with the smell of the eucalypt kept at the ready—a tin in every room of the house.

'Muuum…me foot got caught in me bike!'

'Well, get me the Zam Buk.'

'Muuum…I cut me finger nilly orf!'

'Pass the Zam Buk.'

'Muuum…me toenail's hangin' orf!'

'Well, Zam Buk it back.'

Sometimes Simon joked, 'Me arm's fallen orf!' and Daniel would joke back, 'Stick it back on with Zam Buk!'

But for Hazel the 'I got a cold' called for a different tack and she went from green goo to a clear smear for their chests. The boys called it 'that invisible, stinkin' stuff'. This remedy couldn't be trusted by itself: it needed the help of hot lemon drinks to sweat the sickness out through the night and eucalyptus lollies, to suck in the morning, while she burnt gum leaves, like Grandpa used to, to clear the house out.

Hazel was proud of her strong Grandpa roots and she went along with her mother's home remedies. She was a nurturer and protector. And that was women's business. She was staying clear of toffs in coat-dresses.

But when Simon fell down hard in the playground, the gravel-filled cut was serious. Hazel persevered, bathing it with hot salted water before filling it with Zam Buk, replacing the loose skin like a lid and binding it up with a rag that had been laboriously scalded.

But a tiny grain of gravel lay hidden deep in the wound and when Simon complained of pain in the groin, Hazel knew it was poison.

The white coat glared. 'Youuu people! He's lucky he didn't lose his leg!'

'Youuu people youuu people youuu people' resounded in Hazel's head and her anger rose like sea snakes from a swirling, deep green sea. She cursed herself for missing the grit, hurried from the surgery and retched and retched.

Cabramatta was a small community and although Hazel had met the Morris family, the Westons and the Walkers, who were the other families in Doris Road, she felt safer keeping to herself. She had already taught Daniel and Simon not to tell the neighbours anything.

Jim came to visit from time to time. He hadn't brought a girl home, though, not since Josie. But the love he shared with his nephews seemed to bridge a gap. Jim was just masculine without thinking about it, whereas Eddy had very definite ideas on what a boy should be. And Hazel was pleased to have Jim around to balance them. So the boys had the two men and with the spirit of Grandpa always near, well, she was happy with that.

It had turned cold since Jim's last visit and she was reading a book as she warmed herself in front of the wood stove, when Eddy called out from the living room.

'Haze, can you come 'ere a minute? Jim's arrived!'

Jim was sunk deep in the settee and nursing a cushion when she came into the room. 'What's wrong, Jim?'

But his difficulty in beginning just sank him further into the settee.

'What is it, Jim? What's the matter?'

'It's…um…it's Dad, Hazel.'

They never spoke of their father. They'd lost all contact.

'The gangrene, you know. Well, they had to amputate.'

It hit Hazel like a thunderbolt. 'Where is he?'

'Bea Vista, a servicemen's home.'

'Where's that?'

'Summer Hill.'

The next day, Jim, Hazel, Eddy and Alice slogged up the hill into the wintry drizzle, Eddy carrying John Stanley, Jim piggybacking Simon, and Hazel and Alice tugging Daniel into a sort of take-off position, while they tried to balance their umbrellas.

After reaching Bea Vista, Hazel paused in the foyer and desperately sucked at the air in an attempt to calm the palpitations. The matron offered her a glass of water before she directed her down the long narrow corridor after Alice and Jim, while Eddy stayed behind with the boys.

With his legs amputated from the top of his thighs, Joe could only be propped up for short periods of time in a semi-upright position.

The ward was bare and cold and as he watched his past coming towards him he couldn't hide his joy. Tears filled Alice's eyes as he shook Jim's hand so long and so hard she thought it would break. And when Hazel bent to kiss his cheek he held her face so tight that she almost fell against the bed.

Hazel tried to piece it all together. Billie from La Perouse had told her that if you broke tribal law, spears would be aimed at the wrongdoers' thighs. Her father had invaded another's territory and breached territorial rights, so his thighs were speared by metal blades. The sap from trees oozed no gangrene, though, and he could have kept his legs if the world had stuck to tribal ways.

'Where are my grandsons?' Joe asked, breaking Hazel's thoughts.

The momentary escape as she went to collect the boys from Eddy allowed time for her palpitations to subside. In the waiting room she sipped another glass of water before returning with the boys to Joe's bedside. And Eddy remained in the lobby, out of respect.

'You're the man on our mantelpiece!' Daniel gasped.

'With the funny hat,' piped in Simon.

Nursing John Stanley, Joe had a real laugh for the first time since the war, but he saw the sadness etched into his daughter's face.

'Take a look out of my window, Hazel,' he said gently.

She peered through the misty rain, and there in the distance stood the grey steel arch.

'I told ya they'd build a bridge one day!'

Hazel thought back to the empty gap her father had pointed out so many years before. She had spent years watching the cranes, waiting for the day when the two arcs would be joined. It seemed she was waiting forever, but the day had finally arrived and the arch was closed. But she was left to wait once more for the official opening, waiting to walk across the water as her father said they would.

The Sydney Harbour Bridge had risen like a rainbow, and on opening day clouds had floated above like spirits before evaporating into the blue sky. Flags had danced red, white and blue above the tumultuous crowd, with only a thin ribbon holding them back.

The Governor-General drove up in an open carriage, as black and shiny as his top hat, while military horses glistened, capturing the sun.

Hazel held Eddy's arm and laughed with amazement as a protester rode by on a shiny horse, waved a shiny sword and slashed the official ribbon right in front of the official party. 'What a perfectly democratic Aussie start!' Eddy had laughed.

Then the Premier stepped forward and Eddy lifted Hazel up by the waist, so that she could wave to the workingman's Premier and he'd waved back.

She'd seen him walking through Leichhardt once and her father had told her who he was. 'That's Jack, that's Jack

Lang! Loves ta walk, sometimes all the way from Auburn to Broadway!'

Jack Lang had tipped his hat and grinned. 'Ow ya goin' there, Digger?' She knew her father liked him and she'd seen Grandpa talking to him many times on the corner of Elswick Street and Parramatta Road and he seemed to remember who she was too, even when she was up the street on her own. A man of the people, that's what Grandpa called him.

Hazel moved forward with the crowd and her glee raced along in front of her. 'Hurry up, Eddy. We'll be last across if you don't hurry!' But she had done that funny skip backwards that she did, whenever she was excited. She was wearing a navy and white striped dress and a straw hat with pink flowers on the brim and the flowers bobbed up and down as she skipped. A train of colourful people had surged across the bridge, cheering their city for joining the giant arcs that connected the north side of the city with the south. And their exuberance rose and danced in the arch. And just like everybody on the bridge that day, Hazel loved Sydney with all her heart. That night she wrote in her diary: 19 March, 1932 *The bridge finally opened today, Dad. You were right. Wish you could have walked with us.*

'Well, what do you think of that?' Joe said.

And as she turned back towards him, tears streamed down her face.

Hazel took the boys to see their grandfather each child endowment day. The doctors had taken his legs, but they had given back much more. She had a father again and her palpitations eased.

Joe was the perfect patient, helpful and cheerful. But when he broke into his nasal rendition of 'It's a Long Way to Tipperary', the nurses held their ears. 'Oh, no, not Tipperary!' And when Hazel and Joe sang together 'The Anzac Boys Are We', they scurried for their lives.

Hazel realised this new war in Europe was spilling over and she'd tried to ignore Australia's involvement. But Jim's next lot of bad news hit her like a thunderbolt. 'I'm sorry, Haze, but I've signed up.'

'For the army?'

'I have to leave for training.'

She broke down and cried. She cried for all the times she hadn't been able to. She cried for her mother, for Grandpa. She cried for Jimmy. She cried for Josie. Miss Morphett. And she cried for the chook with the broken neck and her father's legs, chopped off and discarded. 'How could they start another war?' And she collapsed into Jimmy's arms.

She didn't know that she was pregnant, until the 'D' arrived. 'Life goes on, doesn't it Jimmy?' she sighed. 'No matter what.'

Eddy heard the news when he arrived home from work and when Jim relayed Hazel's distress he was glad at the prospect of a new baby, which might drive the war from her thoughts. Jimmy doubted it.

The war overtook Hazel. Everywhere she looked she saw khaki. Everything was khaki. And as Jimmy left for training, he appeared the most khaki of all.

She started to watch the clock, her life revolving around Fred Jones, the postie, who turned the corner into Doris Road between ten and ten-thirty each morning. She'd be at the front gate, waiting. Spot always heard the pedals turning and the whistle blow long before she did and when she heard his bark she'd hurry to the gate, to watch Fred pedalling down the road towards her. She'd guess whenever there was a letter from Jim, because Fred's feet would always go a bit faster.

Fred marvelled at the way a few pages inside an envelope could change a person's life and he revelled in the importance of his duty. He was the bringer of tidings. And as women watched him ride past, their disappointment would catch in his spokes, while telegram stops caused his wheels to seize right up. His fingertips brought the difference between joy and disaster, and in one moment of delivery, lives could turn.

What if he lost a letter, if it blew away in a breeze, or if he held onto a telegram, afraid to deliver it? He understood fully the higher calling of his duty.

Fred Jones was not just another public servant; he was a postman. He had to know when to chat, or when to make a respectful exit. And he knew why they seemed interested in him. Sometimes he was dismissed quickly as his leather bag disclosed its contents, the disappointed in no mood to talk and the joyous too busy reading and already rushing off.

The day after a good delivery was always the best. People would share little snippets of personal news, like 'Billy's accepted Joyce's hand, she's nursin' over there as ya know, gettin' married when he comes home!' or 'They got that shrapnel outa Cecil all right' or 'Frank's training up north with a tree branch cause they run outa guns!' He liked the true-blue compliments. 'Simply 'mazin', me boy got them Anzac biscuits I sent to the front line in Tobruk.' And he'd be overcome with pride in a profession that could accomplish such a feat, delivering support to the soldiers and nurses at the front and hope to the mothers and wives waiting back home on the street. On good days he'd pedal away, ringing his bell and waving a salute.

The clock on Hazel's mantelpiece was polished rosewood with strong black hands that never failed. It ticked louder as the war marched on in time with the heart pumping away in her womb. And she would sit listening to the tick in the late afternoon while the children slept, and watch the hands click round as she waited for Eddy to come home so she could read him Jim's latest news from the training camp.

Hazel had sent Jimmy her book of Byron's poetry, the one Grandpa had given her for her twenty-first, while the boys had sent drawings of Spot, carefully coloured in by Daniel and gaily scribbled by Simon and John Stanley. After talking to the postie, Daniel insisted on separate envelopes with their individual names on the back. And, despite the extra cost, Hazel went along with his wishes on Fred's advice.

A bookmark was stuck against a poem and as Jim prised it away, Josie's face fell out. 'She walks in beauty, like the night… and on that cheek, and o'er that brow, so soft, so calm, yet eloquent, the smiles that win, the tints that glow, but tell of days in goodness spent…'

Tears sprang to his eyes as he read, holding the tiny photograph of Josie, which had hidden itself behind the bookmark. And he turned his life over with the image as he wrote—a *mind at peace with all below, a heart whose love is innocent.* So small that only he could see it, and he thanked Hazel for sending Josie to him, all those years ago.

Hazel huddled with Eddy over the wireless in the winter firelight, straining through the crackle of static to listen to news of the war.

It seemed to escalate. She dreaded news of Jimmy leaving for a war zone and, bulging with new life, she became anxious with all the waiting, waiting for the toll, waiting for the cry of life and waiting for homecomings fraught with shell-shock.

And with the burst of summer, Joe slipped away. It was the morning the Japanese bombed Pearl Harbor. Hazel was still reeling from the shock of the newsflash, when she was called to his ailing side. She walked up the hill with Alice in the soaring heat of the day while Eddy and the boys went to the cool water of the river.

Joe was barely conscious when they arrived, his heart unable to take any more. The room spun around Hazel and she wanted to spin with it, never having to stop or say goodbye, while Alice gently stroked Joe's brow.

'Has the war ended, Alice?' he gasped.

'Yes, Joe, the war is over.'

Hazel stood at the window and, gazing out at the distant arch, she heard voices again rising softly from the past. 'That's where they're going to build a bridge one day'. The tears began to well up. 'Don't be silly, Dad! Who could build a bridge that big?' And a tiny voice trailed away, 'Turncoat, turncoat!'

'Forgive me, Hazel,' he whispered. But before she had time to turn around, his life had closed.

An RAAF plane was flying Jimmy home from the camp for two days' compassionate leave.

Hazel watched the clock on the mantelpiece tick over, while Eddy paced expectantly to the front door and back and Alice pottered about in the kitchen. Then Eddy called the words Hazel and Alice had been waiting for.

'Here he comes! Here comes Jimmy!'

Jim braced himself. Spot was first out the front door, followed by Daniel and Simon, then came Eddy, Hazel, John Stanley and last of all Alice, wiping her hands on her apron and mixing flour with tears.

Everyone was talking at once and Jim felt he had stepped out of a time capsule, back into normality. And he longed for a time before war and longed for Josie to come laughing through the door too.

'How's that little girl of mine?' And he patted Hazel's belly, which had clearly begun to boast life.

But all she could manage was a wan smile, as she followed him inside like a lost puppy.

The evening meal was served with rotating courses of joy and sadness, and everyone rushed about helping. And afterwards, with the children tucked in, they moved out into the warm night air, sipping moonbeams and tears, and brushing off Christmas beetles with streams of laughter.

The boys had woken early, pestering for a day at the river with their Uncle Jimmy and by ten o'clock their patience, like the day, was already hot and sticky.

'If you drink any more tea you'll float away before ya even get ta tha river!' said Daniel, Simon standing staunchly beside him.

So a picnic lunch was quickly packed.

Hazel floated down the river, grateful that Jimmy was home so that together they could put their father to rest.

Early next morning a black shiny car came for them. Mrs Morris had kindly offered to mind the boys, and as the hot car pulled into the cemetery, Eddy wiped Hazel's brow, with Alice muttering, 'The war did it ya know, Hazel. The war did it.'

And as the child-sized coffin was lowered into the deep black hole, Hazel buried a part of herself with it and as each thud of earth smacked down on the coffin lid, it seemed as if a nail was being driven into her own.

She rubbed her hands over her belly, believing that her father's death had made way for this baby's passage, and believing wholeheartedly that Jim would soon be back home again for good. With the bombing of Pearl Harbor, well, she didn't like the Japs' chances. The Yanks would stop them.

The newspapers had become selective in their war correspondence. Jim knew more than his family, but he wasn't saying. The sinking of *HMAS Sydney* off Carnarvon had hit him hard, but he'd managed to camouflage his grave concerns with personal grief, leaving him nothing better to do than keep morale up.

Hazel had already begun to step over the line of reality, accepting and rejecting what she needed to, to keep the war at bay. With Jimmy's departure, a letter arrived for her and as her head bent to read it, something changed.

Dear Hazel

Once more, my condolences for the sad passing of your father.

Although I do not wish to infringe on your privacy at such a time, I feel the urgency of this situation, with your brother soon leaving for the war zone, condones what could rightly be seen as an intrusion.

To get quickly to the point, a will and note of instruction has been found under your father's mattress at Bea Vista. I have forwarded same in accordance with your father's wish that you pass this information to Alice and James. I do hope that the letter reaches its destination, before your dear brother departs. I have also enclosed a Christmas card for you that I found in his bedside table drawer.

Despite your father's disability, he managed to spread much laughter throughout Bea Vista, priceless medicine such laughter, in the middle of so much collective pain. Nursing plays only a small part in the survival of the human spirit. It's some hidden love that keeps people alive beyond normal endurance. Please pardon my indiscretion, but the contents of your father's final testament confirm this.

Sincerely
Matron Alexander
Bea Vista

She handed the papers to Eddy and wandered out into the morning sun, stopping by the gate to pack dirt around the stem of a bright orange poppy and she smiled her first real smile since her father had left Cabramatta.

Eddy came and knelt beside her, and helped her to prop up the long-stemmed flowers. 'Where do you think your father got all that money, Haze?'

'I don't know, Eddy, I don't know.'

'Fifty pounds for each of you! That's more money than I'll ever see.'

'Before the war he could make anything—shoes, kites—even made me a chair once. And could he spin a yarn. Silly bugger he was, silly as a two-bob watch. Just went too far.'

'He left yous no choice.'

'It's just nice to know things in the end. It's nice to see things in his own words. He did love us. And he must have been really sorry. Mum always said that the war did it to him. Guess she was right. But I still can't help blaming the drink.'

Eddy picked a poppy and handed it to her. 'He sure knew how to write a nice note. Somethin' I could never do.'

She looked at her husband kneeling beside her among the flowers. 'Actions speak as loud as words, you know.'

They weren't to know at the time, but the money would be saved until the end of the war to take them on a special journey.

The following day Hazel had an urge to visit her father's grave and as she wandered slowly past the rows of tombstones, she laughed to think that she had spent years silently worrying about her father lying drunk and destitute somewhere after being thrown out by his family, while instead, his life had somehow turned around. Here, among the tombstones, he'd come home.

As she neared his grave she noticed a woman gently patting a plant into the soft earth. Her hair was spiralling over her face but she somehow seemed familiar. At the funeral Hazel had noticed a woman in a fine silk frock, her head covered with a hat and veil, standing away from the family. She'd presumed, with indifference, that it was someone from Bea Vista.

The woman rose, brushed her frock and tossed her hair back from her face and as she turned, her auburn hair danced into the sun.

'Peggy!' Hazel gasped.

SEVENTEEN

NOWHERE TO GO

The day that Joe was chucked out of Cabra he'd wandered around the city streets. Up and down Broadway, weaving along laneways, down to the quay, through the gardens, into the Domain and Hyde Park, and then around again, round and round until his thighs felt like they were going to explode and his heart felt like it would split with the ache. Up and down. In and out. Round and round. Nowhere to go. Nowhere to escape.

As the sun set over the harbour, he slid under a bush and curled up like a sad snake turning in on itself. In the morning he woke to a burst of blinding light. The birds were pecking at the earth, seagulls were hovering and a ferry chugged by on its way to pick up the first passengers. This start of just another day smacked him awake and as the stretch of water overwhelmed him he heard a little girl's voice. 'Take me down to the rocks, Dad.'

Slowly he untied the laces of his shoes and barefoot sidled towards the water. Sitting on a warm flat rock, he dangled his feet into it and watched his life swirling round his ankles as he tried to sing, 'The...the Anzac...the Anzac boys...the Anzac boys are happy...', while a stranger passing by on an early morning walk stopped and tipped his hat.

Joe drenched himself all day in salty spray and shame, before making his way uptown to the Salvation Army shelter for bread and soup. He knew what these soldiers thought of the demon drink. They'd tried to save him at Leichhardt and then at Cabra on many a day, the gentle girl in the bonnet who clutched a timbrel dangling red and yellow ribbons; blood and fire. Salvation. He'd laughed and made some joke about all the blood and fire he'd seen and how the whisky helped him forget it. And he saw once more that sad smile as he turned and walked away. And it didn't matter how much you ribbed the girl with the timbrel, she always came back and she always had a smile and a 'g'day'. Sometimes she'd throw a gentle ribbing back herself and make him laugh.

Now as he watched the distinct uniforms of the brothers and sisters moving among the homeless drunks, red and yellow ribbons began to dance in his face. Blood and fire. Soldiers of the Cross. Demon drink. He had to get away.

He slid back under the bush and curled up.

He woke again to the warm rays of the sun, with the sound of the birds and the calm lapping waves, the sturdy rocks surrounding him, as he looked into the very core of life. He was rolling in and out of nowhere.

He couldn't escape the shame for all the hurt that he'd inflicted on his family. It hung over him like a dark cloud and when the bats flew in that night, they pulled the cloud down with them. He closed his eyes and swore to God that he'd never touch another drink. He'd carry these rotting legs and this rotting brain wherever. He was an Anzac, and had to keep fighting—for Alice, and Hazel, and Jimmy.

In the morning, he splashed cold salt water onto his face and tried to drown himself in hope. 'Dear Soldiers of the Cross,' he prayed, 'find me a job.'

A voice startled him. 'G'day.' It belonged to the stranger who'd tipped his hat that first morning. But his shame wasn't up to a chat and as he turned to escape, his foot slipped on the velvety moss covering the rocks and, with the fine bloke looking on, he went arse over turkey into the drink.

Without considering his smart shoes, the stranger sprang down onto the rock. 'Crikey, I didn't mean to startle ya!' But as he reached for Joe's hand the moss got him too. Joe ducked as this bloke made one almighty splash in beside him. He surfaced, one hand trying to grab his bobbing hat, while Joe tried not to laugh. 'Maybe you'll mind ya own business next time, cobber!'

Water dripped over the stranger's face, as he put his hat back on. 'If a g'day sends ya flying into the drink, ya probably need someone to mind ya business!'

Joe gave a half-hearted laugh and extended his hand. 'Joe Johnson.'

'Sam Garrett.'

And they helped each other out, clambering up the rocks, not knowing whether to shiver or laugh.

'Well, I don't know about you, Joe, but I'm not staying here to dry out. My house is just down the hill. I'll lend ya some dry clothes. It's the least I can do for not minding me own business.'

The house was large but inviting, with a winding pebble path that led to a large partly enclosed verandah. A girl pretty as a picture had fallen asleep over her book, while a cat slept peacefully at her feet. Two red setters had roused and were curiously rubbing themselves against the dripping men and sniffing their wet pants. 'Haven't yous ever seen salt water before?' Joe snapped, which set off a chain reaction with dogs leaping and barking, cat spitting and fleeing and the girl screeching. 'Mummy, come quick! It's Daddy! You never saw such a sight!'

'Now I'm in for it.'

'What about me? I don't even know the woman.'

'Samuel Garrett. What have you been up to? Don't either of you even think about traipsing through the house. There's warm water in the copper and I'll bring you both a towel and a gown. Becky, stop laughing!' And the screen door slammed shut.

Joe could still hear the girl laughing and the dogs yapping over the chatter of his teeth, as he followed Sam around to the back of the house. 'Just minding me own business, trying to escape from the world for a bit and I end up with pneumonia, dogs jumpin' all over me and a strange woman yellin' in me ear.'

With that, the back door swung open and the raging bull came at him again, waving fluffy things at him. 'Get out of those wet clothes while I put the kettle on and fix some bacon and eggs. And, Samuel, you'd better have a good excuse!' She saw Joe laugh. 'You'll need one too, mister.' And then it was Sam's turn to laugh.

Dry once more, Sam opened the door of a large wardrobe. On one side there were shelves of jumpers and cardigans, and on the other there seemed to be dozens of shirts and three of the smartest suits.

'What *is* this?' said Joe. 'A department store?'

Sam held up a pair of pants. 'Sir, these might just fit you.'

'Bit fancy for an old Digger.'

Sam threw a white shirt onto the bed. 'Gallipoli?'

Joe nodded. 'And what do *you* do, rob banks or somethin'?'

Sam laughed. 'Took a gamble. Started up me own furniture business and the wife helped. Smart woman, that one.'

'So what are you gunna tell her? That you fell into the drink trying to save an old Digger?'

'Sounds pretty good to me. If you're smart, you might even get to stay for dinner.'

The bacon and eggs smelt so good Joe had no trouble humbling himself. 'I'm Joe Johnson. If it hadn't been for your brave husband here, I might have drowned. Must have hit a rock when I fell.'

'And so, Joe Johnson, what were you doing down by the water?'

'Fishin'.' Joe's unflinching response impressed Sam, but his bet lay with his wife.

'And do you always fish in your suit?'

Joe started to cough. And, rubbing his arm with his fork, he faked a shiver.

'Samuel, get the rug from the settee while I pour Joe some tea.'

Sam tucked the rug tightly around Joe's knees. 'Warm enough for ya?'

But before Joe could think of a smark-alecky answer they were interrupted by a shrill voice. 'Mum, I want to come in.'

'Samuel, be a dear and bring Becky in.'

He was back a few moments later with Becky in his arms and gently placed her on the settee. 'She doesn't like to miss out on anything. Do you, Princess?'

'Well just because I can't walk properly doesn't mean I can't think.' And she eyed Joe squarely.

'That's what I always say,' was his deadpan response.

Laughter rippled through the house. 'I saw you walk, so you must mean when you're drunk. That's not the same.'

'Never judge a book by its cover. These poor old legs were bayoneted right through in the war. Give me a hell of a time they do. Wobble all over the place.'

'Were you at Gallipoli?'

'I'd rather have been at schoo1.'

'My grandpa was killed in Gallipoli. His name was Samuel Garrett, same as Daddy. Did you know him?'

'Can't say I did.'

'Well, what suburb did you come from?'

'Leichhardt.'

'Leichhardt! Well, Grandpa was from Summer Hill. Ya must have known him.'

This sudden burst of conversation with a stranger surprised Sam and Peggy Garrett as their daughter kept badgering him to talk.

'Can't remember all the names. There were hundreds of us, ya know.' But he saw the little girl's face drop. 'Probly did know ya grandpa. Probly sang with him sometime. Probly shared a smoke. He was brave, I know that. All brave, them blokes at Gallipoli. Names sort of didn't matter because we were one big family. Ya know what I mean?'

Becky was silent. Joe smiled at her and started to sing, 'The Anzac boys are happy…'

But halfway through the song his teeth began to chatter.

'Into bed with you, mister. Samuel, help him into the guest room while I heat up a water bottle. Becky, you shoo those dogs out.'

And this time Joe wasn't acting. He gladly fell into the

flannelette pyjamas and comfortable bed and tugged the thick woolly blankets up around his neck. And, with the addition of a rubber hot water bottle, gladly went to sleep.

Mrs Garrett hung the men's clothes out to dry and Sam left for work, promising to come home early.

She checked on Joe later and found him mumbling. 'Alice…' His forehead was burning up. She went to fetch a cool cloth. And when she returned and gently placed it on his brow, he reached for her hand. 'Hazel, is that you? Ya gotta forgive me, Haze, please. Ya gotta forgive me.' And he fell into a feverish sleep.

Mulling over the names, Peggy Garrett emptied the water from the cold bottle. Alice. Joe Johnson. Hazel. *Hazel Johnson!* And she suddenly dropped the screwtop.

When he woke later in the afternoon, she took him some hot lemon juice. 'So, Mr Johnson, you have a family in Leichhardt?'

He turned away. 'No…no.'

'Do you have somewhere to go?'

'Just down on me luck at the moment. Lost me job. But I'll find something, soon as I get on me way again.'

She tried to lighten the situation. 'Must be hard, with your wobbly legs and all.'

He laughed. 'They're not as wobbly as me head.'

'There's a job going here. Don't know if you'd be interested.'

'A job?'

'I need someone to get a vegetable garden going, I want Becky to have fresh vegies. Ya know what ya getting when they're straight out of the garden. Sam doesn't have time, looking after the business and all, and it would save me hours shopping.'

'What—bit of everything? Spuds, beans, peas, carrots, cabbage, chokoes, maybe some pumpkin and tomatoes?'

'With all that, Joe, I could start makin' me own vegetable soup!'

'Is that all ya'd need me to do?'

'No. I need someone to look after the animals, too, the dogs and the cat. Feed them, brush their coats.'

'Is that all?'

'And someone to stay with Becky when I'm out shopping.'

'Well, I can do that if ya tell her not to pick on me!'

'And there's no need to look for a room. There's quarters up the back, nice and private. Anyway, the job's there if you want it.'

'I'll take it.'

'Only one thing more I forgot to say. Sam and I, well, we're teetotallers.'

'Me too!'

'Oh, that's a relief, because we don't allow drink on the property. It's not a good idea around Becky. Ya never know when she might need us.'

Joe smiled. The Soldiers of the Cross had answered his prayers all right.

When Sam arrived home he heard the news from Becky before he'd even reached the front door.

'Mr Johnson is going to be our new gardener, Daddy. So now there's going to be two of us around that can't walk propIy.'

And as Joe slept, Mrs Garrett took Samuel aside. 'I think he's Hazel Johnson's father,' she said excitedly. 'You remember Hazel, my friend from Nestle's.'

'Hazel Johnson from Nestle's? Of course I remember. I had a soft spot for Hazel. She was one of my best packers.'

'I only met her dad a couple of times. It was such a long time ago, I just can't be sure if it's him or not.'

'Then what makes you suspect?'

'He said he was from Leichhardt and while he was feverish he muttered the name Hazel. It got me thinking. Hazel came from Leichhardt. And her father was at Gallipoli. I remember that because there was always some sort of delicate situation: he had trouble with drink, or getting work, or something. Hazel wouldn't really talk about it, but Josie and I always suspected that something wasn't quite right.'

'Well we can't pry. But I thought a lot of Hazel and if it is her father…she was one of those workers that made a supervisor's life less of a worry.'

Peggy smiled. 'Bit like me?'

Sam kissed her. 'No, not like you at all. You were a worry from day one.'

She laughed. 'Come on, I'll make you some tea. If he is Hazel's father, I think we should watch over him and if he isn't, well he's still a Digger and your dad would want us to look after him.'

'Somehow I get the idea he doesn't want anyone lookin' after him. So let's keep our watching to ourselves.'

Joe recovered and moved out to the quarters, just far enough away from the house for privacy. The yard was made up of a paved courtyard with a stretch of dirt across the back suitable for a garden. The front yard was paved too, with a garden beneath the verandah and a huge cabbage palm on the far side.

Looking about, Joe almost couldn't have been happier. His old legs could handle this, and the fresh salt air wouldn't do his head any harm.

Becky delighted him. Her quick wit and cheeky grin

reminded him of Hazel when she was her age and a girl like that being in a wheelchair, well, it left him no time for self-pity. He could often be found telling her a story as she sat there in the sun. And more than once Peggy had to yell out to him as he screeched her around the courtyard in her wheelchair, like a fire engine racing down Broadway.

Peggy had encouraged Sam to seek out an old Leichhardt Nestle's hand and ask after Hazel. The vague response was that the family had moved away years ago. Didn't know where. Out Chipping Norton way, he thought.

Joe sometimes walked in the early morning with Sam, fearing if he walked off on his own he might end up at the Woolloomooloo pub. However, he'd missed going with him the past few days.

On the last walk Sam had tried to open up the past, disclosing that he'd started out as a factory supervisor at Nestle's and that's where he'd met Peggy. It had hit Joe like a thunderbolt. And he very nearly blurted out Hazel's name. And Peggy? He thought there was something familiar about her. She'd come to the house with Hazel and Josephine. She was the one from Nestle's who ran off and married the supervisor. Joe remembered her wild red hair. He'd teased her about it. He'd also teased the girls about the way they idolised their boss. He'd been envious at the time, because he himself couldn't even hold down a job.

He went back to walking with Sam, but steered clear of any further talk of Nestle's, while Sam went on to explain how he and Peggy had left Sydney, when everyone was being laid off. They'd made their way to a property in the north, but eventually sold up and moved back to Sydney to start the furniture shop.

Joe heaved a sigh of relief. Moving around like that, they'd lost contact. He would have died of shame if they'd found out about him being run out of Cabra, yet their connection to his daughter made them even more special. He had a job now. He wasn't about to let them down. Or shame Hazel again.

The vegetables grew heartily and the red setters had the shiniest coats around. Joe's pride gradually came back and Peggy increased his responsibilities: some reading and writing and storytelling for Becky, just like he'd done with Jimmy and Hazel.

His heart ached for Alice but he could never go back. He could never face his family again. That part was all too late. He just had to keep the shame at bay. And stay away from the pub.

It was years before he fell down.

'Come on, Joe, I've got to get you home.'

'Have a drink. Come on, Sam. One drink with ya old cobber, before they take me legs off.'

EIGHTEEN

DIVINE INTERVENTION

Joe had been pushing Becky around the front yard.

'Faster, Joe,' she yelled.

But suddenly his legs went from under him and he crashed to the pavement. The wheelchair continued on without him, and stopped just short of the cabbage palm.

'Stop muckin' about, Joe. I know ya not hurt. Get up,' Becky laughed.

He tried to stand up, but couldn't.

'Joe, get up!' she yelled.

'I can't.'

Sam and Peggy heard the commotion and went to help, while Joe insisted that he'd be fine. 'I just need to rest up,' he said quietly. 'If ya could carry me to me bunk, Sam. And Peg, if ya 'ave to do somethin' a water bottle ud be nice.'

Sam did as Joe asked and then hurried back into the house to find some aspirin, while Peggy filled the hot water bottle. But as she approached his door with it, she heard moaning. It stopped when she knocked.

The following day Joe was in the garden when he fell against the wheelbarrow. He tried to get up but toppled over and pulled the barrow on top of him. Peggy had been watching him from the kitchen window and she sent Sam to help while she and Becky kept a respectful distance.

Sam carried Joe into the guest room. This time, he wasn't so resistant and Becky's doctor was called to the house to look at *his* legs.

Joe was too sick to fight. He'd known the day would come. The pain had become unbearable and he'd lost weight. And the shame he felt when he thought that he'd rather be dead than without his legs had intensified.

Becky's wheelchair was empty. He managed to drag himself into it, pushed the wheels round and steered it out the gate. The pub wasn't that far.

It didn't take Sam long to find him. The chair stood out with its bright yellow sun painted on the back and lolly-green frogs leaping over its sides. Joe and Becky had painted it, with Peggy yelling, 'Keep the paint on the chair for goodness sake!' But they were both covered.

Sam wheeled Joe down the hill towards the path that led to the harbour. 'Can't take ya home like this, cobber. Bit of fresh air'll sober ya up.'

'Hasn't Peg ever seen a drunk before? I wouldn't hurt a fly, ya know, not anymore. Wouldn't hurt Peg or Becky.'

'I know, Joe. But we don't want Becky to see how upset you are about losing your legs, do we? We'll go home later.'

'I'm a bit silly, that's all. Bit silly in the head. I don't care about me legs, not any more. It'll be a bloody relief to get rid of the blighters. Just think, Sam: no more friggin' pain.'

Sam didn't explain that he also wanted to save Peg the sight. She was only a kid when her dad had died from alcoholic poisoning and that was the reason Sam stayed away from drink. It worried her too much.

Joe looked up at Sam. 'It's not just me legs, ya know.'

'I know that, Joe.'

'I want to work. I want to make up for all the terrible things I've done in me life. I want to die with some dignity.'

'Becky still needs a teacher, Joe. We'll find something.'

Joe's words were becoming more slurred. 'Ya been good to me, cobber. Don't deserve it. Don't deserve nothing.'

Sam stopped pushing the wheelchair and knelt down in front of him. 'Joe, you've been like a grandfather to Becky. She never got to know my dad, or Peggy's. She used to drive me mad asking questions about her grandfather and Gallipoli. You're the grandfather she never had, Joe. You mean a lot to Becky. You've made a big difference to all of us.'

Joe's chest began to heave. 'We had a grandpa. We all need grandpas. You don't know, Sam. Ya don't know what I did to me family.'

'Well life goes on, though. Maybe you'll find your family again.'

'Grandpa's dead and I was chucked outa town. That's how bad I was.'

'But ya gotta forgive yourself. Struth, ya gave up the drink—even with all your pain.'

'Couldn't remember nothin' — whisky sent me crazy. Hurt me own family, but I kept on drinking and lost everything. Even hurt our grandpa.'

'Drink gets into ya blood and ya can't get it out, Joe.'

'I can't let it back in. Betta to be a trunk, than a drunk, 'ey Sam? Can't let it beat me now.'

'Where's your family living?'

Joe appeared to sober up. 'Alice is back at Leichhardt.'

'How do you know that?'

'The grocer I run into told me she was there. He told me she'd been in the shop, planning a party for one of the grand-kids the following Satd'y, so I snuck around to where we used to live, Grandpa's old house. Grocer told me Grandpa had died. Anyways, I saw her in the front yard. Hazel was there too, and two little boys with party hats. Me grandsons. It was a few years ago now; never went again. Upset me too much. He said Hazel was livin' at Cabramatta but didn't know what had happened to Jimmy after his fiancée died.'

'I think it's time to see them.'

'I'm too scared.'

'Come on, Joe. You're an Anzac!'

'It's worse than going to war.'

'It won't be as bad as you think. Let me contact them for ya.'

'You already know me daughter. Hazel Johnson. I should have said, but I was too ashamed of what I done. You were her boss at Nestle's. Always talking about ya, she was, and Peggy used to come to me house.'

'We suspected.'

'Josephine. She was the other, young cobber. To think me son would 'ave married her. The grocer said a horse kicked her.' And Joe hung his head.

'Josephine? Peg's friend? We must have been up north when that happened.'

'I'm going to have to let 'em take me legs. I can't just give up and die without seeing me family again. And they might see me, if ya tell 'em a trunk can't hurt 'em, 'ey, Sam?'

'They might, Joe. They just might.'

Sam went to see Alice at Leichhardt. Peggy was uneasy over how Hazel would feel about their relationship with Joe. It didn't seem right to hit her with too much at once, so they'd decided to keep their side of the story quiet for the time being. Peggy had also felt guilty about losing touch, especially in the light of what had happened to Josie.

Becky wanted to remember Joe as he was, pushing her around the yard like she was a fire engine; not still, in a dark hole. And Sam wanted to remember the cheeky bloke, the day they both fell into the harbour.

Hazel had caught Peggy off guard at the cemetery, but Peggy was overjoyed to see her old friend, and grabbed her by the hand and led her to a grassy patch under a Moreton Bay fig.

Hazel hugged Peggy as if she never wanted to let her go, relieved to find something from the past that she could believe in, as Peggy's hair spiralled and shone and sunbeams danced through the leaves.

'Three boys? And another on the way! You and your Eddy might end up with a football team,' Peggy laughed.

'No, this one's a girl. Grandpa told me I'd end up with one.'

'I remember Grandpa. If he said that, then a girl it is!'

'I just hope she's not as wild as the boys.'

'Don't get your hopes up too much on that front. My Becky! She mightn't be able to walk, but she sure makes up for it in talk. Her mind never stops. Not for one minute. And she goes so fast in that chair of hers, I think I'm going to have a heart attack.'

Hazel laughed and hugged Peggy again, but inside she kicked

herself for being so insensitive. Not fifteen minutes had passed since they'd talked about Becky, and Peggy's inability to conceive again. And the thought of her boys running about, while Becky couldn't, made her vow, *If God intends me to have a football team, I'll knit all the footy socks myself.*

Peggy took Hazel's hand. 'Don't feel sorry for me. I'm blessed, truly blessed. Just as you are with Eddy and your wild tribe.'

Hazel squeezed her hand. 'Let's go and visit Josephine.'

They walked silently passed the gravestones until they reached Josephine's resting place.

'Look who I found, Josie. Peggy. Dear mad Peggy. And her hair is just the same!'

And they hugged each other tight, knowing that Josie would be glad that they'd met.

But as they walked back to Joe's grave, Hazel felt uneasy. Had Josie's divine intervention somehow brought her and Peggy together again? 'How did you know about Dad's funeral? Did you see the death notice in the paper?'

Peggy started to explain. 'Well, it was like this, Haze…'

It was as though her father was still playing games. 'All those years I worried, riddled with guilt, and the best supervisor in the whole wide world takes him home and he ends up being looked after by my best friend!'

Peggy sensed Hazel's agitation and she continued the story, choosing her words carefully. But it didn't seem to help.

'So he managed to give up the drink for you and Sam and Becky? But he couldn't give it up for Mum and me and Jimmy?'

'He didn't do it for us.'

'All those times we begged him. Just stay off the whisky. Stay off the whisky, Dad.'

'Losing everything he loved and the shame of what he did, that's what made him give up the drink.'

'Yeah well, he sure had someone watching over him.'

Peggy tried to cheer things up. 'He wanted to reckon' it was the Soldiers of the Cross, chasing him all the way to Woolloomooloo with their timbrels!'

'The Soldiers of the Cross? Well, why didn't they get to him in Cabra when he was still with us? Gawd struth, they tried hard enough! He always came home from the pub with the *War Cry* tucked under his arm. All we ever wanted was for him to stop drinking. He should have done it for us, that's all I'm sayin'. He could have been happy with *us* all them years. He shoulda been with *us*.'

'He was too riddled with guilt, Haze. He just wanted to die, without bringing yous any more shame.'

'How come you still let him stay, if ya knew what he did to us?'

'Sam brought him home because his dad was killed at Gallipoli, and when we suspected he might be your dad, we offered him a job. He kicked the drink from the day Sam found him. From the day he lost you.'

Hazel ran at her father's grave and started to kick the new headstone. '*Love*?' she screamed, and she kicked again and again and sandstone grains fell onto her shoe. Peggy tried to restrain her and they fell over in the grass. 'Oh, Peg, he hurt us all so much. We ran him out of Cabra, his own family. All them years lost.'

Peggy helped her up. 'Let's go home.'

'I can't.'

'Why not?'

'I think I've broken me toe.'

NINETEEN

CHANGING UNIFORMS

On a cool night, Ellen Isabella was born.

The ambulance that was to take Hazel to the Crown Street Women's Hospital didn't arrive owing to an air-raid exercise, so Eddy was left to lead Hazel through the darkness.

They caught a train from Cabramatta to Central and as Hazel sat in the blacked-out wooden box, she counted the station stops, the pains becoming stronger with each *click-clack* under the track.

Hazel thought that she saw a light. There was a click and a flash and she heard singing. 'Happy birthday to you…' The light danced but flickered out and she found herself leaning on Eddy in a dark open field. It was a moonless night and he was feeling his way along the row of buildings, his panic intensifying with Hazel's moaning as it rose like a ghost riding the blackness.

Every window and doorway had vanished and Eddy tightened

his grip on her arm, pulling her through the dark towards Crown Street, while she longed for her rosewood clock with its gentle ticking.

At last they reached the hospital. Eddy doubled back and forth in search of the entrance, until a sliver of light led him behind the black air-raid cover.

Fear of the dark had blocked out Hazel's pain, but once she was inside the hospital the contractions increased and Ellen Isabella fell into the light with a piercing cry and attacked the world outside with a vengeance.

The following week Eddy came to take his wife and baby daughter home. There was something endearing about a girl baby with a mind of her own and Hazel couldn't help but smile as Ellen squirmed at being bound up in a shawl.

Eddy was in awe of this girl baby, who screwed her eyes shut against the bright light, while Hazel scoffed, 'Don't be silly, Eddy. She's no different from any other baby!'

He had been waiting for this birth. Although he'd promised he wouldn't rush to join up, his time had come. Jim was now in the New Guinea jungle and the Japs weren't going away. But he wasn't as cocky about telling Hazel that he'd enlisted as he'd been when he'd pushed for a workingman's right to a drink.

So he set aside time to make billy-carts for the boys before his departure for training in the Atherton Tablelands.

Daniel waited patiently as his father fitted the little wheels onto the wooden blocks that stuck out from under the fruit boxes, while Simon mucked about beside them with Spot until Daniel's patience ran out. 'Stop knocking Dad's arm, Simon, or we'll never get a ride!'

Simon screwed up his nose and politely tripped over the hammer.

But the brothers joined forces when they took off in the carts down the small incline that swerved into Doris Road with Spot chasing them, barking and snapping at the spinning wheels and flying sparks. Eddy stuck his chest out while Hazel shook her head, unable to stay and watch as Simon, with John Stanley tucked in front, hurtled around the corner and veered straight towards Daniel's cart, which already had two wheels in the grass.

Eddy had shrugged off her apprehension at putting John Stanley in with Simon with his usual 'Boys will be boys!' But in a vain attempt to guide the boy's steering as they powered towards him and criss-crossed the road, he swayed himself into a dangerous squat and, with his backside stuck up in the air, he toppled over.

'Boys will be boys!' Hazel called, still smarting at the thought of Eddy leaving for war, and she kissed the girl baby in her arms and stifled a laugh as he scrambled to his feet and brushed the seat of his pants. But she had barely turned round when she heard a crash followed by John Stanley yelling, 'Look what Daddy done! Look what Daddy done!'

Once more, Eddy lay sprawled in the dirt.

'Ya shoulda got outa the road, Dad!' Simon shouted, and tugged at his arm in a bid to pull him up.

'Ya gotta learn to steer proper, Simon!' Daniel shouted, tugging the other arm, while John Stanley shook his little head.

'Shouldna been playing on the road, Daddy!'

But Daniel and Simon persevered and became expert at manoeuvring, pulling the rope this way and that, to weave and guide the little boxes in whatever direction they desired. Somehow Hazel managed to time John Stanley's naps to coincide with the cart races. And Eddy felt better about leaving when she finally admitted that he'd done something right. 'Keeps the boys outa me hair for hours, those billy-carts,' she said.

The milkman and the baker came in *their* carts before nine in the morning, while the prop man came every second week on washing day, along with the bottle-o. They were all as regular as clockwork, and with motor cars a rarity in Doris Road, Hazel was able to time race-meets and clock-offs quite nicely. Last of the day was the rabbito, who always managed to get the boys inside in time for tea, with every cat in Cabra chasing the stench of the bloodied skins that hung off the back of his cart.

Doris Road was made for boys in billy-carts, with that slight incline, the firm dirt track and the grass patches along the shoulder for accidental landings. But at the sight of the boys dragging out their strange vehicles, birds flew every which way, landed in the stands of gum trees and stayed there until the final race was over.

Hazel laughed at the sight of Daniel hurtling down the road, and singing, 'I like Aeroplane jelly, Aeroplane jelly for me,' his vocal cords unable to catch the whiny, dulcet tones of soprano Joy King, whose childlike rendition reverberated from the wireless in every Australian home.

But after Eddy's departure, the months dragged by as he trained in the heat of the tablelands and Hazel got to be past caring. She knew that the way things were going, he would soon be in New Guinea. War took everybody. It always had done and she guessed it always would. What was the point of fighting it? Hadn't they found Japanese subs in the harbour near Nielsen Park and wasn't there some rumour about Darwin being bombed? Well, she would just stay at home and protect her brood, until Eddy and Jimmy came back. And she would leave the hall light burning for the children so that they would never have to know the dark.

And with the tired months rolling over each other, Christmas came around once more.

Hazel slipped pure silver treys and zacs and dried cherries into the pudding that she was sending Jim in the tin with the Murrumbidgee River on top, while in New Guinea he was surrounded by the stench of death.

Mud squelched in his boots and the giant jungle mosquitoes were eating him alive. Supplies were so bad that his uniform was rotting off his back and his wounds were left infected. Ammunition was running out too and, coming down with a fever, he clutched his photo of Josie and went out on watch. He just wanted the Japs to go away so that he could head back home and tend his beans and potatoes.

But war touches everyone and as his family sat down to Christmas dinner, Jimmy was blown away.

In the far northern tablelands, Eddy smacked blindly at mosquitoes and sank down onto the cold, moonless ground and, with the forest closing in on him, he cursed. 'I took too long.'

Somehow while Jim was alive, Josie seemed to be still about; now all he could feel was Josie lying limp in his arms.

Back in Cabramatta, Alice and Hazel felt it too.

And by the time the hot school holidays came to a close, Fred Jones was returning the Christmas pudding: treys, zacs and dried cherries in place; the Murrumbidgee unscratched. One of the feats of Fred's profession, its attention to detail. Like the army's. Hazel refused to cry that bleak day when he came pedalling slowly up to her gate. But that night she pulled the cord tightly, and the light went out.

Alice received a letter of regret, signed by King George VI of England.

And Fred changed uniforms.

When it was time for Eddy to leave for New Guinea, he stood on the wharf at Woolloomooloo and hugged his mother, Aunt Valma, Alice and Hazel, while the boys asked him questions about the ship. Then he turned on his heels and disappeared into a sea of soldiers.

There was a click and a flash. And the reporter, holding his camera high above the crowd, yelled, 'Good luck, boys! Good luck!'

The men sat with their legs dangling over the side of the ship, and waved casually: some smoking; some gazing. 'Yeah. See ya next Satd'y!' one yelled back.

TWENTY

DISTANT CHARACTERS

The new postie loved to ring his bell and race past the boys in their carts, while Simon tried to catch his bike and Daniel yelled at the top of his voice, 'G'day, postie!'

'G'day, cobber!' the young bloke yelled back.

Samuel Garrett had left for training too, and Hazel and Peggy were left with little time to themselves, while this new postman seemed to come whenever he liked. Fred and the clock on the mantelpiece had always been in time with each other and Hazel missed that. Fred had secured her sense of belonging. To this house. This road. This suburb. This place. He'd left her mail precisely on time, rain, hail or shine and whether she was inside the house or out by the clothesline, he'd alert her with one shrill whistle. With Jimmy gone and Eddy so far away, she had somehow felt safe with Fred about.

There had been a slight drizzle of rain on his last day as a postman, and as she watched him disappearing down the street, she'd barely noticed the black car drive up. She stood there in the wet until the driver approached her.

'I'm Dr Kent, Cabra's new doctor. I'll be keeping an eye on things while the men are away.'

Hazel felt uneasy. 'How do you do? I'm Mrs Palmer,' she answered politely, putting emphasis on the 'Mrs' while looking back down the road after Fred.

Her hands were resting on the gate and he seemed to be staring at the brown and white patches. 'I heard you have four littlies. My surgery is in town, but I don't mind dropping by to check on the children.'

'Thank you, doctor, but I'll contact you in town if need be.'

He tipped his hat and Hazel stood at the gate until his car turned out of Doris Road.

She was on her own. All the whiteness of Eddy and her father couldn't save her. She had fallen into a deep dark hole and the bottom was war. What if Eddy didn't come back? What if the doctor put in a report? She longed for Jimmy and Josie and she longed for Grandpa. And as she went back into the house, she vowed to stay out of sight. Alice could bring a few things for her when she came and she could organise home deliveries. She had chooks, chokoes and a vegie patch. She would only go into Cabra if she really had to and she wouldn't dilly-dally about chatting to shopkeepers or neighbours. She had to give the boys and Ellen Isabella a chance. The welfare had to be kept at bay and if she stayed inside and out of the sun long enough, the brown blotches might fade. From that day on, her social contacts were the distant characters who lived in books.

Alice came to Cabra every Thursday fortnight after collecting her food coupons and pension money. It was good to get out and about, to chat with Hazel and play with her grandchildren. She covered her grief on the train by acting out the lady and wearing her best hat and gloves, knowing the la-dee-da bit only went down the line as far as Cabra. Once she reached the house, she became herself again: meandering barefoot to the river; keeping in touch with the past.

Alice explained the riverbank bushes to the boys while they were on the lookout for rabbit burrows, jellyblubbers, lizards, platypus, possums, tortoises and eels. And as they explored the undergrowth, she taught them to respect every facet of nature, while they poked at blubbers with Spot sniffing at their side.

When they ran off exploring, she'd rest on her favourite log and watch the past drift by: a bobbing rowboat, her and Grandpa grasping oars and Joe pushing them off from the muddy bank, Josie and Jimmy swimming by and Eddy diving off the tree into Hazel's outstretched arms. She felt a strange presence sit beside her whenever she drifted off this way, but Daniel's yell would always bring her back. 'Simon's stuck a blubber!' Or, 'John Stanley's caught in a log!' And she would take them home, shaking her head and hoping that Ellen Isabella would be awake by the time they got there.

Alice was forever pulling adventurous feet out of burrows, or rubbing mud into jellyblubber stings because, despite her nature talks, a rabbit was merely a red rag and bobbing blubbers just waiting for a boy with a stick. But this particular sunny day, after Simon had stuck his fourth Georges River blubber, Eddy was coming face to face with another, not so bobbing, creature in New Guinea.

It was stifling hot and Eddy and Ronnie Russell pulled up in the jeep alongside a river. A unique freshness hung in the air, a monsoon freshness.

They took a chance and jumped into the inviting waters, which bubbled over a huge central rock, but a croc quietly sunning itself on the mud felt even more invited and slid in to join them. Ronnie looked up as its huge tail slithered into the water from the opposite bank, while Eddy floated on his back, oblivious of the silent predator crossing the river towards him. But instead of scrambling safely back onto the bank, Ronnie grabbed a floating branch and, waving it over his head, yelled, 'There's a croc comin' down on ya, Eddy! Swim to me, for Christ's sake!'

Eddy swam like he'd never swum before, not raising his head until he bore down on his mate.

'Go for its eyes! I'll shove this branch in its jaws!' Ronnie yelled.

'Get out, get out, you idiot! Get up the bank!' Eddy yelled back and swam like crazy.

At that moment a submerged bird searching for food found it all too late, as it stared into the croc's eyes. Stretching its snake neck to the surface, the bird skip darted across the water, trying to take off, but the croc was too fast and with one almighty snap of its jaws the bird was gone. The sacrifice offered a split-second's grace, but in his panic to reach the bank, Ronnie's muscles had cramped.

'Come on, Ronnie! Get out!'

'I can't,' he spluttered. 'Can't swim!' And he started to sink.

'Jesus! Fine bloody time to tell a bloke!'

Eddy made one leap, grabbed him in a lifesaver lock and, kicking like hell, made for the bank. They fell over each other in a desperate bid to escape, slipping and sliding in the mud, Eddy dragging Ronnie behind him and yelling, 'What's the matter with ya, ya mug?'

'Me legs are cramped.'

'I'll keep an eye on you, if you don't keep an eye on me,' Eddy puffed as he piggybacked Ronnie towards the jeep.

'And if you don't keep an eye on me, I'll keep an eye on you,' Ronnie puffed back.

Caked with mud, they fell against the jeep and, laughing with relief, Eddy rubbed mud into Ronnie's face. 'I'll give ya cramps!'

'Well, what are mates for?' Ronnie laughed.

They hoisted themselves into the jeep and made a sort of unspoken pact to stick together, no matter what, in the jungle ahead. But as Ronnie closed the jeep door, he nearly jumped out of his seat.

'Look out! Croc!' Eddy yelled, revving the engine with laughter and spinning the wheels so fast that mud flew out in all directions. But from that moment on, they were fair-dinkum mates, taking the mickey out of each other and mucking about in an ongoing effort to keep their spirits up.

Ronnie Russell had been a bushie rouseabout out Cootamundra way, an easygoing blackfella with a cheeky grin and larrikin ways. He laughed at everything that stood in his path and handled the harsh training better than most because the very thought of bellowing, red-faced sergeants made him laugh. He had no recriminations, just a great love for his land. *Life just was,* that's what Ronnie always said.

Their mateship survived the stifling, sticky heat, the mossies and the torrential rains. And they trudged together through the mud-covered months, slipping in bravado, but just when they thought it was time to go home, the dregs of war caught up with them.

Making a routine jaunt through the scrub, Eddy joked about with Ronnie. With the Japanese retreat and the winding down of the war, the jungle had lost some of its threat. The enemy had left New Guinea and the Aussies were looking forward to going home. But in the subsiding gunfire a lost Jap fought his way through the jungle and ventured down to a track, only to find two Aussies coming towards him and laughing raucously.

Already humiliated and crazed by the war, the poor lost bugger thought they were laughing at him and as Eddy stopped for a pee, he ran screaming at Ronnie with his bayonet raised. Ronnie yelled, 'Christ, it's a Jap!'

Eddy turned just as the bayonet tore across his mate's neck.

'Ronnieee!'

But by the time he'd lifted his rifle and fired, it was too late.

Blood seeped slowly into his soles, as he leant over his mate. 'Why didn't ya duck, matey?' he cried. 'Why didn't ya duck?'

Back in Cootamundra, Ronnie Russell's family just kept on coming and, huddled round a campfire, they listened quietly to Eddy's story about the croc and their pact. And one by one they patted his shoulder, as he said repeatedly, 'It was all my fault, ya know. It was all my fault. I was supposed to be keepin' me eye out.'

Then he made the long journey home.

TWENTY-ONE

TOMBOY WITH CURLS

Ellen Isabella had grown up in a town of few men and, with plenty of sunshine and fresh air, Hazel had managed to keep Dr Kent at bay. A family meant a mother, kids and a dog, as far as she was concerned. The single women had been sent away to work at the Lithgow munitions factory and it was mainly the boys too young for war that she saw working, or wandering about. Daniel pointed at a photograph and tried to explain. 'That's Daddy. That's your father!'

But Ellen looked puzzled. She didn't know what a father was.

She was four before her father walked back into her life and even then he was still in the army, coming home for short bursts and disappearing again. She turned five before she could grasp where a father fitted in.

She took Spot up to the back fence and, hiding under the honeysuckle, she tried to explain. 'A soldier has come to live in our house. He's home from the war and his voice is so big! My bed shakes when he snores. When I go to sleep I see soldiers, jumping with guns from Mummy's head.'

Spot sensed Ellen Isabella's distress and he followed her everywhere, growling at any hawkers or stray dogs who ventured near. And he listened with his head on one side to everything she said and jumped up to catch the ragged tennis ball whenever she felt like tossing it.

Ellen also found solace in her gran and she looked forward to her visits. When Gran cuddled, the cuddle kept rolling on and on and she liked poking her fingers into Gran's fat belly. And she loved the way her gran dressed up, as if she was visiting Buckingham Palace. She'd never seen her mother dress up like that.

Gran stood very straight in her silky black dress: her smooth black gloves covering her hands. It fascinated Ellen the way she gently pulled at the tip of each finger to ease the gloves off before folding them neatly together over her shiny black handbag. And she watched the pin with the round white stone, as it was carefully drawn from the felt hat, before the hat and the pin were both placed on the table. Then Gran's silver hair tumbled over the shiny white marbles that danced around her neck. Ellen loved the way they wobbled up and down when her gran laughed.

And she was fascinated when Gran left. She took a round cardboard box from her handbag, lifted the lid and dabbed a fluffy thing into the powdery contents, before patting it all over her face. Powder fairies floated in front of Gran's nose and led her out of the gate.

Daniel and Simon were more interested in the boiled lollies that Gran brought, while Ellen Isabella looked forward to the walk along the river and listening to ants, as Gran told stories about the kingdom inside the earth and opened up a whole new world below the dirt.

Ants lived all along the track leading from Doris Road to the river. And they lived along the bank. Big burgundy ants and small black ones. Ellen knew all the nests and she gave their tiny suburbs names: Cabra Heights, Cabra Glen, Cabra Downs, Cabra Flats and Cabra Waters, gossip spreading from one nest to the next, as she made her way down the winding track that led to a mud flat and a grassy patch under the old gum tree.

Further on, the bank rose and curved into a line of tall pine trees. Sunshine streaked across the inlet in the afternoon, but in the mornings it burst in freely from the other side of the river, where the Aloysius orchard stood.

The far bank had been cleared of trees and sweeping back as far as the eye could see were rows and rows of fruit trees. Still, Ellen preferred her side with its secret places, overhangs, ant nests, rabbit holes, kookaburras, butterflies and mud pies.

Eddy didn't know what to do with a girl. And Ellen didn't know what to do with a father. Soldiers frightened her. They wore big black boots and they came out of a war, with guns and bayonets.

'Now don't go talking to strange men,' Hazel warned.

'Don't wanna. They all got burnt up faces and silly hats,' Ellen scoffed.

But when she saw her father playing cricket with the boys, she gradually inched her way towards them. Eddy noticed her edging closer, but pretended not to and merely changed the direction of his bowling, and when Daniel caught on, he gave the ball a gentle flick and landed it near her feet. But she caught the four of them off guard when she picked the ball up and threw it with such force that it knocked the stumps out.

She loved throwing and catching a ball nearly as much as making up stories. Hazel would watch from the laundry window as Eddy repeatedly threw the ball and moved gradually further back, while Ellen tried to catch it, neither one saying a word, even when a tougher throw ended with a perfect catch.

And so with three boisterous brothers and this true-blue, boys-will-be-boys, sport-doting father, Ellen soon became the youngest tomboy in Cabramatta. But she remained timid and shy in front of others and she still talked to Spot, gossiped to ants and told her doll stories every night.

A tomboy with curls and ribbons made the boys laugh, but Ellen didn't care. The undivided attention that came with curling made her feel special and loved.

On the front verandah, Hazel would towel Ellen's hair dry, before brushing in the sunshine. 'Keep your head still!' was part of the ritual as Ellen tried to stare at the ivory disk with the golden four, which had hung precariously from a rusty nail for as long as she could remember. Hazel would take a fine-tooth comb from the pocket of her neat apron and dip it into a glass of sparkling water, which rested on a brick pier, while Ellen wondered if the ivory disk would ever fall.

Hazel had the gentle hands of a sculptor, the wet comb parting fine strips of hair, as she moved clockwise, dipping, winding and patting, the click of the comb against the glass mesmerising Ellen into a strange, secure world as ringlets spiralled, one after the other, the last tied with a bow and left to bounce over her temple.

Ellen respected her mother's gift for curling and she thanked her lucky stars that she didn't have to have her hair tied up in rags overnight like other girls at school. She couldn't imagine having to do that just for curls, especially when they weren't nearly as tumbly as hers.

She could race off after a ball or climb up a tree, because after the curling ritual, she was free to do what she liked. And she didn't care one bit when her brothers laughed, 'Look at the silly tomboy with curls!'

Hazel's reluctance to leave the house had seen Ellen entrusted to Daniel for her first day at school, and she was bewildered as children clung to their mother's skirts and cried for them not to leave. Daniel merely pointed her in the direction of the kindergarten teacher, Miss Broadhead, and, kicking his football, promptly left. Miss Broadhead led her to a classroom full of brightly coloured toys and shelves of storybooks. While the others cried, she smiled shyly and tried not to show her excitement.

The boys were supposed to walk her home, but more often than not they would run off and chuck their football about, or forget her entirely. Ellen was happy, though, wandering home alone absorbed in her thoughts and wondering why the boys could go barefoot to school and she couldn't. She hated shoes, especially black lace-ups and she pulled them off as soon as she got to the house.

She was a good reader and by the time she'd turned five, she could recite poems with a sensitivity well beyond her years. And she was intuitive, knowing what her mother was going to say before she said it and when her brothers were going to appear or disappear.

Hazel intrigued Ellen, the way she read stories and poems to her each night. 'How come you hardly ever look at the book?'

'I remember the meaning, that's all! When are you ever going to stop asking silly questions and listen instead!'

'I want to learn how to do it.'

'Well, choose a poem and copy it out. You'll never forget if you write things down.'

Hazel wanted her to learn how to concentrate before she taught her the storytelling art, but Ellen insisted on having the poems explained before she agreed to copy them.

'Trust you, Ellen, to want more out of life than to just recite!' laughed Hazel.

The boys thought that she was high-falutin' and couldn't fathom what she was on about when she kept saying the same words over and over again, talking to herself, or Spot.

'Why don't you just stick to playing ball? You're good at that,' jeered John Stanley.

'Yeah, you're not a bad batter—for a girl,' added Simon.

So they took to teasing her because that was easier than fathoming poetry. Eddy still teased Hazel, pulling her apron strings undone whenever he wanted attention, or if she ventured too far into a book and ignored him for hours on end. Sometimes he would go so far as to knock over the coffee table or a vase, just to get her to come back—her air of exasperation better than the hours of complete silence. And although she became tired of replacing a vase or gluing a leg back on, he privately enjoyed this power he had over the written word.

Hazel's withdrawal from life bewildered him, but he never ceased trying to find ways to reach her. Sometimes on a Friday night he would hand her an extra ten shillings and tell her to buy herself a nice new dress, but she would order clothes for the children instead, or get someone to buy her a clock.

Samuel Garrett had been killed in New Guinea. Peggy had

sold the furniture factory and the Woolloomooloo house and taken Becky back to the country up north, close to Samuel's family. There were cousins and animals there and a grandmother for Becky, while Peggy found comfort being close to Sam's kin. She'd promised to write to Hazel, but with joy gone from her and their joint tragedies of war, the letters became few and far between.

Despite Eddy's coaxing, he was invariably left to take the children alone to visit Grandma Palmer and Aunt Valma at Woy Woy, or to work picnics and Christmas parties. He knew that Hazel's isolation was something separate from him, so he respected it and merely retired to his vegetable patch. With his nightmares of war, Ronnie, Jimmy and helplessness, he needed to stick to simple things. *Life just was!* Wasn't that what Ronnie said?

Hazel no longer visited the little stone church with the steeple, but she dressed Ellen up and sent her off to the Salvation Army Sunday school. The lady who collected her each Sunday and walked her home was unobtrusive and Hazel appreciated that.

Ellen loved the holiness of it all and the stories the Sunday school teacher told, as she led little clay donkeys and people in robes across the desert in the raised up sandpit. And she loved the tiny cards given out each Sunday with their holy verses, like 'Suffer Little Children' or 'Blessed Are the Meek' above pictures of a butterfly, an angel, or a delicate flower. And she loved Jesus. He was gentle and kind and he wore sandals instead of black boots and carried a stick or a twig, instead of a gun with a bayonet.

Hazel was not going to make any mistakes. Her children received proper learning and were well mannered and well dressed whenever they went out. She saw to that. But already Ellen had come home from school asking what 'Abo' meant.

Alice had told Hazel that six Aboriginal children from the one family had been barred from Liverpool Primary because one of the mothers didn't want her child mixing with them. That's all it took. One complaint. And Alice said the welfare were still taking part-Aboriginal children from poor families all over Sydney. This was Alice's way of expressing her fear of losing her grandchildren, but she didn't realise that Hazel refused to speak of such things because she was already scared to death.

Hazel kept in touch with the outside world through the newspaper and wireless, while Eddy's concern remained the sporting pages and racing guides.

Gambling was the closest he ever came to wanting anything, with winnings going towards losses and losses being churned back into winnings. As he constantly grinned, 'Gotta speculate to accumulate.' His only other interest was his vegetable garden and nobody, including Spot, was allowed to dig in it. However, the garden was more about regeneration and appreciation than ownership. And while Hazel wanted her own place, it was more to do with having the power to change things.

But as her pigmentation disorder worsened, she was left hiding in somebody else's house, branded like a cow.

Ellen loved her mother's face, full and soft, with cute little brown and white patches, which made her look like a playful puppy or an exotic flower.

She couldn't understand why her mother didn't bring a raincoat and galoshes to school for her when it rained, like the other mothers did, or her lunch if she forgot it. And she couldn't understand why her mother was the only one who never came to the school when she was in a concert, or receiving a special prize, and her sensitivity made her feel inferior and an outcast. She was timid at school and outspoken only in the security of the house.

'Why do we need all these clocks in the house, tick, tick, ticking, when you never go anywhere, Mum?'

At home, she knew that her mother loved her, so she romped with her brothers, climbing trees, chucking balls and looking for snakes. But the boys were soon to outgrow her. They thought it sissy to have a girl hanging about, so they would whack the ball hard at her, or push her into a dirt pit, yelling, 'Snake! Snake!'

And she took all that they dished out and more, because she knew why they were doing it. There was no one else she could be herself with and, besides that, she liked boys' games, so she determined to hang about regardless.

Then suddenly this Dr Kent came to the house and she was being sent away. Something about a Red Cross home at Sans Souci, something about an operation. The boys were being sent to a Red Cross home at Parramatta. To Ellen, it was all confusing.

The reality was that Hazel needed an urgent gall bladder operation. Eddy had to continue working and she would need to convalesce. Alice had fallen down a step and sprained her ankle, rendering her of little help with the children. Hazel was reluctant to burden anyone else, though she had a rare trust in the Red Cross. So Eddy had spoken to the RSL bloke and he'd called them in to help.

He was coming down fast with a bout of malaria and as sweat poured from his brow, he stayed with Hazel just long enough to be assured that she had come through the operation all right, and an ambulance whisked him away to the Ingleburn army hospital to deal once again with the aftermath of war.

The boys ran away from the Parramatta home and made their way towards Leichhardt, but Simon fell head first into a stormwater canal and knocked himself out.

He was taken to Parramatta hospital suffering concussion, while Daniel and John Stanley were returned to the home. A Red Cross lady drove Alice from Leichhardt to see them.

'Why did you boys run away?' Alice demanded.

'They don't put no butter on the bread,' Daniel moaned.

'Yeah!' sneered John Stanley.

So Alice did her best, taking dobs of butter and hobbling back and forth, whenever the Red Cross lady could drive her. And while Eddy wavered between better and worse at Ingleburn, Ellen played with the dolls and vomited over the Sans Souci roundabout.

Hazel convalesced at Strickland House, which sat in the lush parkland surrounding Nielsen Park, the view taking her back in time, right down the harbour as far as the bridge. And, happy to be resting, she sat back and watched the ferries pass.

She pictured her father on the rocks, fishing, the day she and Jimmy had decided to hide in a cave. '*Don't make a sound*,' Jimmy had said. And when she'd tried to tell him about the snake, he'd put his hand over her mouth and, before she could warn him, he'd sat on it. It must have got as big a shock as he did, because it didn't bite, but Jimmy had taken off down the rocks so fast that by the time he'd reached the bottom he couldn't stop. '*A snake, Dad!*' he'd yelled, and knocked him into the water. And when he'd tried to help him out, the fishing line tangled around their ankles.

Hazel smiled to herself as she dozed, but the prodding around by the doctor had prised a buried coffin open and when Hazel returned to Cabramatta, Ellen learnt how to scoff, mimicking her mother and tut-tut-tutting with a tilted head, whenever Eddy broke something, 'Trust men!'

Hazel and Ellen shared a whole heap of these sayings, which made Ellen feel closer to her mother and all grown up. Secure in their love, Eddy ignored them.

TWENTY-TWO

SHAKY FLOORBOARDS

The house in Doris Road became more dilapidated with each passing year but Ellen preferred to play and read up behind the lavatory, where the honeysuckle grew wild.

Eddy had given up long ago getting out of bed in the middle of the night to turn off the hall light. Hazel would only get up and switch it on again. His railway wage didn't go far, but Hazel was determined that the electricity bill wasn't too much to ask, given her modest needs. Eddy, who left for work at five in the morning, was just as determined that his small needs, a beer at the pub Friday nights and a wager on Saturdays, were also respected.

And although each disapproved of the costly needs of the other, neither complained. It would have been futile, with Hazel remaining adamant. 'I need the light and that's all there is to it.'

And Eddy making his position clear in return. 'A workin' man's gotta 'ave his beer Fridy nights and 'is bets on Satdys.'

To Eddy, if a light in the night was all it took to keep his missus happy, he wasn't going to insist otherwise because he knew all the turning off in the world wouldn't make the slightest difference. He only ever switched it off to exert his power briefly and just shrugged when Hazel switched it back on again.

To Hazel, unlike her own father, Eddy was just a silly drunk anyway. After eating his tea and trying a bit of apron pulling on a Friday night, he'd fall asleep with his mouth open. And she wasn't about to complain if a beer and living in perpetual hope of winning was all it took to make him snore contentedly.

Ellen longed for the dapple of sunlight. But the windows were small and perpetually closed and paint had long since gone from the beams. Dull blinds rolled their fawn boredom up and down, while floors sagged with white ants and empty vases gulped air and wished flowers. She could only wait for winter and the crackling fireplace, with sparkles of red, yellow and white and the ritual toasting of bread on forks.

After Jimmy, the house had lost Christmas. There were no puddings with lucky threepences and sixpences, no tree from the river, no silver decorations, no angels. The boys didn't quite understand why, whereas all Ellen had known was a full pillow case at the end of her bed on Christmas morning. That's where she'd found the kaleidoscope, which had taken her swirling into her world of colour.

It was Christmas eve again and Hazel was sick in bed, rejecting Santa Claus and pudding, while Ellen busied herself making brightly coloured crepe paper decorations as a surprise in her effort to brighten up the house. Eddy was out in the garden, digging up potatoes for tomorrow's big dinner before the sun went down, while Simon kicked a football around until he noticed his father moving towards the bean patch.

'I'll take the spuds in, Dad,' he offered kindly, so he wouldn't get roped into picking beans.

'Well, put 'em in the sink and run the tap on 'em.'

The house was unusually quiet and after dropping the potatoes in the sink, he stuck his head around Ellen's bedroom door. 'Whatcha doin'?'

'Makin' decorations!' And she trailed them across the floor. 'Will ya help me put 'em up?'

'Where ya gunna put 'em?'

Drawing the paper chains behind her, she pointed to the living room ceiling.

'I'll havta stand on the table to get 'em up that high!'

They shoved the big wooden table into a corner of the room and he climbed up, while Ellen handed him a long red chain and a roll of sticky tape.

'Where do ya want it?'

'In the corner, as high as ya can get it.'

He pressed the taped chain hard against the wall. 'Okay, now you'll have to push the table to the other side.'

'Well, get down. I can't push it with you standin' on it!'

He jumped and went straight through the floor.

'God, Simon, what 'ave ya done? Get up before Mum comes out!'

'I can't.'

'Stop muckin' about. We'll get in trouble.'

'The bloody board's stuck in me leg!'

She peered down the hole to see the splintered board sticking out of his shin and from under the torn skin a bone glared at her. Blood began to ooze over it, as red as the chain that was hanging its head in the corner.

The colour drained from her. 'Mum's gunna kill us!'

'Jesus, Ellen,' he screamed. 'Get Dad, before I bleed to death!'

Eddy looked up from the beans into Ellen's pale face. 'Simon's stuck in the floor.'

Eddy clutched the colander of beans and raced behind her into the house. 'What happened?'

'He fell through the floor and the board's stuck in his leg.'

Beans rained down over Simon's head, as Eddy peered into the hole in disbelief.

'For God's sake, Dad,' Simon yelled. 'Just get me out!'

Carefully Eddy eased him up, while Simon nursed his shin and the embedded board. 'I think we're gunna need an ambulance, mate. Ellen, run next door and tell Mr Morris.'

'What's all the commotion?' Hazel demanded as she came down the hall. 'What's my table doing over there? And what happened to the floor?'

'It's her fault, pestering me to put up her stupid decorations!'

'Good God, Ellen, what have you done now?'

The ambulance came and took Eddy and Simon. Hazel cleaned up the blood and collapsed back into bed.

'Stinkin' floor,' Ellen cursed, as she tore the red chain from the wall.

As a child, Ellen had slept in her parents' room at the front of the house, first in a cot and then in a narrow bed under the window. With the war, Eddy had only been there for the first few months of her life, so she'd shared the room with her mother.

The second bedroom was small too, way too small for three lively boys, who continually fought over the narrow strips of floor space. So when Eddy had come home from the war, the boys were moved into the room with the dirt floor that ran from the kitchen and across the back of the house. At one end, under the window was a copper and sink and an old sugar-bag for Spot to sleep on, while empty wooden crates leant against the wall near the laundry back door.

The boys chucked the crates into the yard and Eddy repositioned their bunks, the double for the two elder boys just inside the door to the yard, and the single for John Stanley next to the kitchen. The boys were happy with their new space so close to Spot and the yard.

Ellen counted her lucky stars and stared into the night sky from her very own window, pleased that John Stanley had refused to share with a girl. And in the mornings she watched the tiny dust particles floating in on a stream of light that sneaked in at the side of the blind. She imagined the dust to be fairies dancing towards her in beautiful white net dresses. But when the rains came crying to be let in, she missed Gran. Apart from the sky, all she could see from her window was an old paling fence.

And as the children grew older, the floorboards became shakier and Ellen suffered more fear than injury when weakened boards gave way beneath her if she ran too fast down the hall.

Her father would bring home shiny new planks and hammer them over the dark hole, and any grazes smeared with Zam Buk soon healed. But nothing could cover the scars.

The Leichhardt eviction signs had stuck in Hazel's mind, while a fear of indignity loomed over Eddy. For a man's family to be tossed onto the streets was too horrible for words and so with the rent paid early each week and a pact between Hazel and Eddy not to take any complaints to the landlord, he tried to keep his head above water. For Hazel, the very thought of losing her children sent her to her knees, scrubbing the old floorboards every second day, in case the welfare came. And she scrubbed and scrubbed her life away.

'Why doesn't that stupid landlord fix our floor?' Ellen thundered. 'I'll tell him off, if I see him. How would he like to watch his mother falling through the floor and have kids that were too scared to run down their own hall?'

'Anger is a luxury the poor can ill afford, Ellen.'

But this apathy only frustrated her further. 'Well I'll tell him—if he comes round here.'

'No you won't,' said Hazel firmly.

The next day Ellen stayed home from school with an earache and, with a rag tied around her head to keep out the cold and the warmed olive oil trickling from her ear canal onto her ear lobe, she sat under the honeysuckle vine, sucking nectar.

Ellen had been told that she'd been born in a wartime blackout and she fathomed that was why her mother was so frightened of the dark and why there were candles in every room—'just in case of a blackout'—and the hall light was left burning every night. And as she sat sucking honeysuckle sprigs with Spot at her side, she made up a poem, for her mother. There was no way of her knowing about the old potato box.

Don't be afraid of the dark, Mum,
I was with you,
when the war forgot about us

I'm twelve
and you still leave the light on

when you go to sleep
with everybody laughing

you don't explain
But the war has ended, Mum
and thousands lie dead
and nobody lays a wreath on my birthday
at your head
and thousands lie dead

still we're not free,
are we, Mum?

Ellen's earaches got worse. Hazel's home remedies weren't working and she'd become sick at the thought of having to visit the 'D', but it couldn't be put off any longer.

It was eight o'clock when she started to get herself ready. But it was midday when she and Ellen finally left the house and one o'clock before they sat down in Dr Kent's surgery.

'It's common among you people,' he said, peering into Ellen's ear.

On the way home, Ellen asked her mother what he meant by 'you people'.

'Working class…poor people. That's what he meant.'

Ellen suspected from the doctor's and her mother's tone that that *wasn't* what he meant at all.

Dr Kent had scheduled a course of penicillin injections. Hazel was sick for a week after the initial visit, so Daniel had to take Ellen to the surgery for the injections. The penicillin eventually cleared up the infection, but the stirrup bone, which helped bounce sound, disintegrated.

And the Palmer house carried on a war without an enemy, with Hazel pumping empty shells from a tired-out heart.

'I told you to stay out in the yard, Simon! I'm washing!'

It had been raining all week and with the first sign of the sun, Hazel was desperate to have the towels washed and dried.

'But it's Satdy and ya in *my* bedroom!' Simon yelled back. 'And I've got Tommy with me.'

Tommy Weston had moved in with his cousins, down the other end of Doris Road.

He'd brought a pet cockatoo with him and it sat on his shoulder and said, 'Hello cocky,' over and over again. But as Hazel yelled, 'Don't go bringing Tommy and that cocky in here!' Tommy tripped on the step and the bird flew in without him.

At the sound of Hazel's shriek Spot ran in to save her and barked and snapped as the bird squawked and flew madly round the room. Tommy poked his shoulder towards the rafters and tin roof, and yelled, 'Cocky! get down here!' He could see it eyeing Mrs Palmer's head for a possible landing spot, while she tried to balance the load of wet towels on the washing stick. And each time she ducked, hot soapy water ran down her arms and under the sleeves of her frock.

'Get that bird out of here!' she yelled.

But it did land on her head and Spot yapped even louder while Simon and Tommy tried desperately not to laugh, as steamy strands of hair and loose bobby pins fell over her face and the towels plopped back into the copper.

She complained to Eddy, 'We can't keep livin' here. The place is too small.' And he finally put his name down at the Housing Commission.

It was a cool night when a boobook owl woke Hazel. The deep-throated *boobook* was followed by the familiar *karr-er*...

karr-er. But the long-beaked curlews had already flown north. *Karr-er...karr-er.* There it was again.

Hazel felt an overpowering urge to check the hall light. Yet, while the soft light filtered to her bedside, a sense of foreboding wrapped around her. The light flickered and went out. She stumbled in the dark and pulled desperately at the cord. There was a click, but no flash.

She and Alice had waited impatiently for the end of the war. With Eddy and the children, they had not long after made a special journey, a pilgrimage to New Guinea, to pay their respects to Jimmy. Alice had said that Joe would have thought it fitting that his will helped put Jimmy's soul to rest. However, the long hot journey, with Jimmy just another white cross in the rows and rows of memorials to dead soldiers, had taken its toll on Alice.

And it was time for her to go to her son.

Clutching the family photograph of her standing beside Joe, him in uniform, Jimmy and Hazel very still in front, she passed away into the cold, clear night.

Uncle Bert and Aunt Daphne lovingly packed up the remainder of Grandpa's books and took them out to Cabramatta. Hazel already had a good collection, because when Alice had finished reading a book she would automatically pass it on. She knew that's what Grandpa would have wanted.

Alice's books came too and the shelves of stories and poems held up the walls.

Ellen's favourite words came from Shelley.

I am the daughter of Earth and Water,
And the nursling of the Sky;

I pass through the pores of the ocean and shores;
I change, but I cannot die.
For after the rain when with never a stain
The pavilion of Heaven is bare,
And the winds and sunbeams with their convex gleams
Build up the blue dome of air,
I silently laugh at my own cenotaph,
And out of the caverns of rain,
Like a child from the womb, like a ghost from the tomb,
I arise and unbuild it again.

Hazel continued to feel Alice's presence and at the slightest noise she'd call out, '*Is that you, Mum*?' And not a day went by without somebody mentioning her.

'Remember the day Gran brought Jelly home with her?' Ellen said, just as Hazel was about to take another mouthful of mashed potato.

Whenever Alice crossed through the back paddock to their house, she'd stop if there was a grazing horse. '*Here boy*,' she'd call and take a lolly from a brown paper bag and hold it out. '*The kids won't miss one.*'

But one day, the mare she'd named Jelly because she liked jellybeans had decided to follow her. And while she and Hazel were in the living room, Jelly had walked in the back door, across the hard-packed dirt floor of the laundry and the boys' bedroom and clacked up the step and onto the shaky boards of the kitchen floor.

'Oh, my God!' Hazel screamed and Alice's mouth gaped open.

'Shoo! Get out!' Hazel cried.

But Jelly wouldn't budge. And while Alice grabbed the lollies,

Hazel yelled, 'She's gunna fall through the kitchen floor if she moves!'

Alice sized up the situation. There wasn't much room but if Jelly refused to back up, they'd just have to turn her around. And there was an added problem. Since Josie's terrible death, Hazel wouldn't go within coo-ee of a horse.

'If she falls through the floor we'll have to get a crane to lift her out!' she cried.

Alice ignored her and enticed Jelly to turn slowly, feeding her one lolly at a time, but when her rump pressed against the pantry, her head looked like it was going out through the open window. 'Oh,' she sighed. 'Looks like we're gunna have to push her out backwards and steer her towards the copper.'

'The floor's startin' to creak, Mum! Straighten her up. She's standing on the weakest spot!' And she shoved the table against the wall and clambered over it to reach the front of the horse.

Alice kept a lolly down low under Jelly's nose while Hazel pushed her, and gradually she began to move. 'How are we gunna get her to turn?' Hazel cried.

'When we get to the door, you push that side and I'll turn her head this way,' Alice said with false calm as she heard the floor creak under the horse. But Jelly kept taking the lollies from her and backed up until her hind legs found the dirt floor and only her front legs remained in the kitchen.

'Righto, Hazel! Turn her towards the copper,' Alice said triumphantly.

But Hazel, finding herself in a larger space and at the horse's rump, panicked and, to avoid the back of the horse, she climbed under Jelly's belly and pushed the wrong way.

With two quick clops on the kitchen floor Jelly was free, but round the wrong way. And as Alice yelled at Hazel, 'What have you done?' the board beneath her right foot gave way.

'Now you can see why I panicked,' said Hazel, as she helped Alice up and Jelly turned, clopped down the steps and wandered off.

This incident had brought back into focus a traumatic loss and over a pot of tea, Alice consoled Hazel. 'Josie wouldn't want us dwelling on the past, love. She'd be splitting her sides with laughter at my silliness today, don't you think?' And they both laughed until tears ran down their faces.

Alice had prayed that night, 'Dear Josephine, I think we helped things a bit today.'

TWENTY-THREE

LOSING A FRIEND

Ellen's last Christmas present had been a shiny green Malvern Star bike, a girl's bike without that awkward bar the boys had across the top of theirs.

Ellen loved bikes. Her father used to double her to the footy on his, sitting her on the handlebars with the boys riding their bikes alongside. Even while dubbing, her father could still out-ride the boys. Once he doubled her to Leichhardt and back, but now that she had a bike of her own she would be able to ride with the boys to visit Uncle Bert and Aunt Daphne at Gran's old house.

But the boys didn't want their little sister tagging after them when they hung round with the other blokes down at the river. 'Here comes your little sister again!' Bobby Weston would sneer.

There weren't any girls nearby for Ellen to play with and she loved adventures at the river. But the boys became exasperated, Simon then Bobby blurting out, 'Go home, Ellen!'

'Yeah, bugger off, Ellen!'

And she'd pretend to cry until Daniel came to the rescue. 'Ya can stay for ten minutes Ellen, then ya gotta go home.'

And she'd hang about for as long as she could.

The teasing intensified as the boys tried to drive her away. And the next time they agreed to let her ride to Leichhardt with them, they promptly lost her. She had pedalled so fast trying to catch up that her legs had come dangerously close to leaving her body until she caught sight of Daniel away in the distance, appearing to fix the chain of his bike.

But when they rode down to play at the sawdust mill, there she was again, right behind them. She'd watched them swinging high on the rope that dangled from the tin roof covering the sawdust. Tiny grains of sawdust cascaded to the river bank below as they dropped from the rope and as they slid down, the yellow dust tumbled after them.

Ellen had begged for a turn and the boys had finally given it to her. They'd pushed her so hard that her tiny body had swung high into the tin roof and then out wide towards the sky and with her feet almost hitting the tin, she'd screamed, 'Stop pushing, I want to get off!' Fearing that one more push would send her hurtling through the tin and into the sky.

'If ya wanna get off, ya havta drop into the sawdust,' Bobby had yelled.

'It's too far down.'

'Well ya havta drop, or else.'

It was about a twenty-foot drop, but she knew Bobby wouldn't stop pushing. She was high over the sawdust when she closed her eyes and dropped, with a thud, sinking then sliding fast on a cushion of dust until she landed on the bank below. She turned her triumphant face up. But the boys had gone.

She climbed back up to where she had left her bike, only to find that her tyres had been let down and someone had taken her pump. Spot looked at her with his head cocked. 'Come on, Spot. We'll get pumped up at the petrol station.' And she wheeled her bike across the loose gravel, Spot wagging his tail and trotting along beside her.

'It's because I'm a girl.'

Yap!

'They didn't think a girl ud be game to let go of the rope.'

Yap!

'And boys don't like it when girls are as game as them.'

Yap! Yap!

And with her bare feet treading over the sharp stones, Spot knew she was right. One afternoon he'd run beside her as she rode her bike over as many gutters as the boys. So they had coaxed her into a game of cowboys and indians, tied her to a telegraph pole and left. He had yapped and yapped, until a lady came out to see what all the noise was about and untied her, shaking her head and calling them wicked, wicked, wicked boys. But Spot and Ellen knew the boys weren't wicked; they just didn't like her hanging round them. To Ellen, the fun and adventure of outdoor games outweighed the silly teasing of any boys. And it was no use complaining to her mother. 'If you insist on playing with boys, Ellen, you gotta expect to get hurt!' That's what she always said.

Expecting to be teased somehow softened the blows and Ellen's determination not to be shut out of life only made her more stubborn.

Hazel thought she was too much of a tomboy. 'It's about time you started wearing shoes, young lady.'

'What?'

'You heard me. It's about time you started wearing shoes.'

'The boys don't.' She was feeling brave after the sawdust drop.

'Don't answer me back, Miss. You are a young lady now and young ladies don't run around barefoot.'

She didn't bother to ask why. How could playing in shoes make any difference? Anyway, with Daniel and Simon working at the Cabramatta sawmill, she was losing interest in tomboy games, and preferred to pedal off on her own. And she took over Daniel's old job, doing the shopping for her mother, stacking the chrome-plated basket on her bike with groceries from the corner shop, or fruit and meat from town.

After work the boys went down to the makeshift boxing gym, set up in the stationmaster's office on Cabramatta station. This was where all the local blokes learnt to box. The stationmaster had been a district champion in his day and now he gave free lessons in between trains.

And while the boys boxed, Ellen joined the Bjelke-Petersen physical culture class at the Salvation Army hall, learning lady-like precision exercises and fancy marching to bouncing piano tunes.

But one day as she came back from her class, she saw her father disappear around the back of the house with a rifle. He didn't own a rifle, so she wondered what on earth he was doing with it.

She hurried in the front door and confronted her mother. 'What's Dad doing with that gun?'

'It's Spot, Ellen. He's dying.'

'Dying? But can't you do something?'

'Not this time, love. It's old age. He's in a lot of pain.'

'He's not old. He's twelve, like me.'

'No, Ellen. Spot's older than that. Uncle Jimmy got him for Daniel when Simon was born.'

'Spot's *my* dog.'

'It's cruel to let him die in pain.'

'But what's Dad doing with the gun?'

'Spot's crying, Ellen, he's been crying all day with the pain. Listen to him.'

She strained her good ear and heard a mournful howl and her little mouth fell open with shock.

'It's pitiful, love.'

Then a shot rang out. Ellen broke away from her mother and ran to the back door. Her father was carrying a heavy sugar-bag and Spot's tail was poking out of it. She watched horrified as he dropped the bag into a hole beside the lavatory and started to shovel and pat dirt on top. And as her father disappeared up the side path, she ran to the little mound of dirt, threw herself onto it and cried, 'Spot! Spot!'

When the boys came home they made a cross out of an old floorboard and helped Ellen paint SPOT and R.I.P. on it. And the rest of the year passed sadly by.

TWENTY-FOUR

THE FIBRO CASTLE

With Ellen's birthday approaching she wanted one thing only: a party. She had never had one because of her mother's aversion to visitors.

She realised it would be a difficult task so she used gentle persuasion and blackmail, promising to keep her shoes on for good. And reluctantly Hazel agreed, in the hope that Ellen's ladylike ways would quell her fear of the welfare.

So Ellen did what the other kids did and handed out little cards to everyone in her class, inviting them to a party in her backyard. And on the day, she busied herself with the preparations: fairy bread, cup cakes, and chocolate crackles. Her father picked fresh miniature watermelons from his garden, while her mother helped her make a sponge birthday cake with mock cream and decorated it with hundreds and thousands.

Eddy mowed the backyard and Ellen placed a fancy tablecloth

on the soft green grass. And she covered the cloth with bright yellow paper serviettes, cups and plates and, in between, she put party food and jugs of red and green cordial, covered with little beaded doilies. She sat the birthday cake with its thirteen candles in the centre.

But nobody came. Apart from the twins, Annette and Elizabeth.

'But why would they miss a party?' Ellen asked.

'Oh, they all wanted to come,' Annette began awkwardly. 'But they said their mothers wouldn't let them.'

'But why? It's a birthday party.'

'It's because you've got holes in your floors,' Elizabeth mumbled.

'But the invitation said *backyard*!'

The twins fell silent. And when they noticed Ellen's tears, they put their arms around her shoulders.

She tried to smile. 'Well, my best friends are here...that's what matters.'

'And all the more food for us,' said Annette, while Elizabeth tried to smile too.

Hazel found the excuses hard to accept and suspected the holes were only the half of it.

Ellen had felt the rejection deeply and while riding her bike home from the shops the following week with her basket full of lamb chops, sausages and oranges, she heard the bako yelling at his horse.

'Whoa, boy! Whoa!'

She looked around to see his horse and cart bolting down the road towards her, the bako left helpless with his white covered bread basket still over his arm.

Ellen stopped and stood beside her bike, watching the horse gallop towards her. She felt strangely exhilarated as it tried to free itself of the cart, left the roadway and hugged fences, the big wheels skimming the palings. She stood transfixed as the cart toppled from side to side, coughing up loaves of bread, while the horse was constrained by the harness. When it reached her house the cart suddenly kicked sideways and the big wheel burned into the palings as it smashed again and again into the fence. The gate flew off and splintered into a thousand pieces, and the horse broke free and thundered away.

'Why didn't ya move?' the bako yelled, as he rushed towards her. 'Ya lucky the horse skirted round ya!' And as he ran after the horse, Ellen watched its iron shoes clop down hard on the road and send dirt flying in all directions.

Like the baker's horse, she hated constraints, but since the promise to her mother, she had dutifully kept her shoes on. Until one day when she was left no choice. It happened at the park. The boys had just finished footy training and were making bets about how many times they could run around the oval.

'I bet I can run round five times easy without stoppin',' John Stanley boasted.

'I betchas I can run around eight times,' said Simon.

'Well, I betchas I can do ten laps,' said Daniel.

And they ignored Ellen as they pulled their footy boots off.

'Betcha can't,' said Simon.

'I betcha I can,' said John Stanley.

'How much?'

'A hundred quid.'

'Betcha a hundred ya can't.'

'And I betcha a hundred quid, Daniel, you can't do ten laps,' Simon scoffed.

'Yeah? How much didya say ya wanna bet?'

'Hundred quid!'

'Well, I betcha a hundred quid I can!'

'I could do ten,' Ellen piped up. And the boys roared laughing.

'Don't be stupid Ellen,' shouted Simon.

'You couldn't even do one,' John Stanley laughed. But she'd already taken her shoes off.

'Put your shoes on, Ellen, and go home,' said Daniel. And the three boys took off, with Ellen running after them. 'Betcha I can!'

They ignored her and respectively completed their five, eight and ten laps, boasting, 'See, told ya!'

'You owe me a hundred quid.'

'And you owe me a hundred!'

'Yeah? And you both owe *me* a hundred quid!'

Simon and John Stanley went home. Ellen was still running and Daniel hung back.

'You can stop now,' he yelled, jogging up beside her, concerned that his little sister would drop dead at any moment from a heart attack. 'I'll tell 'em that you did ten.'

But Ellen didn't even pause for a toss of the head and ran until she finished the tenth lap. Daniel offered to piggyback her spluttering frame home, but she ran right past him, out of the park and disappeared around the corner.

He picked up her patent leather shoes and dusted them on his pants, muttering to himself, 'Girls are mad, plain mad!'

Hazel didn't bother to ask Ellen why she had collapsed onto her bed and she didn't notice the bare feet because she was waving a letter about. 'It's from the Housing Commission. We've got a house!' But Ellen had already dozed off.

By the next day the excitement had caught up with them all, as they went to inspect the brand new Commission house in South Granville. To Ellen, it was nothing short of a fibro castle, with its inside toilet and separate dining room, painted regal cream. The window frames were dazzling white, while a little beige fence ran around the house and a wrought-iron gate, swung bold maroon back and forth. Windows stretched from the ceiling nearly to the floor, like the windows of a fancy department store. And it looked out towards Duck River.

Hazel and Eddy accepted the house without hesitation, not waiting to check the remaining choices and without fear or favour, Eddy strode off to give immediate notice on the Cabra house to the invisible landlord.

When the two men came face to face, it was difficult to gauge who got the biggest shock. Eddy was endearingly cocky and confident, while the landlord humbly wished him good luck. And Eddy forgot to sling off about getting out before the white ants ate his family.

To beat any chance of this new house slipping through their fingers, Hazel and Eddy packed fervently. And barely had they closed the old door behind them, when Eddy's cocky air paid off. His mates from the railway pulled up in a truck, yelling and cheering and waving a lottery ticket about. 'We won second prize! Two hundred and fifty quid—*each*!'

'You little beauuuty!' he yelled. 'Hazel, get out here! We won the lottery!'

'How many beers ya reckon that'll buy, ay?' yelled Bluey Jarrett. And the railway men waltzed each other through the gate.

Hazel came to see what all the fuss was about and Eddy spun

her out onto the verandah. 'You little beauuuty!' he cried. 'You little beauuuuty!' And with joyous tears in his eyes, he pulled her apron strings undone. 'I told ya I'd win one day! I told ya!'

The next day the boys tossed some extra money in and, with the windfall, Hazel ventured out to buy regal cream venetian blinds that could be angled to let the light in, or shut the world out, and a green velvet-embossed lounge suite to sink into. Then she bought a rosewood table that Ellen could see her face in, with matching chairs and a chiming rosewood clock for the mantelpiece and a pretty picture of gum trees with orange bark peeling black that hugged a winding river.

'Doesn't our house look beauuuutiful?' Ellen cried, throwing her arms around her father's neck and kissing him.

'Well, don't go askin' for anything else. I don't have a brass raaaazoo to me name.' And he turned away to hide the embarrassment of Ellen's sudden, unabashed affection.

Ellen felt safe in her castle, with its strong floorboards, as she skipped and jumped and ran down the hall.

The boys joined the local footy club and she went down to the park to watch them play. She had thought the drawbacks of being a girl were bad enough, but becoming a lady with shoes and pubic hair had really topped it off. Until she saw Kevin Mitchell.

The following week she wore patent leather shoes with silver buckles and pretty pink socks and she pulled her hair back in a ponytail, and tied it up with a matching pink ribbon, while her flared skirt swirled when she walked and her neat pink jumper hugged her neat little breasts.

The boys laughed, but she turned Kevin Mitchell all about.

TWENTY-FIVE

TIME TO ROCK AND ROLL

The year turned over and it was time to rock and roll, a time for football and a time for Daniel to end up in hospital. Simon and John Stanley were the more likely candidates to leave the oval in an ambulance and it wasn't always their fault, of course. A wild cricket ball would bounce away from Daniel, but if the younger boys were anywhere near, it would be drawn to them like a magnet. The last accident occurred when a sixer hit a post and spun off into the outer field and whacked Simon in the back of the head as he stood like a stump, minding his own business and waiting for a catch.

Hazel had come to expect such accidents and hung her resignation in the air, moving under it and sitting there, patiently waiting. But the news of Daniel's accident had caught her off guard.

Stinking of stale sweat and with his mud-caked face contorted in pain, he looked like he'd been dug up from a prehistoric site. His jumper and shorts were stuck to him with mud too and as he tried to sit up and speak with grit caught between his teeth, he was a living dead thing.

The doctor tried to straighten his leg while a nurse held his hand. But as the anaesthetic took effect, the piercing eyes of the nurse disturbed him. He pushed her hand away and muttered, 'Bloody hell!'

Regaining consciousness, he focussed on the same piercing eyes and watched drowsily as the nurse moved about the ward, fluffing pillows and stopping by each patient to smile and talk. Smile and talk. Talk and smile. She was taking forever, fussing over each patient, like his father fussed over each and every one of his vegetable plants. Her deep brown hair looked as though it was happy to be untamed. And as he caught her piercing eyes again, he began to drift off and felt like a new cabbage that had just been found.

'Well, Daniel Palmer, what boyish games have you been playing?'

Maureen O'Reilly, said the badge on the stark white uniform. Her eyes were the eyes of his mother, bold brown, while her teasing cheek tackled him speechless as she whisked the sheets back and moved in for the wash.

'With a body like that, you should learn to take more care of it,' she laughed.

The thermometer bobbed about in his mouth and as she ran the warm soapy washer over his chest, he tried hopelessly to flirt. 'Would ya care to dance?' he joked, sucking back saliva.

Her laugh was like a peal of bells that rang his spine. She patted his plastered leg cheekily, wrung out the washer and flicked it at his behind and, as she read the thermometer, she smiled.

He watched her disappear out the door, probably feeling safe with him in this state, but he wanted to know if her teasing was nursing or flirting, and waited anxiously for her return.

'Where have you been?' he asked boldly.

'There and back!' And she laughed that laugh.

'Well, while you were getting there and back, I might have died.'

She put her finger on the tip of his nose. 'But you didn't.'

'I might have to call matron,' he quipped.

'So call her!' And she smiled broadly as she left the ward.

Matron Higginbotham was a biggish woman, who delighted in roughing up cheeky patients. The ward erupted with male laughter and somebody yelled, 'Matron Higginbotham, Daniel wants you.' And there was more laughter and a simpering voice, 'Where have you been? Where have you been, nursie?'

Daniel chucked his pillows at the offenders, trying to shut them up, but it only prompted further outbursts. He could do nothing but sink back onto his pillowless bed and wait.

But the wait was worth it, because two months after his discharge from hospital, she married him. They had a small wedding and Daniel moved out of the castle. Ellen liked Maureen. That was one brother down.

And as Bill Haley and the Comets began to blast from the Palmers' gramophone, Ellen and Therese Mitchell pushed the furniture back and jived around the house. Kevin Mitchell played guitar in an obscure rock and roll band, while Therese's boyfriend Shane bellowed into a mike.

At the local dances, Ellen and Therese danced with a fervour that was sweeping Australia, like giant spinning tops, twirling their coloured skirts, spinning in and out and if they spun too fast, they skipped clean across the floor into somebody's lap. And a toss over the shoulders, or pull through the legs, could cause an undignified sprawl, with petticoats sailing into the air.

A girl had to know when to lean in and when to lean out.

On Saturday morning the girls starched their petticoats and by Saturday night skirts belled out, rope petticoats, taffeta petticoats, cerise, aqua or yellow, all frilling and frothing, the whole world was flouncing. And all that mattered was having the right twirl.

Whenever the girls danced in the lounge room, Hazel jigged to the beat at the kitchen sink, swirling dishes and splashing her apron, but Eddy hated the blaring sound and hightailed it outside to burrow into his garden.

Hazel had a good sense of colour and Ellen simply loved it, so they enjoyed sitting together to decide which colour enhanced which and what Ellen should wear with what. But for some strange reason Hazel always baulked at the suggestion of red. 'It just doesn't suit you, Ellen,' she'd say.

With her black curls and dark eyes, Ellen knew that it did. 'Blue and green should never be seen, unless there's a colour in between,' she'd chirp cheekily and making sure the colour in between was cerise or hot pink, she ventured as close as she dared to red.

'So why don't you like red, Mum?' she persisted, as she draped the red satin ribbon Kevin had given her around her shiny hair.

'I like earth red and stallion red,' Hazel replied. 'But blood red belongs to the waratah.'

Hazel loved this closeness with her daughter and the excitement of the dance made her feel like a girl again. She would never want Ellen to miss out, but when the girls left the house to meet up with these rock and roll boys, she drank pots of tea and wore a path between her chair and the front window.

Off-stage Kevin was even shyer than Ellen. Over the year since their first meeting, they had graduated from a footy smile and chat, consisting of 'Good game' and 'Thanks', to swimming with the local gang at the Granville baths, the boys doing horse-dives off the tower, and the girls copping the splash; to meeting at the pictures, with the girls in one row and the boys in the row behind; to Kevin walking Ellen home two miles, instead of catching the bus, only to kiss her goodnight at the gate; to the rattle of milk bottles and Hazel's 'Time to come in now, Ellen…' to Kevin and Ellen's relief, as they ran out of things to say.

Ellen still remembered her first kiss and always would. It was in the middle of *A Man Called Peter*, a movie with a strong religious theme. It was a crooked kiss, but that didn't matter. The thrill was in the surprise and the confirmation that she was appealing.

Kevin had gradually progressed along the rows until he found himself next to her. At first it was an innocent touch of elbows that had sent the pulse racing. After that his arm had crept along the back of her seat as she sat stock still, afraid to breathe. Any sudden movement could send that arm into retreat. It had happened once before, when she'd given a little sneeze and frightened the timid arm back into his lap. As shy and innocent as Kevin was, her mother's voice haunted her: 'You can't trust men, you can't trust men, you can't trust men.'

Ellen loved her father, though, and wondered what it was

about him that her mother didn't trust. He was an uncomplicated man. 'Mind your own business and always pay your debts.' That was his philosophy. Oh, and, 'Don't hit anyone smaller than yourself.' As far as he was concerned the worst thing you could call a man was 'bludger'. He grew his own vegetables, said 'g'day' to the locals, was never late and never missed a day of work.

But he drank. And as far as Hazel was concerned, that was teetering on the brink of hell. She'd never told Ellen why.

Hazel's views on the grog were so strong that the less than angelic Palmer boys had no desire whatever to touch the stuff. Around the area, they were just as well known for their boxing prowess as they were for their footy, so when they dropped in to the pub on a hot Saturday arvo and ordered a lemon squash or a cola, no one was silly enough to say anything. While at home, usually just as Eddy was reaching into the ice chest for a cold bottle of beer, Hazel would boast loudly, 'The boys 'ave got the stuff *real* men are made of!'

Friday nights, when Eddy came home drunk and got up to his silly antics, continually pulling Hazel's apron strings undone, the boys couldn't escape their mother's utter frustration, or the deep sadness hiding behind her dismissive words, 'Drink makes anyone silly.' It wasn't their father that they rejected, but the beery state that so upset their mother.

One hot day, Ellen found her own way to respond and, taking two cold bottles of the demon drink from the ice chest, she poured them down the kitchen sink before proudly announcing her victorious act to her father. It was difficult to say who suffered the bigger shock. Eddy gave a disbelieving laugh, while Hazel's mouth gaped open.

She rushed towards the kitchen, as Eddy grabbed Ellen by the arm and pulled her after him.

The sight of his icy cold treats standing empty above a frothing plughole shocked Eddy speechless and, when nobody laughed, Ellen slid behind her mother's big hips. Like Siamese twins, they shuffled round the kitchen, dodging Eddy, who, infuriated and speechless, kept trying to grab this young zealot. But Hazel was too good at protecting her brood and, exasperated, Eddy finally gave up. He'd frightened Ellen half to death, and that was enough. If he'd caught her, he wouldn't have known what to do with her anyway.

But with all the sidestepping and shuffling about, the empty bottles fell off the sink, rolled across the kitchen floor and came to rest at his feet. This final indignation sent him tearing outside to his garden. Ellen watched from behind the screen door as he raised the shovel above his head and smacked it down hard on the vegetable patch, smashing his prize cabbage.

'You must never do that again, Ellen.'

'Don't worry, Mum. I won't.'

Ellen had to listen carefully, because communication in the Palmer house revolved around teasing and not a lot came out.

Tickling was worse than any nightmare. She was left fighting for breath with an overwhelming helplessness, tickled by her father and teased by her brothers, day in and day out. She thought that being a girl had to be the hardest thing in the world and she couldn't wait to be grown up.

Kevin had asked the tired old question that had always left her floundering. 'Where do your black curls and dark brown eyes come from?'

She was sixteen and she wanted an honest answer. She wished

she could proudly say, 'I'm Greek!' or 'My grandfather was Italian.' But her parents had been born in Australia and her grandparents and great-grandparents before them. And every time she pestered her mother for an explanation, she would only laugh. 'Tell them that you're Jewish.' And she'd wave her hand, in a dismissive way, as if it was totally inconsequential.

Ellen knew that her mother was Aboriginal, but why wouldn't she just say it? Kids had more than once called out 'Abo' when she'd ridden past on her bike and way back in sixth class she had come home, spluttering with exasperation. 'I'm sick of kids asking me the same question, over and over, as if they already know the answer and just want me to admit to something. They're all so smug with their fly-spot freckles!'

'What did you tell them?' Hazel asked anxiously.

'I told them that my father was Chinese and my mother was a Pygmy.'

Hazel laughed. 'Oh, Ellen, you're a funny one.' And she hurried off.

But as the years passed, her confusion caught up with her frustration and she felt more and more alienated. Who was she? And why wouldn't her mother tell her the truth?

She began to feel inferior and shamed, realising that she'd always had to watch what she said and comply with her mother's 'What will the neighbours say?' She'd had to be twice as polite as other kids and she'd been warned never to complain, tell anybody anything, or make trouble. If she spoke back to her mother or raised her voice, it was the same refrain. 'Anger is a luxury the poor can ill afford, Ellen!' And it pounded around in her brain.

She knew that her mother loved her, but why hadn't she ever gone to her school? And at the Town Hall four years in a row, when she'd been awarded the Bjelke-Petersen Champion Girl for Physical Culture, there was no sign of her.

Ellen's ear infections had left her partially deaf and she constantly struggled to hear an explanation as to why her mother didn't leave the house. But there wasn't any. She could only talk to her father about gardening or sport. Any other subject merely resulted in tickling, so without her mother's help, the mystery would remain just that.

And as she lay helplessly in her bed, gazing at the *Women's Weekly* pictures she'd stuck to her wall, the Melbourne Olympic swimmers smiled down at her, just as they had two years before, when she'd crouched in front of the family's new television set.

Her father had bought it with his big win at the races. Her mother had wanted the winnings to go towards a deposit on the house. She kept saying, 'Commission houses don't need much deposit, ya know Eddy.'

But she was talked down. 'Don't be silly, Hazel. There'd be rates and painting and repairing. We wouldn't be able to afford it. Better to let the Commission do all that. How 'bout a television set instead?'

Ellen remembered her mother hanging her head, while she herself had nearly fallen off her chair with excitement. 'You can buy that one you saw advertised in the paper, on time payment. You know, the one you liked, in that cabinet thing that looked like a good piece of furniture. Probly be first in the street to have one! We'll be able to see the Olympic races, John Devitt and all them other swimmers and when that's over, you'll have something to watch during the day, all them new shows!' John Devitt lived down the end of the street and Ellen had seen him training at Granny baths.

Her mother's consent had eventually been swayed by the idea

of watching pictures within the safe confines of the house. Her father, on the other hand, couldn't hide his glee at the thought of watching the horses race right round the track, sitting in his chair with a cold beer and not having to go to the pub or the course. So the television set in the rosewood cabinet arrived in time for the swimming. And so did Mr Hay their neighbour, who'd gone to school with John Devitt. Eddy had wanted to invite the whole neighbourhood in, but after getting Hazel to agree to Mr Hay, he didn't want to scare her off having the set before it had been given a chance.

Now, as Ellen dozed off, the swimmers smiled down at her, Dawnie, Lorraine, Henricks, Devitt and Rose taking over her thoughts, just as they had before, bringing joy to the house again.

Ellen was glad that the Olympics had come to Melbourne and as she sank deeper into sleep, she smiled at the memory of Mr Hay hugging her mother and her mother letting him, when the boy from Granny baths had won.

She went to work at Slazengers after that. It meant travelling all the way from Granville to Alexandria, but at fifteen meeting famous tennis players and golfers made the peak-hour trains bearable and the filing and tea-making less boring.

The summer weekends continued to draw her to the baths, where she would swim and dive till tea time, while in the winter months she played basketball and religiously followed Kevin's football team about. On Saturday nights, summer and winter, she'd watch 'Bandstand' with Therese before Kevin and Shane picked them up for a rock-and-roll dance, or the pictures.

At dances, alcohol was taboo and pubs were for drunken oldies. Bodgies and widgies hung around milk bars, swigging cola or sucking milkshakes, motorbikes hugging the gutter, lined up like mothers waiting outside the school grounds for their kids.

Shane had a Zephyr Six and sometimes they would drive up to The Entrance and go fishing, or south to Wattamolla or Garie Beach to surf. Kevin would take his guitar and Shane would try to get the girls to sing. They were pretty hopeless and they sang out of key and out of tune. Ellen was sixteen and, on the surface, life was simple and sweet.

But after the excitement of the Olympic Games, hope seemed to have disappeared from the Palmer house. The hall light still shone right through the night, but things were left more or less undone. Simon joked about it. 'Never do today what you can put off until tomorrow, that's the motto in this house.'

It was Housing Commission and you weren't supposed to fiddle with things. The house belonged to the government and there were government rules. If anything broke you had to report it and it had to be properly fixed, by the right people, under the correct contracts. To Eddy's way of thinking, he only paid the rent, it wasn't his house and there was no way he was going to battle with red tape. So he left repairs undone.

The Palmers weren't ones to complain, so they steered clear of trouble and if they had to register a fault, it was never followed up. The neighbours kept telling Eddy that if he didn't complain the Housing Commission would never come, but it wasn't the Palmer way.

Once, the tap over the kitchen sink broke and after four months of turning it on and off with pliers, the Commission plumber finally came. And when the light switch broke in Ellen's bedroom, her mother merely gave her a torch. She'd shone her way into bed for six or seven weeks, waiting for the government electrician.

This tolerance of things left unfixed dragged Ellen down and clocks ticked throughout the house out of kilter, alarms going off day and night, with only Hazel knowing why and which clock was right. 'I'm a busy woman, Ellen. Housework never stops and I haven't got time to run round looking for the time. I need a clock with an alarm in every room, to help remind me of all the things I have to do.'

'But why are they all on different times? An alarm went off at five this morning!'

'You just take note of the clock on the mantelpiece and leave the rest to me.'

The war had knocked the life out of Eddy and although physically strong, he'd become a man of few words, with no way of showing his feelings. Everything stayed inside. Jimmy. Ronnie. Lost mates. Bugles blowing. Killing. Blood. Hate.

Back in his garden, Eddy couldn't kill an ant, but he'd come back when Jimmy and Ronnie hadn't, and his guilt was continually turned over with the soil.

Down at the RSL the dutiful recitation 'We will remember them' was as close as many soldiers got to their feelings. A beer and a laugh covered broken hearts and, with their manliness hanging in the balance, tears were left in gut trenches.

So in some ways, the house was still at war, with empty hopeless shells being fired at nobody in particular. And nothing much got done, or said.

Hazel drifted further into her books and away from Eddy, while he sipped beer and guzzled sport, or followed the sun around the yard. He dragged an old kitchen chair behind him, with the vegetable garden in tow and eventually taking up most of the yard: choko and pumpkin vines running down the fence; the peas and beans chasing each other up and down tracks.

The contrast between her father's inside hands and outside hands fascinated Ellen. Clumsy inside hands seemed destined to break everything before them, yet once outside they tucked plants tenderly back into their beds of soil.

Eddy had taught her the secrets of gardening, but he left her to her own devices when she started nurturing flowers.

Hazel still dreamed of her very own house, a house that she could decorate and change about without having to ask for Housing Commission approval and when she wasn't busy with housework, or reading, you could find her with a book of graph paper, designing. House plans in newspapers were never quite right and she would discuss this with Ellen, while she made fine pencil lines on the grids before her. And she'd talk about how she would change the Granville house if it belonged to her and not the Commission. 'Now if this was my house, I'd knock that wall down between the dining and lounge rooms and I'd make an arch and I'd make the dining room window a door, and run a beautiful verandah right along the northern side to catch the morning sun.'

And she'd show Ellen a plan that she'd cut from the newspaper. 'Look at this. Only a man would design a kitchen like that, with not enough light and the door opening into the middle of the room and wasting space.' And she would set to, improving the design.

She became an expert, with graph book after graph book discarded as she worked on her plans. 'Why don't men ask women? That's what I'd like to know. We're the ones that have to work in the house!' And before Ellen could escape, she would add what Ellen had heard a thousand times before 'Men should never be left to design a woman's house.'

But despite Hazel's criticisms of men, she respected and loved Eddy, and the boys made her laugh and lit up her life. Her family came first and it was only after all the housework was done that she'd disappear into her own world. She had a quirky sense of humour and because she was usually kind, her criticism was taken in everyone's stride. If trouble came in through the door she would swish her straw broom and sweep it back out. 'No good crying over spilt milk!' she'd say or, 'Don't just sit there: get up and fight!'

And she still had poetry. She would cut little verses out of the newspaper—*Lines of Comfort* or *Quiet Moment* or *Thought for the Day*. And she'd pencilled one of these verses onto the back of a graph book.

The world may mock at your vision
and destroy the thing you saw
and crucify your ambitions
yet this is the Ancient Law
'Defeat is no misfortune
failures are not what they seem
And success, as the Gods regard it,
is won by a shattered dream.'

Eddy knew how much a house of her own meant to Hazel, but there was no way he could afford it, not on his salary. So he continued buying lottery tickets and swore that he'd win the big one, one day. 'Ya gotta speculate to accumulate, Haze!'

He wanted to win, more than anything. He was a good punter and his Saturday bets never got out of hand. And rather than start an argument, Hazel put up with the dreadful nasal sound on the wireless that went on like swearing losers, and disappeared into her room with a good book, while in the lounge room Eddy followed the nags.

But Hazel's fear of authority culminated in twenty years of piled up receipts, filling chests of drawers that surrounded her chair.

To escape the blaring Saturday wireless, the boys would go to the oval, Ellen to Therese's house and Eddy was left smiling at his good fortune.

Ellen wove in and out of life, outgrowing Granny baths, petticoats and popcorn, while Simon and John Stanley ended up as rouseabouts on a property out west, and Daniel continued to saw at the Cabra timber yard.

Hazel hadn't badgered the boys about the failings of men. She accepted their wildness. It was Ellen she worried about. She believed she had a lot of Alice in her. 'Never love a man too much!' That had been the length and breadth of Ellen's sex education, whenever any topic touched even remotely on romance.

But Ellen still wanted to know who she really was and where she came from. And she became increasingly frustrated by her mother's refusal to explain.

Kevin Mitchell and his family had moved to Dubbo so she started to travel to the city by herself on Saturday arvo. She went to see foreign movies, like Ingmar Bergman's *Wild Strawberries*. She couldn't explain to anyone how art made her soar. Passion. Fine thoughts. She wanted to get away from the Housing Commission. She wanted to be free. But more than anything she wanted the truth and she wanted trust.

After the movie she would sometimes walk down to the Botanic Gardens and on up to the rock called Mrs Macquarie's Chair, overlooking the harbour and the great steel arch and she'd sit there, letting the salt air fill her lungs, while she thought about the city's past.

It was autumn again, and as she wandered around Circular Quay towards the Rocks area, the sound of soft jazz lulled her into a sandstone coffee shop. 'Rosies' was carved into a stone block above the door. She asked for hot chocolate, because she didn't know coffee. Teapots in crocheted cozies were all she knew. But with the strong chocolate aroma seeping into her nostrils and the mellow music into her soul, she somehow felt at home and with an added sense of freedom she kicked her shoes off under the long checked tablecloth. She'd found a place where people made their own music.

And a whole new world opened up. Men in corduroy and suede, with desert boots of beige, tan, chocolate brown, black or deep olive green, all looking very Greenwich Village. The women with their dark stockings, tight skirts and stretched mohair jumpers, free of lipstick and rouge, hair parted down the middle and tied in two, looking more American Indian.

Ellen adopted both the Village colours and the Indian look, foregoing her bouncing ponytail and girly pink lips and she began to feel comfortable in this room of autumn leaves, rustling in time to another season.

One cool Saturday as the musicians paused for a break, she pushed her cup aside and prepared to leave, but the drummer pulled up a chair, spun it round backwards, sat down on it, and faced her. She held his enchanting stare and waited for what seemed forever for him to speak.

'I've noticed you in here a few times,' he said, looking deep into her eyes.

'I like the music,' she said into the empty cup, as she twirled it on its saucer.

'Excuse me for staring, but there's something different about you.'

She lifted her gaze from the rim of the saucer to the rim of his polo neck.

'You seem shy. Yet you can come in here by yourself?'

'Oh, that's because I'm really just stopping off on my way home from a movie.'

'You go to the movies by yourself?'

'Not everyone likes what I like.'

'Most of this crowd travel in groups.'

'Why?'

'They're uni students.'

'Does that mean I'm not allowed in?'

The drummer laughed. 'Hey, if you're not afraid of strange places, or strange people, would you come with me to a TV recording next Saturday? I could do with some objective support.'

'I live at Granville.' Ellen feared this might put him off, being western suburbs and quite a way out from town.

'Well I'm at Sutherland, so I'll scoot across and pick you up. It's a long way round, but who cares? We'll have dinner afterwards, listen to some jazz and then I'll drive you home. Okay?'

With that, he took out a notebook and handed it to her. 'Could you write down your name and address for me?' And he peered at the page as she obliged in her best handwriting, before he took the book back. 'Ellen 'ey? Ellen Palmer. Well, I'm Matt Wilson.' Then he stood up to leave. 'I'll pick you up at five o'clock. Saturday.'

She moved towards the exit, trying to appear unaffected, but she knocked over a chair and as she quickly bent to pick it up, she heard the most incredible pounding. It was coming from her heart.

She liked his cool sophistication and there was something more. She couldn't quite put her finger on it, but she felt a strange sense of trust.

'He won't turn up,' Hazel sniffed.

But Ellen dressed, the wireless blaring with Dakota Statton singing, 'Gee, it's cosy in the park tonight...' And she sang along, out of tune, at the top of her voice.

'Jazz musician?' Eddy called out in disgust. 'Too worldly for you, Ellen.'

'He won't come,' Hazel repeated.

There was a knock on the door and Ellen called, 'Would you get that for me, Mum?'

TWENTY-SIX

OUTSIDE MORNING

A full moon sprayed its misty beams across the park, as the red sports car slunk up to the edge of the lapping harbour. The engine purred off. The mellow voice of Ella Fitzgerald drifted onto the night air as Matt Wilson sat back from the radio and Ellen snuggled into his arms like a soft possum. Together they watched the coloured night lights slow dancing on the water. Winter had passed with a warm glow.

Matt and Ellen had grown close over the past few months, but she was young and less worldly than he and he wasn't about to rush her into anything that she wasn't ready for, or that he wasn't ready for either. And as he brushed strands of dark hair from her cool cheek, her gentle kiss interrupted his thoughts. He was happy to hold her, while Ellen snuggled further into the warmth of his chest and felt as if she could stay there forever.

His day job as a park ranger was close to home in more ways

than one. The Royal National Park bordered Kerala Road, where he lived with his parents, Charlie and Barbara Wilson.

Ellen had been to the park and Matt had pointed out native plants and animals as they walked a bush track to reach the river bank and a bulky line of rowboats. 'Which one?' he'd asked, and she'd pointed to the boat with the flaky blue paint.

It had skimmed into the water, Matt steadying it, before he plunged the oars into the plate of murky glass, while Ellen heel-nudged her mud-speckled sandshoes off and leant over the bow in her wet socks, to ripple the water's surface with her fingertips.

But when a huge jelly fish blubbed under the boat and surfaced within an inch of her trailing fingers she jumped back so fast that she tipped the boat and as Matt tried to catch her before she went over the side, they both fell into the ruffled water. With the boat upside down and the oars floating off in different directions, it was a ridiculous sight: Matt's shirt ballooning out like a child's dinky float and Ellen's crooked sunglasses dripping water, with him trying to right the boat and her trying not to laugh as she rescued the oars.

They'd left dry clothes in the boatshed and not long after, shivering, they locked the river out.

Hazel had made it clear that she expected Ellen home at a decent hour. And now, as the last ferry disappeared from view, Matt backed the small red car away from the harbour and as they cruised along the highway the wind rushed through Ellen's hair and she slipped her shoes off.

When the car finally rolled into the kerb in front of Ellen's house, Matt noticed the silhouetted figure behind the tilted venetian blinds. Ellen noticed too and she exchanged a knowing smile with him and gave him a quick kiss goodnight.

Reaching the gate, she turned to wave.

'You'd look beautiful in white,' he called.

Matt had invited her to lunch at his house the following day. She was to meet his grandmother, who was visiting from the Hawkesbury. But his parting comment the night before had left her uncertain. How could she marry when she felt so isolated from herself? All she could see were the lines of straight telegraph poles as she looked down the street, with their overhead wires leading nowhere. She wanted to follow them, wanted to go to the end of the line and as far into herself as it took, to find her past.

She wanted to be taken seriously, not teased. She had longed for a man who would listen and talk back, not down. And now there was Matt. 'Always do what feels right for you, Ellen,' he said. A simple philosophy she preferred to her mother's vacillations.

She respected her mother's teachings, but the contradictions made her baulk. Ellen wanted to enjoy the spontaneous side of who she was.

Hazel loved Ellen's nature and she believed in what Gran had taught them both, but she began to fear the free spirit more each day. That free spirit that had taken Josephine and Jimmy from her, that free spirit that had trapped Gran. Love and devotion. She never wanted Ellen to suffer what she and Gran and Joe had suffered. And then there was the fear the British had of free spirits that had made it neccessary for her to hide her face. But while she tried desperately to protect Ellen, she just couldn't escape. Her love for Grandpa and Alice went way too deep. The conflict had no way out.

And her collection of odd things started to take over the house. Ellen had only herself to blame for the pebbles and rocks.

Whenever she'd gone to the river, she'd brought some home and Hazel had placed them neatly beside her chair, until the pile of rocks made it look like a cave. Now cardboard cylinders were stacked up in a corner of the kitchen and when Ellen asked why, Hazel replied, 'I need them. I have my reasons and it's nothing to do with you.' Ellen loved her mother dearly and there was nothing she could say. But a feeling of helplessness weighed down on her like a concrete block.

Ellen may not have known where she came from, but she knew what she believed in, and the things her beloved gran had taught. 'The truth is in that big tree there; it's in that plant, that berry, that rock. It's in the song of the birds. Listen, Ellen. That's where truth is. It's in the sun and it's in the moon. It's in outside morning and evening frost. Other than that, things get twisted.'

The Wilson house in Kerala Road was surrounded by trees and shrubs. Bush flowers fell over the verandah and grevillea brushed shoulders along the meandering path, while cheeky honeysuckle hung over the fence and beckoned.

This homeliness was foreign to Ellen. The gate to her mother's house clearly said, *no hawkers*. It was meant to keep trespassers out, and the cold steps leading to the empty porch yelled, *Don't come any further and whatever you do, don't sit down*. With her mother to guard it, they had no need of a sheriff. That house was her mother's territory, entry only by invitation.

'Ellen, this is my grandma,' Matt said softly.

She had the patchwork face of Ellen's mother. And as she took her hand firmly she clasped it and leaned forward, her eyes prying into Ellen's. In a shroud of silence she stared long and hard before unclasping her hand. 'Call me Essie,' she whispered.

Ellen felt grounded. Earthed. It was as if Matt's grandma had taken her to another place, connecting her somewhere. Matt knew when to leave Ellen with her thoughts, so he joined his parents on the couch, while Essie showed them the edible berries she'd found at the park end of Kerala Road.

Ellen watched in silence as Essie stroked the berries and spoke of them with reverence, as if she had opened the Bible at Genesis. And she held them in cupped hands as if holding a crystal ball, the future and the past resting there.

And as Matt listened to his grandma, Ellen saw hers down by the river with a pocket full of berries, explaining what different plants were used for, as they crouched over nests and listened to ants. 'That one over there, lilly pilly, baby apples, good for ya belly, dem ones.'

Ellen was quiet during dinner. Later, she joined the others on the verandah as Essie began to tell stories. 'Burra…that's eel, came along the river bank…' And Ellen saw her mother and her mother before her. Wrapped up in a story, and a face.

Essie's waianya was there too. And Yerrabana.

'Make them take me with you, Yerrabana!'

River waianya could never catch her sprightly son, so she'd taken to calling him Yerrabana, language name for this way, on the move, never in one place. When Essie got upset she'd slip back into tongue.

'Shoosh, Essie. Don't let 'em hear you callin' me that. You'll get in trouble for not speakin' English!'

'I wanna be with ya, Yerrabana.'

'I gotta think. I gotta think how to stop 'em from takin' me.'

'If they take ya away, ya won't see waianya, or me, again. I'll be here all by meself, with no one to look out for me.'

'You'll be all right, Essie. I'll come back for ya. Tell waianya I'll come back, all right?'

'But what if I get caught talkin' to waianya through the fence?'

Jack felt helpless. 'Let me think, Essie, let me think. Where's Daisy?'

'I dunno.'

Daisy was older than Essie, but with an unfortunate gammy leg, one a little shorter than the other, she'd been in the orphanage longer than most. When Essie and Jack had arrived, Daisy promised Jack she'd look after his little sister when he was off in the boys' quarters. So she helped Essie with her lessons and began to watch out for Mrs Biggs when Jack and Essie met up to talk to waianya through the fence.

'Go and find 'er and tell 'er I said she's gotta look after ya, till I can think of somethin'.'

He tried playing up when the people came to meet him. He tried limping and puffing as though there was something seriously wrong with him. But it didn't work. And when the people left unruffled, he tried crying, begging Mrs Biggs to let his sister go with him to the new house. But Mrs Biggs ignored his plea. 'The paperwork's already been done for Essie. She's going to a rich family to help with the littlies. Your kindly people just want a boy to carry on the name and help in the garden and they're only eligible for one. That's just the way it is.'

'But I want Essie with me!'

'That's not possible, Jack. You don't want to keep her in the orphanage, do you, when she's got such a lovely home to go to? And you've got a lovely home to go to, as well. Be grateful. You don't want to stay in the orphanage forever. This will give you both a chance to assimilate.'

'But why can't we assimilate with our mother?'

'Now, look, we've been through all that before. You don't

have a proper father and your mother isn't well; she's not in a position to care for you. Besides, you and Essie had a white father, makes you both half-castes, and your mother's people have gone from the river. There's no place for you and Essie to go to. It's hard when there's no father. I'm doing what's best, you'll see.'

'We had fathers at the river!'

'Well, they've all gone now.'

Jack was angry. 'What about Essie? She's only little.'

'She'll have a good home.'

'But I won't be allowed to visit 'er?'

'Maybe you will, Jack, we'll see.'

But Jack Wilson knew in his heart that Mrs Biggs would never see. And he was right. She had no intention of discussing such a thing with new parents. No further contact was part of all arrangements. The children soon settled. It was just two more half-castes she'd found proper placements for, with proper people.

Daisy tried to console Essie, who was yelling to Jack from behind a locked dormitory window as the horse and cart took off. Jack couldn't look back and, fighting tears, he stared at the reins as they steered him into a world without hope. He was delivered to his new home and a few minutes later the horse and cart left.

The people were kindly, but he couldn't talk.

'We weren't blessed with a child of our own.' Mrs Smith tried to explain. 'But if you let us, we can look after you and love you just the same.'

'And your name will be like ours too, Jack. You'll be a Smith, like us,' said Mr Smith proudly.

The following morning Jack stared glumly into a bowl of porridge, while Mr and Mrs Smith tried to coax him into eating.

'You can have more sugar if you want,' said Mrs Smith.

'Or, there's bread and jam,' said Mr Smith.

'What about Essie?'

The Smiths went silent.

'Essie Wilson, me little sister. Yous left her behind!'

'We were told your sister had already gone to a good home,' Mrs Smith said warmly.

'She's still there! The old hag's lyin'!' And he shoved the porridge across the table. 'I don't wanna be a Smith; I wanna be a Wilson, like Essie. She'll never find me if I'm a Smith. I'm a burramatta boy!'

Mr Smith smiled. 'You mean Parramatta, Jack.'

'Burramatta! Burramatta! Matta's place of water, burra eel, food, see! Yous changed it, just like yous wanna change me name. I'm Yerrabana Wilson, burramatta boy!'

Mrs Smith looked helplessly to her husband, with pleading in her eyes.

'Well, Yerrabana, what if I go to burramatta tomorrow to see what I can find out about your sister?'

'Rules are that we're not allowed to inform,' Mrs Biggs said coldly. 'The good people are arriving from England and have been delayed, but the papers are all signed and I cannot divulge where Essie will be going. They're the rules, and if families that barely meet the financial requirements can't abide by them, then we're forced to look again at their placement.'

Mr Smith made his way home, knowing there was no way he could console Jack.

A week later, instead of going to school, Jack hitched a ride by climbing into the back of a goods cart on its way to Parramatta. He jumped off near the orphanage. He knew what time Essie would be in the yard, hanging out the washing and loitering near the fence where waianya sometimes came.

But she wasn't there. Nor was Daisy. He pressed his face against the fence and called towards the dormitory window, 'Essie! Essie!'

But somebody grabbed him. It was Andy, the old gardener. 'What are ya doin' here, Jack?'

'I wanna see Essie.'

'Essie's gone.'

'Gone? But I gotta find her.'

'Ya know they don't tell no one where the kids go. But if ya ask me, Jack, she's lucky. Ya friend Daisy'll probly never get out!'

Jack could feel tears welling in his eyes, but he didn't want Andy to see them.

'Well, I'm gunna wait behind that tree, till me mother comes. She'll be comin'; she would 'ave heard 'bout Essie and me.'

Andy had turned a blind eye whenever the river woman in the employ of the Murphys had sneaked up to the fence to talk to her kids. 'Jack, I got somethin' painful I 'ave to tell ya. I 'ave to tell ya cause I don't want ya waitin' round here forever an' gettin' into any more trouble.'

Jack looked up at him and wondered what could be more painful than losing his sister.

'Ya know they moved them last ones, them ones from the river. Well, ya mother, she came to see Essie. I saw 'em talkin'. Essie was pretty upset, must 'ave been tellin' her about you goin' away and how they were sending her somewhere else. Anyways, I see ya mother stagger, see, and Essie was yelling, "Don't go way and leave me, waianya." By the time I got to ya mother, Jack, she'd fallen down in the long grass. And she was dyin'. Her last words to me were, "Find 'im for Essie." I'm real sorry, Jack, but ya should know somethin' like that. I can't do nothin', cause Mrs Biggs burns them papers once she finds places, and with me own missus gone…well, I'm just a gardener, Jack.'

He didn't know that waianya's spirit had passed into him, to begin a journey.

Jack ran off towards the river. There was nobody there. He ran back and forth along the bank, searching, until he finally fell down exhausted. It was an hour later when Andy found him.

'Jack,' Andy gently shook the sobbing boy. 'Jack, this bloke 'ere is gunna give ya a ride back to Sydney; 'is name's Stan. You tell 'im where ya gotta get off. Ya gotta go back to ya new place, or you'll end up back with Mrs Biggs and ya might never get away.'

The sun was setting by the time he had walked from the main cart road to the little back street in Leichhardt. He'd prepared himself for a whipping but was shocked by the sight of Mr and Mrs Smith rushing towards him, calling out, 'Jack, thank God you're back!'

He could have taken the punishment, but this strange behaviour overwhelmed him and he burst into tears. 'Waianya's gone,' he sobbed. 'I'll never see her again and Essie's gone too.'

Essie had gone, but though Andy didn't know it, she'd been drawn back. She was there the day Jack had come to rescue her, returned like an ill-fitting frock. Sydney's heat had been a shock to the English missus, who had a faint heart, and the English mister, well, he'd smacked his own face so hard trying to ward off the mossies and flies that it was still puffy when he went to book their fares back to England.

Mrs Biggs kept Essie inside, well away from the fence, because Jack had sworn in his parting words that he would come back to get his sister. Essie knew that her waianya wouldn't be coming back, so she had little inclination to loiter by the fence, waiting for a mother that couldn't come and a brother who wouldn't know that she'd been returned and probably couldn't come anyway.

To make matters worse, Mrs Biggs had found out about the encounter between Jack and Andy Jones from Stan, when he came looking for some recompense for taking Jack back into Sydney. And although Mrs Biggs didn't want to lose Andy, his intimate knowledge of orphanage business embarrassed her. Placements were confidential and an old, caring man like Andy could upset that. So she organised a position for him tending vegetables at the Parramatta Government House, which made her feel quite noble, as she delivered her harsh warning. 'You're not to come near the orphanage again, Mr Jones, not if you want to keep the good position I've procured for you at Government House. Do you understand me fully?' And she warned Daisy, 'If you go telling every Tom, Dick and Harry that Essie is back, I'll send her away again. Have you got that?'

Mrs Biggs was secretly pleased with Essie's return. She'd enjoyed showing her off to officials when they came, her chest swelling with pride as Essie revealed how well she could read and write. Mrs Biggs enjoyed the extra praise for Essie's perfect manners and good nature, adding excitedly that the girl could also spin and sew and wasn't at all averse to work. 'She almost begs me to let her hang out the washing!'

She was so pleased with her protégée that she decided to

employ her in the house and Essie was given a bunk space closed in at one end of the back verandah. She began with menial tasks: scrubbing, darning, doing the vegetables. But as she got older, Mrs Biggs taught her how to cook properly and she felt very important, ordering and stacking ingredients in Mrs Biggs' own pantry.

Mr Biggs had been fatally thrown from a horse, chasing Aborigines from the river. Her son Harold was away at school and when he came home for holidays, he wasn't allowed to mix with the orphans and Essie spent any spare time she had with Daisy.

Harold had never taken much notice of Essie, but lately she'd noticed him watching her. She smiled to herself, believing him to be impressed with her grown-up skills and importance in the house. But to Harold, Essie was the maid. He just liked the way bumps were beginning to push her apron bib out, making him feel funny down the front of his pants.

Since losing waianya and her Yerrabana, Essie had longed to be loved. So when Harold began to tease her and kiss her behind Mrs Biggs' back, she let him. But one night he crept into her bunk and did something she knew that he shouldn't have. He said it was their special love secret. But when her stomach began to swell, he went away to college.

Essie gave birth to a healthy girl, with eyes as dark as the night she was born in, before she quietly passed from this life.

Essie Wilson was buried at Daisy's request down by Duck River. And as her baby lay sleeping in Mrs Biggs, arms, Daisy sobbed, 'Yerrabana, Yerrabana, Yerrabana.' Mrs Biggs hung her head. She'd told her years ago that Jack had died.

She was sick with guilt and when Daisy insisted on keeping the baby, Mrs Biggs brought them both into the house, upon

Daisy's promise to treat the baby as her own and keep everything else quiet. Daisy became the new cook and a mother overnight.

She named the baby Essie, after the child's child-mother. And Minnie, language name for dark night. Essie Minnie Wilson. For Yerrabana.

And as Essie grew, Daisy took her down to the river to collect berries for jam and yams to bake. And she'd tell her river stories and sing a river song, in language. She passed on to Essie all that was left of the river and in the evenings they read maps and river stories and drew river pictures with platypus, duck, tortoise and eel, and koala, bat, possum and crow, in tall gum trees. Sometimes they drew women digging the banks for yam and sometimes they drew the men putting hollowed out logs into the water to catch eel. And they drew wild flowers and all the flowers of the banksia, because they tasted so sweet.

With one final turn of the soil, Andy Jones died, and waianya's spirit passed into his grandson, who had begun to do carpentry jobs at the orphanage.

Essie had been instantly attracted to young Charlie Jones and they met, when they could, down by the river with Daisy watching out.

And before too long, on Essie's sixteenth birthday, he asked her to marry him, and promised to build her a house.

Mrs Biggs had encouraged the friendship and was more than happy with old Andy's grandson. She'd been hoping for the day when Essie could assimilate through marriage with a nice white boy, so her efforts and guilt could be put to rest.

Daisy was happy too, but she was scared of losing her daughter. Since Essie's birth, she'd called herself Daisy Wilson and she'd told Essie that she was hers. And she'd imagined that

Yerrabana was her river brother; telling Essie how he'd been taken away, and swearing to hang onto the Wilson name, so that one day they could all be together again. She'd kept the story going right up to the night before Essie was leaving her to get married. In the beginning she did it to keep her friend alive, while minding the name for Yerrabana, but she'd ended up believing that she had a brother and a daughter who belonged only to her.

On the eve of the wedding, Essie tried to console her as the story of the child-mother tumbled out and Daisy trembled at the memory of her sibling friends.

Charlie was so moved by Essie's and Daisy's distress that he searched desperately for a way to mend the link and when the preacher announced Mrs Essie Wilson-Jones his wife and Daisy and Mrs Biggs cried.

And with Mrs Biggs' influence and help from a land grant, Charlie procured a block, big enough for a little farm overlooking the Hawkesbury River. Essie was ecstatic. Her own home. Her own place. Her own river. Just her and Charlie. And Daisy and Mrs Biggs coming to visit.

The next day Ellen confronted Matt. 'Why didn't you tell me about your grandma?'

'The first time I saw you I knew that we were connected that way. But you didn't seem to twig, so I didn't say anything. When I met your mum I knew for sure. She looks so much like Grandma. But some people don't like to say. I sensed your struggle to understand, but it was up to your mum to tell you; not me. I thought if you just met Grandma like that, you'd see the resemblance and work things out for yourself. I thought it might give you something to talk to your mum about. I wasn't trying to hide anything, Ellen. On the contrary, I was trying to bring things out without hurting anyone.'

'She looked at me as though she already knew. Did you tell her about my mum, without even talking it over with me?'

'No. It was probably just like when I met you: some sort of spiritual connection.'

Ellen sighed, 'I did feel something. And now I want to go and see Uncle Bert and Aunt Daphne. Can you take me over to Leichhardt?'

She was nervous when the car pulled up outside the house and as she and Matt were welcomed inside, she blurted out, 'I had dinner at Matt's place last night. His grandma is down from the Hawkesbury.'

'That's nice, dear,' smiled Aunt Daphne.

'She's an Aboriginal woman. Like me.'

'So your mum finally got around to telling you, did she Ellen?' she said, innocently.

'Yes,' Ellen lied.

'She was only trying to protect yous, ya know,' said Uncle Bert.

'Why did she have to do that?'

'Well it was like this, Ellen. Your great-grandfather's name was Yerrabana Wilson, but he was taken to an orphanage and given the name "Jack". My parents adopted him a long time before I was born. They were told there was no birth date, no family details, only a sister, who'd already been adopted out. But they said all Jack talked about was his sister Essie and his waianya, that's mother. He insisted that he wasn't an orphan and he kept telling them his grandfather was Wil Wil, from Duck River. He told them that's why his last name was Wilson. And when he refused to be called Jack Smith, they let him be, hoping he'd change his mind later.

'But nothing changed, until a note arrived informing them that his little sister had died in an accident. All he said was, "You can call me Jack Smith now, if you like." When Mum and Dad insisted the matron show them his file, they only found one flimsy piece of paper with a few flimsy words—'taken from mother—address unknown'. It was Jack who told them that she'd died later.'

Feeling that something strange was happening, Matt made a quiet exit to the back steps of the house. He'd watched Ellen struggling with her search, but somehow now he was being edged into her secret, ancestral space.

Bert sensed Ellen's confusion and thought it was time to lighten the load. 'They thought if he forgot what was black, he would turn white!' And he laughed. 'But none of it worked, because ya great-grandpa married an Aborigine anyways.' And he laughed again with a deep belly laugh, his lightheartedness drawing Matt back into the room. 'And now here's you two. Matt Wilson, eh?'

Matt looked quizzical. 'My grandma's name is Essie Wilson.'

Bert stared at Matt. 'Jack had a sister, but she died when she was just a girl. He didn't have anyone else.'

'You can't beat the intricate workings of basic instincts, can you, dear?' Aunt Daphne concluded as she glanced towards Matt and slipped her arm through her husband's. 'Show Ellen the album you found on the top bookshelf. I found the key to unlock it in your grandma's dressing table drawer.'

Bert wandered quietly off, came back with the album, and turned to the time-worn photograph of Isabella. 'That's your great-grandmother, Ellen. I was only a boy when Jack met her, but I still remember how happy he was.' And Ellen listened with fascination, as Bert reminisced about the time when Jack had met his Isabella.

'They met on the shore of Shark Bay—that's Nielsen Park now…'

And as Bert's voice faded, Ellen squeezed Matt's hand. 'Where did great-grandpa come from?'

'He was a Darug boy from Duck River, Watagora clan. He also talked of catching eels along the Georges River, round Cabramatta way. And he remembered being in a canoe, on a river that led to little islands and the beginning of the sea. His mother told him he was going to the place of Whale Dreaming.'

'He was from Duck River?'

'Well it *was* a river once, till all the factories round there turned it into a creek!'

'We used to swim in Duck River, just down the road from our place. Anyways that's what Mum always called it. I wondered why everyone else called it Duck Creek.'

'Your place all right!' And he laughed. 'You Sydney mob never did wander too far from home.'

'It all seems so strange, Uncle Bert.'

'Not so strange, Ellen. Lots of spirits round here. Imagine what Duck River must have been like thousands of years ago. Lots of spirits round here for sure.'

Ellen remembered the tug the creek had had upon her. Her mother kept telling her that it wasn't safe to swim there. 'They killed the river, Ellen. Ya used to be able to swim all day, before the oil refinery came and all those smelly factories. It's dead water now. Ya not to swim there.'

But Ellen still went, swimming where others wouldn't, in

among what was left of the mangroves, sunning herself on the sloping clay bank, while flames and dirty smoke shot into the sky from the refinery. *'They've killed the river, Ellen...killed the river... killed the river.'* Ellen had shut the warning out, and tunnelled her vision to where two old trees blocked out the roads. She'd imagined another time. But one day as she splashed about, a dead dog floated by. That was the last time she swam there.

The Georges River held fonder memories. Swimming there had always been fun, a family affair with siblings, Gran and live dogs. Her mother often told wonderful stories. 'I remember the time...', her voice trailing off only after the mention of Jimmy and Josie. 'Just think, Ellen. If they were still here, you'd have cousins to splash about with.'

Matt wandered outside again and sat on the bench under the Moreton Bay fig. His grandma had ducks all through her house. Porcelain ducks flying across the lounge room wall, duck plaques and duck figurines. She even had a duck tile in the bathroom.

Inside, Bert was continuing the story. 'Your great-grandpa had such vivid memories. We were down Balmain one day fishing, and two old fishermen went past in a rowboat. Jack wasn't one for saying much and he watched that old boat until it was practically out of sight before he spoke. "I remember an old man in a canoe...he paddled me up the river towards the sea...showed me where ta get mud oysters and told me how he used to take bush food to the beginning of the waters, to meet with the short tails, the fish people, and how the fish people used to come to the long tails, possum people, with food from the sea and how there'd be singing and dancing and big corroborees." Jack said he'd always remember that day because the old man was so sad, shaking his head and muttering, "No more, no more short tails."'

'What happened to the river people, Uncle Bert?'

'Some of you still about. Darug land flowed right through here, along the lower Hawkesbury and up the slopes of the Blue Mountains.'

'Why did it all have to be such a secret?'

'Your mum was scared of the welfare. She hung onto you kids like grim death, wanted to give yous all a chance.'

'But why didn't she tell me the truth?'

'Kids let things slip. I remember the time ya brother, Simon I think it was, got caught at the park with a kid who'd nicked a horse. Your mother was so petrified she told your father to keep his nose out, that she'd look after things with the police and the welfare. Eddy was tellin' me later, "For a woman I can't get to go out, she sure splashed a lot of talcum powder on in her rush to meet them other blokes."'

Bert laughed. 'Apparently she dressed you up, with ya father yelling, "What are ya takin' her for? Court's no place for a girl and what bloody difference is a doll tucked under her arm gunna make?" That's when ya mum told him to keep his nose out. Ya dad said he couldn't tell which one was the doll, by the time yous raced out the door!'

'But why was Mum always so scared, if she wasn't doing anything wrong?'

Bert hung his head.

'Well this is the fifties and I'm proud of who I am and my mother shouldn't have to hide in the house! It's like stopping the sun!'

'The spirits are still here, Ellen, and time is still engraved in the rocks. I'm proud to live in such an old place. No other city on earth like it.'

'Tell me more about Nielsen Park.'

'Isabella was a domestic at Vaucluse House. The Wentworths lived there then. Her mum had died when she was only three.

'The littlest Wentworth girl had taken a shine to Isabella. She was the wild one of the family and Mrs Wentworth had seen the merit in making Isabella the little girl's nanny.

'Jack said Isabella used to make him laugh, imitating the plummy voice of the head chambermaid—"Now Isabella, don't disappoint us. You are being promoted from domestic to nanny." And so she was allowed to take the girl for walks along the shore. And that's how she met Jack. I'll never forget the day he came home and told us about her.

'Edith Wentworth believed that the love match was all her doing and when her mother informed her that the family were going on a long trip to England, she fretted about Isabella being left all alone.

'Jack told me how that little one told her mother she wasn't going on any trips with the family, unless Isabella was allowed to marry Jack.'

'They must have been close, this girl and Isabella?'

'Jack said the girl was like a daughter to Isabella.'

'So there's a happy ending to the story?'

'Until Isabella had Alice. Then she worried herself to death.'

'Why?'

'She was scared of losing her. Whole clans of her people had died.'

'How old was Gran, then, when her mother died?'

'Alice...she was three too. Isabella had lost all her family and the more she loved Jack and Alice, the more worried she became. And the constant checks on her by the welfare type people only made her worse. I know, because I was there. It was just before Alice's third birthday, that's when she died. Her last words to Jack were, "Hang onto Alice. She belongin' Sydney." Her untimely death devastated Jack, but he kept some smithing jobs around the La Perouse area, so he could catch up from time to time with the families from the south coast who'd taken Isabella down there with them when she was little, after her mum had died. He used to take me and Isabella and Alice and then your mum out to La Perouse in the horse and cart. Never stopped loving his Isabella.'

There were tears in Bert's old eyes. 'Your great-grandfather was a good man. He was my big brother, my father too. When Mum and Dad died, they left him the house and he looked after me.'

Ellen agreed to pass the key and the locked album on to Hazel. But it had been locked up for so long, she felt reluctant to confront her mother with it. When and if the time was right she would, but otherwise she was just happy to know who she really was for the first time in her life. The wedding was planned for May and Essie Wilson was coming down from the river.

She wished her gran could be there too and she hugged Uncle Bert because he'd been so close to them all and she kissed his crinkled brow, when he whispered, 'There's happy spirits all around you, Ellen. I can feel them.'

Grandma Wilson felt them too. Before Matt met Ellen, her beloved Charlie had died, but his spirit had remained close by. Now there was something even stronger surrounding her grandson.

She could feel the power of it, as she sat on the verandah with him, just hours before the wedding. They were laughing about how he'd hated having a hyphenated name at school and how her Charlie and Matt's dad, Charlie, had both agreed that they'd all drop the Jones, because it was too common anyway.

It was the perfect opening for Matt. 'What was your mother's name, Grandma?'

'Daisy,' she replied innocently.

'Did you have any brothers or sisters?'

'No, just me and me mum.' She was feeling it again, this strange power.

And Matt was left with only the notion that he and Ellen were strangely entwined.

Eddy had found it hard to come to terms with his daughter marrying a man who showed his feelings through music. He'd presumed she would one day marry a footballer or a cricketer. The closest Eddy ever allowed himself to music was at the pub, when the men crooned, 'It's a Long Way to Tipperary'. Flowers and music were in the same fairy basket as far as he was concerned. But, despite that, he liked Matt all right and Ellen seemed happy and that was all that really counted.

Ellen felt whole. Uplifted. And only now did she feel she had the right to share Matt's life. She felt close to everybody, even the ticket collector down at Granville station, when he nodded g'day with his eyelids.

Kerala Road ran down to the rocks at the edge of the National Park, where they'd found their bush altar. Ellen kicked aside her new shoes. She wanted to feel the earth beneath her feet and with her delicate white dress sweeping down over her ankles, she thought nobody would notice or care, not even her mother, because now she was being made honourable, a Mrs, and surely shoes didn't matter.

Surrounded by banksia, wattle and waratahs, Ellen waited. Matt's friends from Rosies were getting ready to play a jazz version of the bridal march and as she waited she gazed into the deep red of a waratah and remembered the sad story of the loyal wonga pigeon, passed down to Gran by Isabella. 'Long ago all waratahs were white…' And tears came to Ellen's eyes as she pictured the pigeon with its torn chest flying frantically from waratah bush to waratah bush, leaving behind blood-stained blossoms as she searched for her mate. And Gran's voice faded away, 'Waratahs are tainted with the blood of the brave…'

'Smell the bush, Ellen,' Matt whispered, as he reached for her hand and she screwed up her nose like a possum.

'Do you take this woman…'

And Matt kissed his bride, before everyone meandered back down the track to the house.

Essie Wilson began to sing as Daisy had taught her, tapping her flat palms against her thighs, rocking her hips in time with her shuffling feet, sweeping Ellen's happiness up, as the cheery chatter merged the present with a resurrected past. Hazel hummed and tapped her thighs too, while a kookaburra sat on a fence and watched them all pass.

Back at the house Bert edged his way towards Essie. 'Matt looks a lot like Ellen's great-grandfather.'

'It's so strange, Bert, but all I can see in Ellen is myself.'

'His name was Jack Wilson. He was in an orphanage at Parramatta, before my parents adopted him.'

'How strange. I came from there, but I don't remember any *Jack* Wilson.'

'He was probably there before your time.'

‘My mother Daisy was there before me. My real mother died when I was born.’

‘Did she have a brother?’

‘Yes, she had a brother, but his name wasn’t Jack. It was Yerrabana.’

Tears sprang into Bert’s eyes. *Yerrabana?* ‘Yerrabana was my brother.’

TWENTY-SEVEN

VIETNAM

Hazel tried to hold back the war in Vietnam, but it came anyway. Australian troops were flown out in jungle khaki. She refused to hear talk of it and disappeared into a book. But her heart cried out for all the young boys being sent to fight.

Simon and John Stanley were out west shearing on a huge sheep property and Hazel hoped they'd stay there. Daniel was still at the timber yards, but she was pestering Eddy to get him a job with the railway, because some transport workers were always needed at home in times of war.

Charlie and Barbara Wilson had retired from Sutherland to the Hawkesbury to be with Essie, and left the younger Wilsons to look after the house in Kerala Road, the garden and nearby bush: the perfect surrounds for Matt and Ellen's new daughter.

Minnie Hazel had been born with eyes like round black moons on a starless night, eyes as distant, yet familiar, as Essie Minnie's and Nana Hazel's.

The winters had turned into springs, the springs into summers, and the summers into autumns. Ellen knew who she was and knew who her mother was and her mother's mother and she knew that her mother's mother's parents were Jack and Isabella. And she knew Matt's grandma's side. The first Essie Wilson was her great-great-aunt and she'd discovered with wonder and awe that Matt was her third cousin. She knew her father's side too. The first Sydney Palmers. She had black and white ancestral beginnings. And now there was Minnie Hazel. And Matt, a man touched by spirits and music.

Falling through floors had scared Ellen once, but nothing did now.

'My foot won't reach the pedal,' Minnie complained to her father, as she bent sideways off the little drum stool and gave the big bass drum a kick. She just as quickly tired of the kettle drums, preferring to sit on the floor with the bongos, her tiny shoulders jigging up and down with each beat.

Ellen took her often to Rosies to hear Matt play, but late nights were out. Instead, Minnie would find herself tucked up in bed with Ellen reading, or at Nana Palmer's, with Hazel reading. Either way she didn't mind, but deep down she wanted to be out there to watch and hear the music being made.

But the air at Rosies began to feel tense. Ellen felt it and so did Matt. During the breaks the usually laid-back crowd became talkative, chairs shifted and the Sydney Uni students merged with the New South Wales Uni students, the coffee shop became more crowded each day, and people hung about on the street outside, some walking off, some coming back in.

It was the war. Two regular battalions had already been sent to Vietnam, and now the Libs were bringing in conscription.

Most of the regulars at Rosies were registered for National Service, with their lives in a ballot box.

They marched verbally into the war, questioned it, studied it, tossed it all about, but little came out that made any sense.

Ellen couldn't help but heave a sigh of relief that Matt was out of the birthday bracket for the call-up. Hazel heaved an even greater one, not just for Matt but for Daniel, Simon and John Stanley. But the Palmer boys had enlisted without telling her. And now they didn't know how to break the news.

'The timber's drying up round this way,' Daniel began shakily, while Simon came in real quick-like. 'An' smelly sheep are gettin' up my nose.'

'We're not white feather blokes ya know, Mum. Me mates are goin' and if we stick together, brothers an' all…'

John Stanley's tactlessness brought it all out into the open and left his brothers floundering for words, 'Umm, well, Mum, we wanna go,' Daniel stumbled. But she turned her back on him, hurried to the security of the back room, and closed the door.

The boys dragged their feet as they made their way to the front gate, Daniel half turning back towards the house. Then, like scamps running to try and dodge having their bottoms smacked, they hurried down the street.

Hazel refused to discuss the war with Eddy and sunk back into her books, while he went back to tending his plants.

But she began to stock the house with groceries: tins of this and tins of that, rolls of toilet paper and rectangular boxes of paper tissues, while Eddy became more and more exasperated. 'What are ya doin', Hazel, wastin' money on things we don't need?'

‘I know what I’m doing. Ya mind ya own business! It’s stock. Tins last forever.’

‘Well, what’s all the dunny paper for? Ya got a pain in the belly?’

‘Don’t be stupid. You know that one of the first things that gets rationed is paper. And whatever happens, war or no war, I’m not going back to cutting up newspaper and stickin’ it on string!’

So the light in the hall that stayed on all night slithered into a vast cave, with paper tunnels waiting to be unravelled and rectangular volcanoes about to erupt, while night light splashed across hilltops of tomato soup and camp pie. Outside, ticking clocks beat to different times and different tunes, and kept watch, and from every corner of the house they ticked away Hazel Palmer’s life.

The first of the conscripts were called up. Ben the actor, who was studying playwrights and dreaming of directing off-Broadway, his number came up. And Andrew, the rugby player who spoke like one with that rough edge around his mates, and sauntered like a footballer with that confident swagger around the girls, but who had confessed to Matt his dream of playing the sax, his number came up and the demonstrations continued.

These boys had been regulars at Rosies. And that’s where Simon had met Hatsuhana. Ellen had been checking Hatsuhana’s essay for English mistakes and they were chuckling over a funny misinterpretation, when Simon had appeared out of nowhere. ‘I’m lookin’ for Professor Elly.’

For years Hazel had kept up a resistance fight, for the loss of Jimmy. And Ellen had to search under cups and saucers at Woolworths for the *Made in England* stamp, rejecting what she could of the *Made in Japan*. But now she hoped that her friendship with Hatsuhana might soften her mother's grief.

Hazel was hesitant when Ellen's happy chatter turned to Hatsuhana, but Ellen persisted and her mother's curiosity got the better of her when Simon mentioned her too. She slowly began to ask questions and her resistance slowly subsided. Hatsuhana was just another young girl and Ellen and Simon liked her.

Simon and Hatsuhana had liked one another straight off. Hatsuhana was intrigued by his manly demeanour and silly teasing, while he loved the way she covered her mouth and laughed at everything he said, even when it wasn't all that funny. And Simon went more often to Rosies, jamming on the drums with Matt, while Ellen poked fun at them and Hatsuhana laughed. And each time he left, he found he was counting the days until he could get back there again, with Hatsuhana waiting anxiously for his return but reluctant to show it.

'When is Simon coming back?'

'Saturday after next.'

'Oh, Saturday after next? I think I will be very busy studying.'

Daniel sometimes dropped into Rosies with Maureen. But he ignored Simon's attempts to lure him into jamming. Daniel was the strong silent type, even more so since Maureen had suffered a miscarriage, and Simon and John Stanley were still the Palmer larrikins.

The group at Rosies had sat talking together, that last Saturday before Ben, Andrew, Simon, Daniel and John Stanley were to leave for training. At their farewell, Matt gave Simon his old harmonica. 'It's small enough to stick in ya pocket.' And he gave Daniel a used drumstick for good luck. Ellen gave Simon *Stories of Wise Women and Faithful Wives*, with a Japanese illustration of 'Hatsuhana in prayer under the Gongen waterfall at Hakonen'.

But she'd made the mistake of showing John Stanley the day that she'd bought it. 'Don't go giving me any silly poetry, Ellen,' he said, or charms to take to war. I got enough to carry with me rifle!'

So as John Stanley stood among the wellwishers at Rosies, thinking he'd escaped all this sissy stuff, he was surprised by a drum roll and Ellen thrusting a bunch of snapdragons into his hand and Simon kissing him on the forehead. He clipped Simon's ear with the snapdragons, and sent the flowers yapping across the floor then he grabbed Ellen and twirled her round and round, until she was so dizzy she toppled over.

Over the years she'd taken her brothers for granted, but now, she found herself taking a long hard look. Simon and John Stanley were both larrikins, but in outward appearance they were as different as chalk and cheese. Simon had a rugged physique, with his chest thrust forward, head half-cocked, cheeky grin and swaggering gait, a grin coming out from the corners of the eyes and the mouth, the blackest of hair flopped over deep-set brown eyes and olive skin, and his was voice rich and deep.

John Stanley on the other hand, had tight curly brown hair with a reddish tint, eyes that darted and nose freckles that laughed. His voice, though, was a monotone of indifference.

And Daniel was dark and silent as the night.

Hatsuhana was as calm as Simon was active, but she'd run off with him on the spur of the moment to the Registry Office to get married.

John Stanley liked Gwen Carruthers, but he found it hard to talk.

Now all three brothers were going to war.

TWENTY-EIGHT

THE MORATORIUM

Within three months of leaving Australia, Simon's hand was blown away along with his pipe-dream of making music, which now lay scattered in bits and pieces across some jungle. There would be no more football and no more pleasing his father.

The buzz in the coffee shop back home grew louder. Henry, who hugged the far corner and avoided attention, his intense eyes and bohemian good looks grabbing it anyway, now sat up front, stirring everyone to action. His kid brother had been killed in Phuoc Tuy. 'So, are we just gonna sit back and watch another lot go? We gotta stick together, shake the government up. We don't want any more kid brothers comin' home in boxes!'

And his little group surged into the Domain with the other demonstrators, PEACE surfing in on a wave of placards, as voices cracked over megaphones and arms shot into the air like a volley of arrows.

By sunset the park was empty, and on the edge of the Domain, the Art Gallery with its tall Ionian columns looked like a deserted Greek temple. Onlookers had left its steps and the pigeons had returned to squat on frescoes and bronze horses, and wait for the bats to draw the dark cap of night over the monument before folding in the park.

Matt returned to his niche at Rosies, but when Simon was shipped back from the war, he and Hatsuhana no longer came. Simon had found himself caught between wars at Rosies. So he and Hatsuhana had set up house near Ellen and Matt, and walked with them in the surrounding bushland rather than hang around coffee shops in times of tired waiting, waiting for news of Daniel and John Stanley, good news.

At first Hazel had been reluctant to accept Hatsuhana as a family member, because she saw it as a problem. But just by being around, this new daughter-in-law reminded her that her years of conscientious objection were less to do with hatred than grief. And just to see Simon beaming, she'd warmed to the dear girl, grateful that her son had a love to bring him back home, unlike Jimmy.

And Simon had come home. Bolder. It was his way of coping and he'd managed to con an office job in the army, where he could keep tabs on the Vietnam vets, which was about as close as he could get to Daniel and John Stanley.

Nothing was going to stand in his way. True, he was no good for rugby, but he started to train the local kids' soccer team, with Hatsuhana handing out the oranges.

But more and more boys were being called up to be set down in a strange land, and to kill; they were fed hate in their army slop dishes. Others had joined the conscientious objectors in gaol. Matt wanted to do something but he didn't know what, so he became restless and disillusioned. Ellen noticed it and so did Minnie Hazel.

'You don't bang bongos, you tap 'em. Haven't ya learnt anything, Minnie?'

'Silly dwums,' she sniffed. And she toddled off, giving a little side kick to the drum as she left.

'She's right, Ellen. What good is a man playing drums?'

'You're not thinking of joining up? Not after what happened to Simon?'

'Not the army.'

'Well, what do you want, Matt?'

'There's a group of entertainers going to Vietnam.'

'Isn't that supporting the war?'

'It's doing my bit the only way I can.'

'You'd be putting yourself in danger. And for what? Drumming up morale, before the boys go missing or get their hands blown off?'

'Well at least I'd be safe. Not like your brothers. Banging a drum is nothin' compared to what they've had to face!'

Ellen fell silent.

'Don't worry. The army will keep me away from the action. I'm just a drummer.'

'They know better than that, Matt. They'll be happy to have you off the streets!'

'Yeah well, they can teach me what bravery is all about.'

'You don't have to go to Vietnam for that, you know.' And she hurried into the kitchen and ran cold water into the kettle, as she called back over her shoulder, 'Do what you believe in, okay?

That's what my brothers did and it's what you've always told me.'

Minnie came wandering back in and climbed up onto her father's lap. He hated the thought of leaving her, but he hated war and inactivity more. He wanted to find Daniel and John Stanley before it was too late.

Hazel was in two minds. She was worried half to death for Matt, but the thought of him going to her boys brought the first sign of relief anyone had seen in her in ages. If only Matt could be there for them when they came out from the jungle. But the thought of him going anywhere near war brought on the palpitations too. 'Don't forget, you've got Ellen and Minnie to come back to!'

'I won't be taking any silly chances, Mum.'

'They always get mail through to the front and back again. Make sure that you stay in contact, Matt; no good worrying Ellen and Minnie. And remember to watch out for Daniel and John Stanley. John Stanley's always been a bugger for wandering off on his own, so he's probably lost in the jungle.' Before he could say anything, she continued. 'I won't send parcels, just letters and cards. Parcels can cause problems for the posties.' She could still see Fred's face the day he'd pedalled slowly up to her gate and handed her the pudding.

He opened out a map and explained gently. 'See this spot here? That's where I'll be. And I promise, cross my heart, that I'll stay in contact with you and Ellen and Minnie.'

But Hazel stayed at home when Ellen, Minnie and Eddy went to the airport to see him off. These days she didn't even venture into the backyard, not since the boys had left for war. Eddy hung the washing on the line and it was Eddy who checked the letterbox each day. The neighbourhood children knew that Mrs

Palmer lived there, but they never saw her now, so they made up stories about what she looked like. Hazel was unaware of the interest her solitude caused, but she would have giggled with delight at their vivid and sometimes grotesque imaginings.

'She's a witch! She's got hair growing out of her face and her toenails are so long that they scrape along the floor. She's locked in that back room and she can't get out! I saw her. I looked through the window.'

The day of Ellen's wedding, the neighbours had stood silently in their front gardens, while children congregated on the footpaths, all waiting for the bride to come sweeping out. But when she appeared and gave a friendly wave, she'd noticed that all eyes were averted towards her mother. Unaware that anyone but Ellen existed on this special day, Hazel trailed happily in her daughter's radiance. Cars moved off, white ribbons flapped and the mother of the bride disappeared like a celebrity with no need of fans. Ellen had smiled at the realisation that her mother had become an enigma, stepping out rarely from the pages of a book, and even then still wrapped up in the story.

To reassure Hazel and Ellen that he was safe, Matt sent home a tape. 'I'm sitting cross-legged on me skinny bunk and I've even got a wardrobe. Well, you women probably wouldn't call it a wardrobe…' And he sent another, jamming with some of the blokes. 'We're sitting in the blazing sun under banana trees.' But in his attempt to sound lighthearted, he unwittingly captured a sound beyond the bongo beat, in the distance between peace and war. Ellen had picked it up—distant gunfire and what sounded like a bomb going off. She kept the tape from her mother, and waited anxiously for her brothers' and Matt's return.

And good news followed. Matt had made contact with Daniel. 'His eyes are sort of glazed over, Ellen. He was glad to see me all right, but there's a kinda stony indifference and he wasn't interested in anything.' Ellen sensed an immense sadness in Matt's voice and she wondered if Daniel would ever be the same again. She wondered if Matt would too. He didn't have the heart to tell her that Daniel had become separated from John Stanley and hadn't seen him for weeks.

Eventually Matt came home. Back in Sydney the harbour sparkled and yachts drifted a million nautical miles from war, their colourful spinnakers billowing out with a fresh breeze, daubs of swaying colour sailing across the smooth blue canvas of the sea, brushing the lush green of Shark Island and Clifton Gardens. And the weeks crawled by, until the day of the May march.

Ellen and Minnie watched as hundreds of demonstrators surged towards them, sweeping the gutter like council cleaners on a Friday arvo. Then Minnie saw Matt. '*Daddy!*'

Matt waved, but Minnie puzzled over the serious look on his face, because she thought it was a parade. People were walking arm in arm, calling out, chanting and singing, while others waved banners or carried big flags with writing on them. And when she waved, they waved back.

'Where's Daddy going?'

'Only around the block. He'll be back soon.'

She stared after the streaming line of people. 'Which way, Mummy?' she asked, shifting from one foot to the other.

Ellen pointed off into the distance and Minnie continued to watch, until Matt appeared across the long stretch of grass. She pulled her hand from Ellen's and started to run towards him, but with her head down and watching her legs pick up speed, she ran a little off course, threw her arms around the leg of a startled stranger and caused a double fall.

'Minnie!' Matt called, hurrying towards her.

She picked herself up and, ignoring the poor stranger lying sprawled in the grass, she ran to him.

Ellen was left to apologise. She hurried to rescue the man still lying there and as she bent over him to see if he was all right, he sat bolt upright and started to laugh. It was Henry, the protester who'd fired up the little group at Rosies. After narrowly escaping arrest by the police, to be bowled over by Minnie was light relief. And with Ellen trying to tug him to his feet, Minnie's laughter rang out across the park, as he pretended to slip and slide on the grass.

The national moratorium was scheduled for the fourth of July, with people from all around the country making a stand against America's and Australia's involvement in Vietnam.

'The marches are becoming dangerous. I don't want you there, Ellen.' Matt said. 'Not on the fourth! There'll be any number of violent arrests.'

Minnie's wide searching eyes as she listened to her parents reminded Ellen of the innocence of John Stanley's. She wrapped her arms around her daughter. 'We'll stay home if you promise to be careful, Matt. We want you to come back home safe, don't we Minnie?' Minnie nodded solemnly.

And on the day set down for the demonstration, the normally picturesque harbour turned grey. Yachts scurried and tossed their way towards the sheltered bays, before black, swooping clouds obliterated them from view, and the huge steel arch vanished.

Thousands and thousands of Sydneysiders marched on the Domain, while thousands more marched in every city of Australia. NO TO VIETNAM! There were violent clashes from Darwin to Hobart. And, despite Matt's promise, he and Henry ended up in gaol.

But by November, it was all beginning to pay off. The 8th Battalion was coming home, a first ray of hope. Daniel was the second. He was coming home too, and he'd found his brother wandering out of the jungle, just as his mother had predicted. But, because John Stanley had got himself lost, he'd insisted on making up the time, and the sergeant major wasn't arguing with that. So Daniel had to leave him behind.

Matt and Ellen waited patiently at the airport with Eddy and Simon standing beside them and Minnie jigging about, until the aircraft came into view.

It roared like the devil along the tarmac, before gliding to a graceful halt, its majestic wings glistening in the sun as it rested like a stretching pelican.

Daniel had been seated next to some bloke from Campbelltown, who'd tried to strike up a conversation. 'Back to work Mondy, building trade, just pray the weather's good when we hit Sydney, and it betta bloody stay that way, 'cause I spent more dough than I shoulda in Singapore! Always the way, aint it, when ya go on holidys?'

He'd been sent home on a passenger plane, so as he disembarked, there was no twenty-one gun salute. No brass band. It was as if he was returning from a camp, or a weekend away. No tickertape parade. No army major.

The small group stopped by Rosies, where WELCOME HOME DANIEL had been strung across the door and his favourite tune, 'Take the A-Train', drifted out onto the street. His friends waited inside. But to Matt and Ellen, it suddenly seemed such a hollow welcome. It was a relief to have Daniel back, but John Stanley wasn't there, or Henry's kid brother, or Dick Sawtell from the far table, who'd hung himself.

Although Daniel was pleased to be there, a part of him, the part that he couldn't share, ached to be alone. Simon understood when he promptly left the welcome home to make his way to his mother's house.

Hazel was shocked by the change in her eldest son. He was distant, unreachable, even more so than Simon. 'How's John Stanley?'

Having to face her without his kid brother was bad enough, but the anxious look on his poor mother's face caused a rough manner he'd never had before.

His voice had developed a gravel edge, deeper and lower than Maureen remembered, a monotone and his lips twisted up at the corners. The vowels dead. And gentle intimacies she'd enjoyed with Daniel before the war had turned into grabbed buttocks or tit, out of nowhere, as if he was trying to drag her down to some depth so that he could have her there to share his pain.

Maureen hung on desperately to the rare tender moments that gave her a glimpse of the Daniel she'd married. She did what she could to make him feel secure, while she prayed for the old Daniel to come back.

But three months after his return, the army transferred him to Townsville, without her. It was to be two long months before all the paperwork was completed, and she could join him, two long months of Daniel waiting alone, waiting for his kid brother to get back home.

She had waited alone too in the army barracks, worrying about how Daniel was coping, while the veteran in the house next door began to rant and rave, day and night, at his wife and tiny daughter, until Maureen could take no more of it. She begged the army padre to do something and chase up her transfer to Townsville.

Matt had changed too. He disappeared deep into himself and wanted to stay there. The distance between music and war had become too great, improvisations shuffling on, while he searched the faces that came and went, looking for John Stanley and the men who wouldn't hear the music again.

Over the years, Rosies had become a sort of club, without anybody noticing. The regulars had got to know each other intimately, their moves in and out of relationships, bad habits, beliefs and dreams, food quirks, how many sugars, who liked their coffee iced or hot. But the war had burst in like a dud grenade and regulars stopped coming. The happy sounds that had brought them all together ceased. Matt lost the desire to improvise and a wedge lodged itself between him and Ellen.

The continual waiting for John Stanley to come home weighed heavily on the whole family.

When Matt was away, Ellen had turned to study, to shut herself off from the war. A new prime minister had been voted in and with his fair-go philosophy and education for all, she felt she finally had a chance. She was accepted into Sydney University, and wanted to teach. But Matt couldn't let go of the war.

'You're fighting a lost cause, Ellen!' It went against his grain to interfere with her beliefs, but after what he'd seen in Vietnam, he couldn't stop himself. 'Nobody wants to know about Sydney's Aboriginal history. Sydney's a thriving city now. The past is the past!'

'You expect me just to turn my back? Forget our ancestors and thousands of years? Is that what you expect, Matt?'

Silently he'd watched Hazel withdraw further and further

into herself. And he wanted to save Ellen from that, just as desperately as he wanted to save her from the bitterness that comes with speaking out.

'The bottom line is that we're human beings first. Different belief systems, that's all. It can be dangerous, speaking up; like opposing the Vietnam war. You just have to reconcile the differences.'

'Like Mum had to? What's changed then, Matt?'

And she left. Her mother would understand.

'Matt's right, in a way, Ellen, but…well, if ya gut burns, ya havta fight,' she said.

'This is a different kind of war, Mum. We shouldn't havta cover up who we really are, so others can feel all right. I'm not gunna let Gran just fade away, as if she never really existed. I'm not gunna let Great Grandpa and Isabella fade away as if they never really existed. As if the Cadi people never existed, or Watagora, as if Darug never existed. I'm not gunna do that.' Her voice softened. 'What are you crying for?'

'Well, if you feel that way, do what I couldn't. Go to that university.'

'I don't know anyone from around here that's been. The only uni students I've ever met are the ones at Rosies and they're all sort of middle class. What if I'm meant to stay where I belong?'

'Your great-grandpa once told me, "You belong everywhere, everyone belongs, in the great scheme of things." Everyone plays a part, a small part, whatever it is. You belong, Ellen, and if you've got somethin' to say, say it.'

Ellen hugged her and laughed. 'I thought unis only took the kids from private schools. You know, the ones that wander round Parramatta wearing posh-looking uniforms, all the time, even when they go to the pictures.'

‘I missed out on a scholarship, love. In my day Aborigines and the working class didn’t know what a university looked like. But it’s different now. You’ve got a chance.’ And she rummaged in a drawer and handed her a clipping from a newspaper.

Ellen took it from her, and read the words slowly.

> *If you have come here to help me, you are wasting your time. But if you have come because your liberation is bound up with mine, then let us work together.* Lilla Watson (activist).

‘I’ll do it,’ she cried. ‘For you, Mum. We’ll make up for that lost scholarship, eh?’

‘No, do it for yourself, Ellen. Your spirit, not mine. That way it’ll work.’

‘You know, it wasn’t long ago I didn’t know that that beautiful old building on Parramatta Road was the university. My friends at Rosies told me. Did you know that anyone can just walk in there and look round and look at the books in the library? Did you know that, Mum?’

‘Well, it wouldn’t have made much difference to me. Working class don’t like going where they feel they don’t belong.’

Ellen looked around the room. She’d never known her mother to venture much further than these four walls, and it saddened her. Was this the *only* place her mother felt she belonged?

‘I would have gone there if I’d known,’ she said, mechanically.

‘No you wouldn’t have,’ Hazel laughed.

No. I guess I wouldn’t. And she thought about how brave she must have been to walk into Rosies by herself that very first time. But she couldn’t kid herself. She would never have walked in through the tall iron gates of that beautiful building on Parramatta Road, not without being invited.

'You know, there were some really clever kids at our school, but they just sort of dropped out. Doesn't make sense, does it? It shouldn't matter where a brain comes from.'

'Well that makes sense to you and me...but it's all about privilege.'

'Yeah well I just hope Labor stick to their promise...or I'm out!'

'Course they will. Labour's never forgotten the working class!'

But Hazel found it hard to understand. It was like a long lost dream, like boiling water to a cool stream. Eddy wondered what all the fuss was about and why a girl, let alone a married woman and a mother, would even bother. And he was afraid. Afraid of her mixing with all those rich, snobby kids. Afraid she would look down upon him, and he would lose her respect. His unspoken fears compounded with Ellen's own as she wrote

my dad is not a school teacher, my dad is not a bank,
my dad is on the railways, my dad has had no breaks
my dad knows no Shakespeare
but I'll be doing a B.A., I'll be visiting cultural centres
nearly every other day
And I'm wondering—
when I'm finished, will anybody care
or will they jeer, instead of cheer
if I step up—
without my dad?

She would never forget that first day, the day she crossed over and walked in through the gate of what looked like a castle. She had stood on the grass and drawn energy from the earth and soaked in the dream, before wandering up to the magnificent old building with its bell tower and grassed quadrangle.

In the evenings, she listened happily to her mother recite and read from the classics, with the same animated face she had loved as a child. It seemed she knew most of the writings by heart, the poetry, the stories, the characters, protagonists, antagonists, and well into the evening, while Minnie slept, Ellen would listen and discuss the philosophy behind the story, the philosophy behind life and she'd watch with fascination as her mother came alive. And the stories helped to relieve the worry of John Stanley.

Hazel had stepped in and out of these places many times. The characters were her friends and acquaintances; she'd been inside their houses, worshipped in their churches, strolled through their gardens. Ellen had been there too, but she hadn't realised that she'd been walking in the classics, because that's all there ever was in the house. She'd remembered the stories, but had forgotten the authors and although she wasn't sure who wrote what, she knew what the author was trying to say. Whereas she'd noticed that many students went about sprouting a Dickens here and an Austen there, as though they were their second best friends, without even knowing the story. Others dissected pages with such cold deliberation that she felt sick inside.

'Repetition, third paragraph.'

'Page forty-four...description slows the pace.'

'Style isn't sustained...rhythm, page fifty-six, doesn't seem to flow as well as it did on pages fifty-four and five.'

Ellen felt out of place in this institution of high ceilings, with its professors, doctors without stethoscopes and the arrogance of the young who knew everything before the professors even opened their mouths. But she loved the learning atmosphere and the exchange of thoughts and most of all she felt akin to Yeats and his belief in *spiritus mundi*, the universal link with everybody belonging some place.

It was the age of Aquarius and it suited her right down to her bare feet. With long, swinging skirts of delicate cheesecloth, flowing blouses all smocking-stitched, beads bouncing and arms piled high with books, she tried to feel at peace with herself. Between lectures she sat among the hedges and cut herself off from discussions of war.

The mere mention of Vietnam caused her to fret for John Stanley. So she'd put her opposition to one side for the time being. She needed to do something to take her mind off the war. She wanted to mend Sydney's broken link with its past.

Mother's totem. Father's totem. Clan totem. Personal totem. Country. Heavens. Creation. Death. Birth. The cycles of weather and the cycles of life. Language of mark. Language of art. People, flora and fauna unmistakably defined, where they belonged, where they'd come from. Yet no two people exactly alike. But her totem was gone, swept away with the wind and the rain. Was a part of her submerged in Duck River, or etched into a rock? She had sunned herself on the banks of the river, she'd splashed about in her own people's graves. She had sat on the cliffs at Bondi, running her fingers along Murubora enclaves.

And as her passion spilled into her tutorials and essays, she was advised to keep it out. But she challenged one eminent professor. 'Sir, how do you apply logic to deep heartbreak?'

A hush had come over the tutorial and with all eyes following her, she'd walked out, and, as she hurried off campus, her thoughts turned to Matt. He'd tried to warn her. 'Just because your heart is in the right place, don't expect people to recognise it, Ellen. In fact, because of it you could get crushed. There's no way back.'

The minute Ellen's body swam into summer, it tanned. 'Gawd struth! You look like an Abo,' strangers would laugh. Yet, in winter, when the colour faded, she just as quickly heard the sneer, 'You don't look Aboriginal to me.' But it didn't change what she felt inside. She'd grown up on Darug land, like her mother and her mother's mother and her mother's mother's father and her mother's mother's father's mother and father and so on and on. And she had to stand up for Isabella. Who could understand, if Matt didn't?

But once again she heard his voice: 'Deep down we're all the same, good and bad, kind and cruel. We're all human beings. That's the gist of it.'

'So to hell with everything else?'

'All you have to do is understand that point. We're still who we are; nobody can change that.'

'It's deeper than that, Matt! I'm proud of where I come from. How can you turn your back? I can't just let a part of me die, like if I were to lose John Stanley. I want to keep Duck River alive. I want to say, "Hey, don't forget who was here before you!"'

And that was the day she had stormed off and left him.

'I have to do something to try and mend the link,' she had yelled back over her shoulder, as she bundled Minnie into the car.

'Do what you have to,' Matt whispered, as the car shot off down the street.

Her words 'mend the broken link' resounded off the empty walls and Matt knew that he had to let her go, if he wanted her to come back.

As the wheels turned the dirt over in the street, Ellen's heart cried, 'I want the link back.'

'Nana's always asking me to come for a holiday. She'll be happy I decided you could come too,' Minnie said with a chirp, trying to cheer her mother up.

And Ellen's repressed sorrow gushed forth for her proud strong roots, locked up in an album and in laced-up boots. The thought of her mother hiding from the world caused a deep sorrow. Others could say, 'I'm Scottish!' or 'I'm Irish!' or 'I'm Italian!' While Ellen had to search for the right to her birth.

Hazel listened to Ellen as she stroked her daughter's hair.

'I remember that day you caught the beautiful butterfly on the honeysuckle and brought it in to show me. It was turquoise, midnight blue and velvety black. You wanted to keep the beauty by cutting off its wings. "Won't it just grow some more, like when we pick peas in Daddy's garden?" you asked me.'

'And you said, *you can't pull the wings off a butterfly and expect it to fly away*! I remember, Mum.'

'I want you to go back to your class, Ellen. Show our resilience. And one day, you can teach or write about your ancestry.'

She kissed her mother and slept long and sound into the night.

She worked hard at university. Matt waited. He waited for the day she would come back and do what she was destined to. He loved the passion of this woman and she had a way with words. He loved Hazel for planting that in her, and he loved Eddy too, for his quiet cultivation.

Ellen was right, though. The war had changed Matt. He had things to work through himself and for now it was best this way.

He'd listened to the dying, while he played music and watched poor boys slip away. He'd kept on playing, John Stanley still not home and children with limbs torn off. He couldn't go back to Ellen's way. It scared him, this fight for recognition. And he feared that Ellen and Minnie would get hurt.

Ellen completed her teacher training at La Perouse Primary and it was the Aboriginal students that kept her going. She'd learnt so much from them and, like Matt with Vietnam, she couldn't walk away.

'Stanza…stanza eh? Now there's a good word,' said Pete, with his head cocked to the side and his eyes searching the ceiling. Pete was keen to learn new words. He had a cheeky grin and there was no mistaking the gait that stomped out, *I'm proud to be who I am.*

'So duz that mean if I were sittin' next to a whitefella on the bus, I could ask 'im to read the last stanza of 'is paper to me?'

Ellen explained the proper technical use of the word 'stanza' in poetry, while Pete listened closely.

'Oh, right! So if the whitefella on the bus was readin' a book of poems, I could say somethin' to him 'bout the last stanza?'

'Right!' She was taken by surprise at his apparent interest in this one tiny word.

'Boy, wouldn't that bowl 'im over? A kid knowin' a word like that! And do ya know what I'd say, when he asked me where I'd learnt it?' Pete stuck his chest out. 'I'd say, I learnt it from me Aboriginal teacher!'

The students had a gift for storytelling and she'd entered their stories in a writing competition. And now, as she stood on the stage, congratulating those who'd taken out the three top prizes in the metropolitan region and those who'd received encouragement awards, she looked on proudly, as each student stepped forward to receive a certificate.

Billy, who had been taken from his family when he was five years old, smiled at her. He'd told her once that he could still see his parents running down the railway platform, screaming after him as the train and the welfare people chugged him away to another town, placed him in an institution and destroyed all family ties, before a foster family brought him to Sydney. He made his way now to the raised platform and accepted his certificate with tears in his eyes.

He shook Ellen's hand. 'This is tha first time I ever got a certificate in me whole life,' and he sobbed for a past he hadn't been allowed to cry for.

Ellen watched him leave the stage and soon he was laughing as his mates patted him on the back and the girls hugged him and shook his hand. And he laughed and laughed.

TWENTY-NINE

HAZEL'S FAREWELL

Matt had begun to write his own songs. Ellen was right. She'd stood up and been counted. Played her small part, like he had in Vietnam. Like her mother before her, she'd said, 'That's all anybody has to do. Play a part. Their own small part. To connect up with the universe.'

And she realised that Matt was right too, when he'd said, 'We're all pretty much the same.' She looked once more around the hall and stepped back from the microphone. She smiled down at Billy, who grinned broadly back, while Pete yelled, 'Nice stanza, Miss!'

Matt suddenly felt Hazel's presence and he hugged Minnie Hazel. Ellen gazed down at them and felt something too. 'Thank you, everyone,' she called into the mike, the crickets outside picking up the echo of her voice and flying with it into the void of night.

The humming ceased and she heard Gran's voice, *'Listen to the sounds, Ellen.'* There was something wrong. She had to go to her mother.

Matt sensed the urgency too and warmed up the engine of the cold car, turning it over with gentle pumps to the acccelerator, and with Minnie asleep in Ellen's arms he turned the wheel towards Granville.

Hazel had slipped into her warm book, and silver strands of her once dark hair softly veiled the words of Yeats.

Eddy sat watching a cricket replay. The game was piss-weak, so he'd got up to make a cuppa and as he passed by Hazel's reading nook he shook his head. There she was, asleep with her head in a book again. He called to her from the doorway, as he did every night. 'Hey, Gertie, ya goin' ta bed?'

That had become a term of endearment over the years, and one of his few ways of voicing affection. But tonight there was no stir, or the usual slight wave of her hand, and he took one step inside the room and called again. A little louder. 'Hey, Gertie...it's past ya bedtime!'

There was still no stirring. He moved closer. 'Gertie,' he almost whispered, as he reached out to shake her arm. But he was confronted with the full force of death. He wanted to hurl her book out the window and hold his wife, but he backed away, afraid to pull her out of the pages. 'Rain has interrupted play,' a voice droned on from the television, as he fumbled to switch it off.

He was wandering towards the gate when Ellen and Matt arrived, the front door wide open as usual on such a hot night.

'What's the matter, Dad?' Ellen asked anxiously.

'Gertie's gone into the book.'

Ellen rushed into the house.

Eddy nodded Matt towards the couch and as he lay Minnie down, he heard Ellen's gut-wrenching cry. 'How could you die like this?' And Hazel's book came flying out the door. 'You should have waited for John Stanley to come home!' And as Matt rushed in, the bookcase crashed to the floor. 'Why did you have to hide all your life?'

The sight of Hazel's lifeless body, her beloved books scattered about it as Ellen's grief raged, was almost too much for Matt to bear. He held Ellen tight, and as his eyes rested on Hazel's drooped head, old wounds seemed almost a mountain range, rising through grey mist, as her hair floated down its slopes, finer than rain.

Because of Hazel's self-imposed exile, nobody but family came. No wreaths. No bouquets. No cards of sorrow. But interspersed with the grief was an immeasurable joy. John Stanley was coming home.

Eddy tried to make some sense of an unfathomable love, as Hazel was lowered into the Darug earth.

The room was a nightmare and Ellen shook her head. Drawers were bursting with receipts, cards and letters, while *Thought for the Day*, *Quiet Moments* and *Lines of Comfort* that had been neatly cut from newspapers and boxes of goodness knows what lay in dusty cupboards and lonely corners, age-yellow, poured from wooden drawers and tired old shoeboxes.

She began the arduous task. And as she opened each tight drawer and removed lids from shaky boxes, all her mother's fears swarmed out. 1948, 1927, 1934, a clock that had stopped ticking, a sagging matress, a cold iron, folding house payments, bills creased shut. And always her mother's warning voice, 'Don't forget the receipt, Ellen!'

She kicked a box and sent papers flying across the floor, but in all the disarray, one letter caught her attention. It was unmailed, stamped, with her mother's handwriting on it: 'Jim Johnson, Johnson Farm, Chipping Norton.' It had a Santa Claus drawn on the back and the year 1944 printed in bold ink. She slit the seal and opened it. Inside was a Christmas card and a letter, which she carefully unfolded.

Dear Jim,

Merry Christmas! The army are adamant about the sniper, but they make so many mistakes. Why, just the other day it was in the paper, a man turned up after his family thought he'd been dead for years. Dog tags got mixed up and he suffered from amnesia. They'd buried some other poor soldier in his name.

Well, when you come walking through the door, the only thing you'll have to confront will be my relief.

Ellen looks a lot like you. Your spirit too. I'm grateful to Dad for making way for her. Along with the letter and the will, well, he made his retribution. The army returned the Christmas pudding. I don't write to the New Guinea address anymore. I write to Chipping Norton. Your fifty pounds from Dad is still in your account, waiting for you. When you come back, you'll be able to start up your farm again. Peas are fetching more now than they were before the war. Who knows? You could end up rich!

The boys are waiting patiently for you to come back too. Eddy told them you'd gone on the big boat to heaven, but I set them straight. I told them the big boat would be bringing you back home some day. Simon and John Stanley are as wild as ever. There's always one of them having an accident. Lucky Daniel is around to pick up the pieces. I think they need their Uncle Jimmy though!

Mum's fine. Won't talk about you. You know how she believes that if you cling to the dead, you hold them back. But she knows in her heart that a sniper didn't get you. She's like me. Never trusted the government. But we'll all have a great big laugh when you come through the door. We'll be a proper family again, without any guilt, for once. We've got Dad to thank for that. Even if he was always as mad as a meat-axe!

We couldn't do any more than we did, Jimmy. Mum would have been dead by now if it wasn't for you. I'd be dead too. We were both just lucky that you came home when you did!

I came back from the dead. Remember the old potato-box? And Dad did too. Never touched a drink again, Peggy said. So if we can come back, why can't you?

I guess we both know that Josie won't be coming. I still see her waving your letter and smiling. But at night, I can't get her out of the paspalum. If you come back Jimmy, we could visit Josie's grave and let her know that things turned out all right. But, whatever you do, don't come home with shell-shock!

I still see them coming you know. The tanks in Dad's head. He's telling me to get out of the way, but I can't, because Mum has fallen down in the dirt. They come all night. The enemy are on the top, screaming at Dad to go to the asylum and yelling down at me to give them my kids. I'm yelling, 'Run kids, run!' And they can run pretty fast.

You can't trust anyone these days so I stay inside. Eddy doesn't understand. He's a good man, as you well know, but he just doesn't understand. Nobody knows what I'm really thinking, because I don't tell them. It's better that way.

I just tell Eddy and Mum that there are reasons for everything I do, and not to worry about it. They both think I'm mad. But I'm not. I'm just good at pretending. Spent my childhood doing it, so they wouldn't cart Dad off. So I've got pretty good at pretending. I'm an expert now. I even pretend to believe you're dead, for a bit of a laugh.

The baby's crying, I have to go. Love as always,

Your sister,

Hazel.

PS I'll let you in on my secret before you come home. I just live in other people's stories, because it's safe inside the pages. I hate it when Eddy tries to pull me out. So when you come home, just let me be.

The sun was beginning to set, light filtering shadows in through the venetian blinds and Ellen sat on the floor with the flimsy remnants of her mother's life.

And Ellen understood at last. Life was in the story, and the story wrapped itself around life. Her mother had merely turned over a tired page.

Nobody had known her mother, why she had withdrawn like a bird that had lost its song. But before she died, her pain had revealed itself.

In the quiet of the day, she had begun to moan, and that cold shudder that comes with the sound of a howling dog had overcome Ellen.

'What's wrong, Mum?'

But Hazel had looked surprised and smiled warmly. 'Nothing, love!'

'But you were moaning.'

'Was I? But I'm not in any pain!'

'Why were you moaning then?'

And Hazel had given one of her little laughs. 'That wasn't moaning, Ellen. I was just thinking on the past.'

Ellen wiped her eyes and opened the Christmas card. It

wasn't addressed 'To Jimmy from Hazel', as she'd expected; it was 'To Alice, Hazel and Jimmy, from Joe Johnson 1941'.

Joe Johnson, her grandfather. The one who'd fought at Gallipoli.

She read the verse:

Dear Santa Claus, These gifts we pray
For others on this Christmas Day:
For all the world the gift of peace,
That wars both hot and cold may cease,
That everywhere men may be free
As God intended them to be.
Leave happiness in larger store
Than folks have ever had before,
Deliver these on Christmas eve
And we won't care what we receive.

EPILOGUE

Out across the misty water, Ellen saw a spirit holding Minnie's hand, and leading her into a lost dream; stories on stone carpets and ochre on floating bark, a kingfisher's song, a kookaburra's laugh, emus in the bush and footprints in rocks, the river and the sea; a blacksmith, a child-mother and a mermaid.

And as the mist cleared, the sun danced. Waianya's dying words, 'Find 'im for Essie.'

Distant cousins, as distant as the Blue Mountains, had married Duck River back up and waianya's spirit had come to rest with Minnie Hazel.

And as Minnie smiled up at Ellen and Matt, her dark eyes beamed hope. Hers would be a new story.